TARGETS
DOWN

**Center Point
Large Print**

Also by Bob Hamer
and available from Center Point Large Print:

Enemies Among Us

**This Large Print Book carries the
Seal of Approval of N.A.V.H.**

TARGETS DOWN

BOB HAMER

CENTER POINT PUBLISHING
THORNDIKE, MAINE

ISBN: 978-1-61173-111-8

Library of Congress Cataloging-in-Publication Data

Hamer, Bob.
    Targets down / Bob Hamer.
    p. cm.
    ISBN 978-1-61173-111-8 (lib. bdg. : alk. paper)
    1. United States. Federal Bureau of Investigation—Fiction.
    2. Undercover operations—Fiction. 3. Organized crime—Fiction.
    4. Sex crimes—Fiction. 5. Large type books. I. Title.
PS3608.A57T37 2011
813′.6—dc22

                                                      2011012679

CHAPTER ONE

The powerful hand gripped the silenced Russian-made weapon, and the tattooed arm straightened. As the teenager talked to the killer's two associates in the darkened parking lot, she had no idea she was about to be erased by the threat behind her. It was all so impersonal, but career criminals operated on a different plain. Morality was never an issue; expediency was. The Ukrainian girl was a liability and thus expendable.

The ever-constant traffic on Ventura Boulevard masked the sounds of the two muted gunshots fired in rapid succession. From just a few feet away, either shot to the back of the head was fatal. Before anyone exited the rear door to the Russian Veil, the three men threw the limp body into the bed of the pickup truck and were gone: another anonymous victim of Los Angeles street justice, a judicial system lacking due process or fairness. Even a quest for freedom was a capital offense.

MATT HOGAN STOOD IN front of the mirror admiring his greased biker-hair look. His rugged battle-scarred features were in sharp contrast to the metrosexuals parading up and down the Sunset Strip on any Saturday evening. The undercover agent then sprayed a 70 percent solution of alcohol on the left side of his powerful neck. He carefully placed the Tinsley transfer, blotted the paper, waited a few seconds, and just as carefully removed the transfer. Satisfied with his work, he finished with a dash of baby powder to aid in drying the large prison-like tattoo. A movie studio German "SS" now complemented the stubble. But even clean shaven, Matt could be a menacing figure, a no-holds-barred, man's man.

If it's true, the hotter the fire the stronger the steel, then Hogan was as strong as they came. A member of the FBI's small cadre of undercover agents, he successfully played the role of contract killer, drug dealer, and when cleaned up, a sophisticated white-collar criminal. A psychologist described him as a "synthesist," a person who could void himself of his own personality and take on the characteristics, mind-set, and mannerisms of whatever the part required. Matt was good, maybe too good. Sometimes even he questioned who he was.

Working undercover meant more than a fake driver's license and a fictitious name. It was living life as a liar for hours, days, even months at a time. It meant becoming one of them without becoming one of them. Distance offered detachment, but when you went undercover, it became personal. It was getting close to people you will ultimately betray and probing the darkest side of humanity, including your own. Unlike Hollywood, there were no retakes; a botched line, a missed mark, a mistake could mean instant death. Matt Hogan walked in the flames many times; he experienced the fire.

As he began writing the letters H-A-T-E on the fingers of his right hand, Steve Barnett walked into the Joint Terrorism Task Force locker room.

"Well, if it isn't the Mary Kay of the FBI," said Steve. "You enjoy putting on makeup way too much. I hope you aren't switching sides on me."

"Don't ask. Don't tell," said Matt concentrating on his artwork.

"Why don't you just pierce your ear and grow a ponytail, like every other undercover agent I know?"

"Caitlin won't let me. She's got a pretty strict dress code around the house. In fact, these biker undercover assignments keep me sleeping on the couch until I take a shower."

"I guess that's why she's been spending so many nights with me at my place."

"In your dreams, big guy. I know for a fact she doesn't date the follicly challenged with a bad weave."

Steve pulled out a comb and began to rake his sparse locks styled in a weak comb-over. "That's how much you know. I'm a Hair Club for Men honor graduate, and she loves to run her fingers through these amber waves."

Matt didn't even look up, still writing on his fingers. "I'm surprised you're awake. Isn't this way past your bedtime?"

Steve looked in the mirror, moving his face even closer, carefully examining his skin, searching for tell-tale signs of aging. "These late nights are causing all kinds of wrinkles."

"I'm not sure eight hours of sleep or Mary Kay will help," said Matt without cracking a smile.

"What about Botox?"

"Yeah, that might fill in a few of those deep crevices around the eyes, but you still don't have a shot with any skirt rated higher than a three or four."

"You're probably right. I keep hoping my near-perfect shooting scores at the Leisure World pistol range will attract some blue-hair with money, but I'm even striking out there." Steve paused, turned serious, and then said almost in a whisper, "Dwayne said we're ready to start the briefing when you are."

An FBI office is like a locker room with the requisite jock snapping and sarcastic sniping. The thin-skinned need not apply. A sense of humor is almost a requirement, sometimes the sicker the better. Those on the outside would never understand or appreciate the need to talk or act the way grown men in law enforcement do. Those in the military understand. Those on the front lines fighting evil know the need. It brings a sense of relief from the tensions the real world throws at you every day, the constant reminders of your mortality. It also brings a sense of camaraderie. You can't count on judges, lawyers, lawmakers, or administrators. Like the combat soldier or Marine, you can only count on the man next to you on the urban battlefield.

Matt blew on his fingers to accelerate the drying time of the ink from the tattoo makeup pen and followed Steve to the room at the end of the long hallway.

CHAPTER TWO

Darkness blanketed the hilltop road. This section of the mountain pass didn't burden taxpayers with streetlights, and only a faint glimmer of illumination from Los Angeles's San Fernando Valley could be seen through the thick, damp fog. It was well past ten, and Lydia Mitchell was hopeful she could make it home by the eleven o'clock news. Her two young daughters would be asleep, and her macho FBI agent husband, exhausted from just a few hours of babysitting, would probably be stretched out on his favorite leather recliner in the family room. Lydia valued her volunteer work at the community food bank. She chafed, however, at the late-evening committee meetings at various members' homes.

Her husband's Mustang sputtered as she pulled from the Laurel Hills development off Mulholland Drive, and now the car seemed even more irritated as she tried to accelerate up a small rise in the road. The twenty-eight-year-old brunette glanced at the fuel gauge. Of course it registered full; she just filled the tank earlier in the evening. Flip babied his car and always insisted on brand-name gasoline, but Lydia thought his obsession was silly—after all, gas is gas. The local independent dealer a few blocks from her home always beat the Mobil and the Shell on opposite corners by several pennies so she filled up, saving nearly ninety-seven cents. Now she wondered if her frugality was a mistake. *Would cheap gas cause all this clanking?* She wasn't looking forward to explaining to her husband why she entrusted his "precious pony" to off-brand fuel.

She rounded the bend of this two-lane road, and a fire team of coyotes greeted her. The animals stopped in the middle of the road, four pairs of eyes glowing in her headlights, and they stared as if telling the Mustang it had no right to be trespassing. When the engine sputtered, the animals raced into the roadside underbrush, giving way to the machine belching its dinner.

Lydia drove another mile, and the car continued to cough, more frequently as the trip progressed. Her efforts at variously giving it more gas and taking her foot off the pedal were ineffective. Eventually it died. She struggled to steer the vehicle to the side of the road, resting it just off the pavement. Frustration began to build.

Fishing through her purse, she found her cell phone lodged at the bottom hidden beneath her wallet, checkbook, and an assortment of cosmetics. She opened the door to activate the dome light, and the alarm signaled the keys were still in the ignition. The annoying sound only added to her frustration. She looked down at the phone pad and, using the speed dial feature, called home, hoping her husband could provide answers and a rescue. Closing the car door to silence the alarm, she waited for the sound of the familiar ring of her home phone. Nothing. She opened the door, the alarm sounded, and she tried again, speed dialing her home number. Her efforts were futile as she realized she was out of her cell phone provider's service area.

"Great!" she muttered, "Now what?"

She knew absolutely nothing about cars, so even raising the hood to examine the engine was a useless gesture. She tried the cell phone one more time but to no avail. The heavy fog was a mist-like rain, and the windows were quickly covered in moisture, obscuring her visibility even more.

Fear began to envelope her. She was unfamiliar with this section of town and had little idea of where to seek help. Was it safe to start walking in either direction? Maybe a cop would stop to help a stranded motorist, but this seldom-traveled section of the road offered little hope. She couldn't wait here all night. She knew somewhere on this road there were homes, but she could see no lights behind gated entrances. Her friend's home was several miles back. She hated the thought of walking that far in the dampness and the dark. Was it even safe to leave Flip's car? Maybe if she walked a little way in either direction she could at least get cell phone coverage.

Just as she was about to exit the car, she saw the reflection of headlights in her rearview mirror. A chill ran down her spine. This seemed like a scene from a cheap Hollywood horror movie—a dark, lonely road, and a stranded female who became tomorrow's headline. Always the drama queen, as her husband liked to point out, she tried to squelch her fear.

She took a deep breath and watched the vehicle approach. Her heart began to pound; her palms began to sweat. Should she flag down the motorist? Before she could even decide, the car passed. At first it was a feeling of relief, then confusion, and finally irritation. She was safe but still stranded. As she began to capture a second thought, the car stopped and made a u-turn in the road. She watched the car slowly return. Her heart was almost pounding through her chest, and her hands were shaking.

The vehicle pulled alongside the Mustang. The driver's side window of the dark blue Chrysler 300 retreated into the door frame, and a warm, black face appeared.

Lydia relaxed and breathed a sigh of relief. The driver was Benjamin Hobbs, a minister from a church in Baldwin Hills, who also worked at the food bank and was at tonight's meeting.

"Need some help?"

"Oh, thank God, it's you. My car stalled, and I can't get cell-phone coverage. I wasn't sure what to do."

"Let me pull over, and let's see if I can get it started," said Ben.

Lydia exited the Mustang as Ben pulled his car to the side of the road, parking near a large tree whose low-hanging branches almost concealed the Chrysler.

A tall, lean man with dark chocolate skin, Ben Hobbs played basketball in college in the mid-eighties. Still athletic, he bounded across the street to Lydia's car.

"Glad I turned around. I couldn't see inside the car but wanted to make sure no one was stranded.

Course, wanted to be careful, thought I might find a couple attempting to violate the Seventh Commandment."

Lydia smiled as the mist fell gently on her shoulder-length hair. "I'm glad you took a chance. I think I got some bad gas this evening. My husband insists on brand names, but in the interest of good stewardship, I went cheap, and it may have cost me."

Ben laughed. "Maybe I can help. I know God wants to reward the wise steward."

Just as Lydia was about to hand him the keys to the Mustang, she spied a dark Dodge Ram Mega-Cab stop short a hundred yards from her location. She knew it was a Dodge because a similar model sat in her driveway at home. It was her husband's surveillance vehicle.

Three men exited the truck, grabbed a large limp object from the bed of the pickup, and heaved it over the side of the road. The men quickly returned to the truck and sped off, now heading toward Lydia and Ben, almost clipping them as they stood by the side of the road.

"Crazy kids," barked Ben.

Before Lydia could respond, the truck skidded to a stop. The driver threw the vehicle into reverse and raced back toward Lydia's car, tires spinning on the wet, slick pavement, water spitting in all directions. Three men jumped from the truck.

The driver was short and powerful. His head was shaved, and Lydia could see a tattoo on the left side of his neck. The other two were much taller, one muscular but both menacing, wearing dark knit caps, which they immediately pulled down over their faces as they exited the muddied pickup. Both arms of the largest of the three were covered in tattoos. The other wore a long-sleeve black Harley-Davidson shirt which would have concealed any markings.

Initially paralyzed with fear, Lydia stood by as the men moved with ferocious speed toward Benjamin Hobbs. She then screamed as the three men attacked and began to pummel Ben with their fists and feet. She watched as the minister attempted to fend them off, but following a blow to the windpipe, he quickly collapsed. The kicks were made with blinding speed; steel-toed Doc Marten boots their weapons of choice.

Ben curled his body into a fetal position, unable to protest, craving a breath, and attempting to ward off the blows.

Lydia's pleas for the men to stop fell on deaf ears; they evidenced no intention of stopping. She tried to intervene, grabbing the driver by the arm, but he used his free arm landing a devastating punch to her face, shattering her nose.

The men were too quick, too powerful, too many. When the driver's left foot landed a well-placed strike to the head, Ben's body went limp.

The brutal, random, and spontaneous assault took less than a minute. The largest of the three men grabbed a silenced 9 mm from his waistband and pumped two shots into the minister's dead body. He then walked over to Lydia and fired two more rounds.

CHAPTER THREE

Eight men and two women, all casually dressed, surrounded the large table centered in the Joint Terrorism Task Force conference room. Dwayne Washington stood at the far end. His shaved head and recently cultivated goatee earned him the nickname Shaft because of his resemblance to Samuel L. Jackson's character in the movie. The Georgetown graduate joined the Bureau after completing a master's degree program in international studies and brought the requisite credibility to his position as the supervisory special agent for a diverse collection of law enforcement professionals.

Composed primarily of FBI agents with floating representatives from the Department of Homeland Security, DEA, the Los Angeles Sheriff's Office, and the Los Angeles Police Department, the squad was created a year earlier.

Their mission statement looked simple enough on the written page but more difficult to implement: identify the criminal activities of terrorists and those who supported terrorism, whether foreign or domestic. Individuals selected for the assignment were successful agents weaned on investigating traditional street crimes—bank robbery, kidnapping, extortion, and drugs. They were used to "runnin' and gunnin'" not "snoopin' and poopin'," preparing reports for some administrative black hole never to be read again. They enjoyed the chase, the confrontation, and the ultimate conviction. Their successes were public and, more often than not, exploited by Washington bureaucrats.

"Okay, let's get started," said Dwayne. "Steve is passing out the ops order."

As Steve Barnett walked around the room passing out a multi-page operations order detailing the night's agenda, one of the agents whispered under his breath, "Kiss up," just as Steve passed. Steve swatted the older agent in the back of his head, and everyone joined in nervous laughter. Any buy-bust was cause for preemptive alarm, and often during the briefings the tension was as thick as a San Francisco fog. Tonight was no different. Midnight ops were a blessing and a curse. The same darkness concealing the agents could just as easily hide the criminal intent of those playing for the other side.

"Matt, you want to fill us in," said Dwayne.

"Yeah," said Matt, "sorry about the hour. I don't like late-night drug deals any more than the rest of you, but I couldn't convince Tweedledum to do it any earlier. My guess is the precursors showed up this morning, and he knew it would take most of the day to cook a new batch. Whatever we're buying should be fresh."

"Just make sure it's evidentiary in nature. I'd hate to miss Leno cause your boy's shooting blanks," said a smiling Danny Garcia, a sergeant with LAPD who was leaning back balancing himself on two legs of his chair.

"Bobby Himmler is a wannabe neo-Nazi who wasn't smart enough to even be considered for the Aryan Brotherhood during his most recent prison stint. He hung out with the AB while away on the government-funded vacation but never made it into the inner circle. He's weak. If he's fighting a big-boned woman, bet the broad. He's been out about a year and is back slinging crystal meth. I picked up a sample earlier in the week, and it graded out almost pure. As a drug dealer this guy is for real. As a neo-Nazi we aren't sure. He has a prior narcotics conviction so, if he delivers tonight, he's looking at a double-up."

Dwayne interjected, "For you locals new to the task force, under the federal sentencing guidelines a prior drug conviction gets you twice the punishment with a subsequent slam."

"So our boy is looking at twenty at Chez Fed once he produces the product," said Matt.

Somebody whistled and added, "I love those federal guidelines."

Matt continued, "Bobby brags about his dealings with various neo-Nazi groups so we're hoping an arrest will provide him suitable incentive to join our side."

"From everything I've read, Bobby's not well respected in those circles because of his drug dealings," said Danny Garcia.

"You're right, Danny. He's more accepted in the biker community, but he can pass if he has to. If he doesn't work out for us, we'll pass him along to someone working outlaw motorcycle gangs, or we'll send him on another all-expense-paid trip courtesy of the Bureau of Prisons. It's a win-win for us, but we prefer his cooperation," said Dwayne.

"There's a cowboy bar in North Hollywood called Saddle-Up. The address is in the ops order. That's where I met him the last time. He's comfortable there. We did the sample in my pickup truck so I don't see a problem doing it the same way this time. But be flexible; he may want to move it into the bar."

"If he does, I'm out," said Dwayne. "I think that place still has a 'No Coloreds Allowed' on the front door."

"You ever hear of Darius Rucker?" said Steve.

"Yeah, Hootie and the Blowfish," said Dwayne.

"Man, we're in the twenty-first century. Hootie was hot when Bill Clinton was servicing White House interns. Darius has gone country. You and your people are welcome in almost any redneck bar in the Valley," said Steve with a broad smile.

"Dwayne's right; it's pretty white," said Matt. "But Dwayne, if you hear shots fired, you're welcome to join in the fray. I will do my best to keep it in the parking lot. I'm only picking up five ounces at $800 apiece so I'm not sure he'll think this is worth a rip. He believes my buyers are looking for a regular score each week so I want to keep it simple and so will he. Besides I won't be able to get an iPod-quality recording if all the negotiations are done with country and western music blasting in the background."

Someone asked, "Will he be alone?"

"He came alone the last time. I assume he'll be by himself tonight. It's not like he's running with a crew. I seldom trust the word of a convicted felon, but he said he wouldn't be bringing any friends, and I promised him no new faces."

"Yeah, but you're lying. Maybe he is too," came a comment from the back of the room.

"Good point," said Matt as he sat down.

"We're set to go at 11:30 so everybody be on station within the hour," said Dwayne who finished up the briefing with the admin details and the obligatory review of the FBI shooting policy. Even in the FBI the lawyers always had the last word.

Matt remained as everyone casually filed out of the conference room. With the hint of a smirk on his face, he prepared to enter his element, the dark side where shadow warriors love to dwell. He was humming "Folsom Prison Blues" as he opened the black plastic case containing the back-up miniature recording device. He inserted the batteries and checked to make sure it was operational. Too many times the devices failed, and he was taking no chances this evening. Once he was satisfied the device worked, he strapped it on and prepared for the next adrenaline rush.

CHAPTER FOUR

Flashing red and blue lights lit up the night. Three LAPD units from the North Hollywood Division were on the scene, and the homicide detectives, summoned from their homes, were only a few minutes out. A patrol sergeant requested an illumination truck which was in route. The truck would provide enough candle power to rival a night game at Dodger Stadium. The crime scene would then be exposed, and investigators would soon begin pouring over every inch of the area. Yellow tape already surrounded a large area encompassing the Mustang and the deceased body. What little traffic frequented the mountain road was rerouted.

A teenage couple, well past the girl's curfew, came upon the scene almost fifteen minutes after the attack. As the teen's car rounded the bend, the headlights swept the road. The driver and his passenger immediately focused on Benjamin Hobbs's limp body lying in the road, his head resting in a large pool of darkened blood. The seventeen-year-old high school football player slammed on his brakes, and on the rain-slick pavement his vehicle pulled left away from the minister, coming to a halt on the other side of the road. The girl screamed as her boyfriend jumped from the car to survey the scene. Within seconds he discovered Lydia unconscious behind her Mustang, lying in the loose gravel bordering the blacktop, her body clinging to life. Both bodies were soaked from the heavy mist that would wash away what little evidence might be available to the crime scene technicians.

The football player stayed with the bodies while his girlfriend drove his car to the fire station just east of Laurel Canyon almost three miles away.

The paramedics responded immediately, and the police arrived on the scene within minutes of their call.

The first officers on the scene identified both Lydia and the minister from their respective driver's licenses and vehicle registrations. There was nothing on either of the two victims to link them or to identify Lydia as the wife of an FBI agent.

By the time the homicide detectives arrived, the ambulance had taken Lydia to the nearest trauma center, and she had yet to regain consciousness. Without her help it was doubtful even the best investigators would be able to piece together the crime scene puzzle. It didn't take much experience to determine Benjamin Hobbs was savagely beaten and shot but a motive remained unclear.

CHA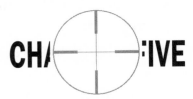IVE

Matt drove the 2009 Ford F-150 FX2 Sport truck into the parking lot of the Saddle-Up. The vehicle with a dark shadow-gray exterior was forfeited to the FBI a year earlier, seized from a Long Beach meth dealer who used the truck to transport three kilograms of the white crystalline product. The black leather-trimmed captain's chairs provided all the comfort Matt needed to negotiate tonight's deal. His appreciation for stupid criminals with good taste grew with each forfeited piece of property now at his disposal.

The vehicle's seizure was the result of a slick law enforcement cooperative effort. A court-authorized FBI wiretap on the conversations of a member of the Mongols motorcycle gang identified the pickup's owner as a conduit between the bikers and the Aryan Brotherhood at Folsom State Prison. The FBI arranged for a Highway Patrol unit to pull the truck over on a bogus traffic violation. Knowing in advance the driver had two outstanding warrants for failure to appear on several speeding tickets, the driver was arrested. The drugs were "discovered" during a routine inventory of the vehicle. The FBI successfully "walled off" the subsequent seizure of the drugs without disclosing the wiretap which successfully ran for several more months.

The Bureau's top tech agents retooled the interior of the pickup, concealing hidden cameras and microphones making the front seat a recording studio almost as perfect as the ones used in Nashville to record the songs Matt blasted on the Shaker 1000 audio sound system. Tonight Matt was featuring Charlie Daniels and planned to have "Uneasy Rider" playing in the background as Bobby Himmler entered the truck to begin negotiating the next step in his quest to lose his freedom. Matt would provide a clue. The song was cued to the line, "He's an undercover agent for the FBI."

The parking lot on this weeknight was about half full, and Matt parked toward the back, away from the other vehicles, giving his surveillance agents a clear shot at observing the imminent transaction. Although the parking area was dark, a lone light at the far end of the lot would provide enough illumination to silhouette Matt and Himmler, highlighting the activities inside the cab of the truck.

Dwayne and Steve Barnett were northeast of the location just on the other side of a six-foot block wall separating the Saddle-Up from a run-down office building. The other agents were placed strategically throughout the lot and in front of the bar observing the comings and goings of the patrons.

Although the squad surrounded the venue, Matt wasn't about to delegate his safety to others. Personal safety was a personal responsibility. Too many times while undercover the axiom became a reality: when seconds count, help is minutes away.

Danny Garcia had the point and was parked just down the street from the main entrance to the bar. Even though drug dealers aren't known for their punctuality, Danny surprised the cover team when he reported Bobby Himmler was pulling into the driveway at precisely 11:30 p.m., as promised. Himmler's Buick Riviera with gray primer and a broken front headlight made him an easy spot, and Danny first caught a glimpse of the vehicle when it rounded the corner at the end of the block.

"He's alone," reported Danny.

Matt spotted Himmler as soon as he pulled into the parking lot and watched the drug dealer circling the lot, carefully looking into every vehicle, obviously trying to detect any law enforcement activity. Matt's men were pro-fessionals and were well concealed. Apparently, when Himmler was satisfied the lot was clear, he parked his car next to Matt's truck and hopped into the cab.

"I thought maybe you didn't see me," said Matt turning down the radio after providing the clue. "I saw you circle a couple of times and almost flashed my headlights."

"Just checking the lot. I learned my lesson. I'm not getting caught again," said Himmler in a quick-paced staccato voice.

"Again? You been away?" asked Matt feigning surprise.

"Yeah, did a nickel. I had an old lady who lied. She said she wasn't coming back until Sunday. When she came home Saturday night, she found someone else keeping her side of the bed warm. Turns out she had a friend on some drug task force, and she made a phone call."

"Ouch!" Matt laughed. "The wrath of a scorned female."

The pencil thin meth addict ran his fingers through his greasy, long brown hair. It was obvious Himmler sampled his latest cooking achievement. He was jerking, twitching, and more nervous than when they dealt earlier in the week. This apparent anxiety was not the result of tonight's larger transaction but could only be attributed to an addict who recently used. Matt watched Himmler's eyes as they darted back and forth, and his hands continually scratching his dry skin.

"I learned my lesson. Can't be too careful in this line of work. Wanna make sure neither one of us is sucking heat," said the agitated dealer followed by a nervous lick of his lips.

"I know I'm clean, but I like a careful man. It makes me want to deal with you again and again. Assuming you can put it together this time," said Matt.

"I can put it together. Just make sure you hold up your end of the bargain. You bring Mr. Green?" asked Himmler.

"Four thousand in old bills, just like you asked, but I need to see the product first."

"We're not playin' those games. It's always the same with you people. I've got the product. Show me the money, or I'm taking my business inside. Everybody knows Bobby Himmler's got the best ice in town. I can move it all tonight. So get on or get movin'." Himmler's voice deepened, and there was a hard edge to his demand.

"Bright boy like you wanna piece it out all evening? Go right ahead, if that's your play. Doesn't seem like the move of a careful man. All you gotta do is show me the product, and you've got it sold in one move, one cash transaction. Five-o may be workin' the Saddle-Up this evening, and your next cash transaction might be coming up with enough bail money to spring you from county."

"You like playing it tough, don't you?"

Matt was in fact playing. If he appeared too eager to complete the deal, Himmler might suspect the eagerness as the sign of an inexperienced undercover cop. Matt needed to play, at least a little. He really didn't suspect Himmler of trying to steal a flash roll of $4,000. Although $4,000 to a tweeker was big money, even Himmler was smart enough to understand the concept of deferred gratification. He could rip Matt for a lot more after a few successful smaller transactions. The fact remained, Himmler was a capable manufacturer of crystal methamphetamine. Matt was convinced his new friend in the passenger seat had the drugs so maybe it was time to move the deal along. It was getting late, and he knew his team was hoping to get home before the early morning commuter rush.

"The first time's the hardest," said Matt. "Once this one goes down, we'll laugh about how we both played hardball tonight, and soon we'll be sending everything UPS with an automatic withdrawal from my checking account."

Himmler offered a calming laugh and started to reach inside his tattered blue sweatshirt zipped halfway.

Matt tensed, suspecting Himmler might be going for a weapon. The undercover agent prepared to attack, carefully watching Himmler's hands.

"I've got what you . . ."

He froze in midsentence as a black-and-white LAPD patrol unit entered the parking lot.

"Cops, man!" shouted a paranoid Himmler who sprang from the passenger seat and began running toward the northwest corner of the parking lot.

It was a stupid move only a longtime addict, suffering from delusions, would make.

"Wait!" shouted Matt.

But Himmler was out of the truck and on foot before Matt could reassure him. Tonight's transaction just became a live-action video game!

Ironically, the patrol unit missed the entire episode and drove out of the lot, completing its nightly routine cruise around the parking lots of every bar on its beat.

"We got a rabbit. Northwest corner. I'm gonna try to catch him," said Matt, hoping the transmitter was working and Dwayne understood what was happening.

Matt jumped from the cab and pursued.

CHAPTER SIX

Matt watched Himmler race into the darkness, the fog partially obscuring the twice-convicted felon. High on meth, his rail-thin legs pumped overtime getting him to the far end of the parking lot in near record time. He reached the six-foot block wall and scaled it like a recruit fresh from boot camp. Within seconds he was over the top and heading down an alley with no other goal than to elude the cops whom he assumed to be following close behind.

Matt almost admired the burst of energy the methamphetamines gave the addicted drug dealer. Matt was forced to summon strength from the long hours of conditioning, balanced diet, and clean living just to maintain the pace. Matt's pursuit may not have been wise, and he questioned whether he should call it off. He had no way of communicating with anyone on the surveillance team. Himmler could have a gun and might just think Matt was a pursuing cop. Of course, he was, but it made sense for Matt to join Himmler in fleeing the perceived police assault. Matt knew Himmler was "holding." Maybe if Matt could also appear to be evading the cops, Himmler would welcome a coconspirator in the race to freedom, and they could consummate the drug transaction in other than the comfort of the pickup.

Matt scaled the wall, and as he was coming down the other side, he caught a glimpse of Himmler fleeing down the trash-strewn alley. Filth covered almost every inch of the cratered blacktop. Potholes were as plentiful as a bombed-out street in Baghdad. Debris was blowing from the winds bringing in a cold front from Alaska, and rats claimed possession of the immediate neighborhood.

Himmler hit a hole, and a cacophony of vulgarity spewed loudly into the night air. He hit the ground hard and tumbled in the garbage. Unable to get up, he was crawling for cover when Matt caught up.

"Man, I hit a hole. I think I busted my leg. It hurts, man," cried Himmler.

"Let me help you. Why'd you take off?"

"The cops, man. I'm not stickin' around when uncle makes the scene," said a winded Himmler who was obviously in pain.

Matt helped Himmler to his feet. He took Bobby's arm and placed it around his shoulder, serving as support so Himmler could limp to the rear entrance of an abandoned building. The smell of stale urine greeted them. The two men sat on the stoop, a street light a hundred feet at the end of the alley providing illumination. Matt rattled the door pretending to turn the knob. "It's locked. Let me take a look at that ankle," intent on limiting another escape attempt knowing the shoe provided at least some support to the injured ankle.

Matt removed Himmler's shoe and pulled down a filthy white sweat sock with more holes than Swiss cheese.

"Big time dope dealer like you ought to be able to afford some new socks. Put something new on your feet before you put something up your nose," said Matt.

Himmler winced. "Is it broken?"

"Yeah, it's broken. The toes are supposed to point the same direction as the knee cap," said Matt. "The bone didn't break the skin, but I'm guessing you broke it in a couple of places."

Himmler moaned as if the mere diagnosis by an amateur physician brought more pain.

"Probably need to get some ice on it as soon as we can until we can get you to a doctor. But I'm not sure the Popsicle man is coming around here anytime soon."

"Those cops spoiled everything," Himmler moaned.

"That crystal is making you paranoid. Those boys in blue were on routine patrol, just cruising the lot. You bounced too soon," said Matt.

"You can't be too careful when you're holding product. I had to protect my investment."

"Well then let's get back to business. You got my stuff?" asked Matt.

"Yeah, it's right here, but I'm not sure this is the time or the place. My ankle's busted. You said so yourself."

Matt pulled out a wad of bills totaling $4,000 and watched Himmler's eyes. What had previously been darting back and forth were now focused on the undercover agent's flash.

"If I wheel you into the ER, it's gonna look better with a pocketful of hundreds than a bagful of a controlled substance guaranteeing a government-imposed vacation. Those hospitals have reporting requirements," said Matt.

Himmler reached into his sweatshirt and pulled out a large clear-plastic Ziploc bag. Even in the dim light Matt could see the contents—five ounces of a white crystalline substance, known variously on the street as meth, speed, ice, crystal. Bobby Himmler, criminal genius, just violated Title 21 of the US Code, Section 841, possession with intent to distribute. In law enforcement circles, he was now "bought and paid for."

Matt grabbed the bag and began to examine it. "Looks good, my friend."

Before Himmler could respond, Matt heard the faint sound of familiar voices as Dwayne and Steve made their way up the alley.

"Somebody's coming. Get me out of here," cried a panicked Himmler. He started to rise, seeking Matt's help in finding a safe refuge.

Matt shoved the handicapped tweeker back onto the step. "Relax. The run's over."

"What?"

"Dwayne, Steve, we're over here," shouted Matt. Matt turned long enough to see Dwayne and Steve running toward him with their guns drawn. In that brief instant Himmler reached further inside his sweatshirt and pulled from beneath the tattered clothing a screwdriver with an eight-inch blade.

When Matt glanced back at his capture, he spied the reflection off what little light the alley offered. Instantly Matt knew it was a potential weapon, and before Himmler could react, Matt lifted his right leg and did a sweeping kick, knocking the tool from Himmler's hand. When Matt's leg landed, he twisted at the waist and followed with a powerful left hook to Himmler's chin.

Dwayne and Steve arrived on the scene in time to see a collapsed Himmler lying in a limp pile. Matt was rubbing his left hand attempting to ward off the pain, hoping he hadn't broken his hand again.

"Why do I always go to the face? I know better," said Matt.

"You okay?" asked Dwayne.

"Yeah," said Matt handing Dwayne the bag of crystal meth. "Didn't exactly go as planned, but it ended the way we hoped, one in custody. This looks pretty good to the naked eye. I'm sure the lab rats will confirm it's the real thing."

The wind whipped up again, and trash began to blow everywhere. Bending over to grab the limp Himmler, Matt said, "Help me get this piece of garbage out of here before we drive down property values."

CHAPTER SEVEN

The emergency room was buzzing with excitement on what should have been a quiet weeknight. Police vehicles flooded the parking lot of the hospital which was permanently half-finished. The Valley medical facility seemed always to be in some type of building project mode. Construction equipment forced most visitors to park at the far end of the lot. Matt and Dwayne maneuvered around the orange cones and construction tape and arrived just as the ambulance pulled into the driveway. The two quickly exited their car. They could hear the loud cries of anguish from inside the ambulance. When the paramedic opened the rear door, Steve Barnett exited first.

"He's been whining ever since he woke up. What a baby, claiming police brutality, wants to sue everyone from the president on down," said Steve. "Of course, when the paramedic turned his head, I guess the fact I cracked his ankle with a clipboard may have enhanced his chances of prevailing in the lawsuit, but you gotta have witnesses to win in court, and I'm not talking."

The two paramedics pulled the gurney from the back of the ambulance, and the folding legs automatically opened. Himmler's left hand was handcuffed to the gurney, and ice packs surrounded the ankle.

As the paramedics wheeled the detained drug dealer past Matt and Dwayne, Himmler spotted Matt. "That was entrapment. You'll never make this stick and I'll have your badge. You had no reason to kick me or hit me. You broke my ankle. You're nothing but savages, all of you. I will own you by the time this is over."

Himmler's whine was almost a blubbering cry.

"Nice try, slick," said Matt. "But I was wired and not on homemade meth. It's all recorded, Bobby, so you might want to re-think your defense."

Himmler screamed obscenities. Dwayne, Steve, and Matt laughed at the blue-streak tirade, "The machine's still running, Bobby. Want to say anything else for the benefit of the jury?"

The automatic double doors opened as the paramedics moved the gurney into the emergency room.

Steve got serious. "You turned off the machine, right? I mean you just didn't record what I told you about whacking his ankle with a clipboard?"

"No, it's off. Wait let me check." Matt reached inside his shirt acting as if he were checking the machine. "Oh, no. I forgot to turn it off."

"Matt, no, please tell me you're kidding. Hey, I was just teasing about hitting his ankle. Really I was just teasing. I meant it as a joke. It was all for show. I would never taunt or injure a prisoner. You know me better than that. I put the highest priority on the rights of the prisoner."

Matt looked serious then broke into a smile. "It was off in the alley after you guys cuffed him."

Steve sighed heavily.

"So did you really crack him on the ankle?"

"Of course."

CHAPTER EIGHT

Once inside the ER, the uniformed law enforcement presence was obvious. Four police officers and two detectives were speaking to a doctor.

"Hate to see this place on a weekend. Seems like a lot of cops for a weeknight," said Matt to Dwayne, who agreed with Matt's observation. "You might want to badge them and check it out. We don't need an incident here if we just happen to have people from rival biker gangs showing up in the ER."

When Matt peered to his left, he saw a familiar face sitting in the waiting room of the main lobby. Philip Mitchell had his eyes closed with his face tilted toward heaven as if in prayer. Matt tapped Dwayne on the arm and pointed toward Flip, as he was called in the office. Flip Mitchell worked in the Special Operations Group, known in the FBI as SOG, the surveillance squad. He was team leader of a six-man unit, given the radio designation the "sixties."

"Flip, what's going on? What brings you here in the middle of the night?" asked Matt.

Flip opened his eyes and looked toward the voice. He stared for a few seconds, trying to come to grips with the situation. When he realized Matt Hogan called his name, he stood up and walked over to Matt and Dwayne.

"It's Lydia. She was shot tonight when her car broke down on Mulholland. The attackers killed a minister she works with. They rushed her into surgery. She's in the recovery room now. She hasn't regained consciousness so we don't have the real story yet."

Matt grabbed Flip and gave him a hug. He didn't say another word, but Flip knew the sincerity of a man who confronted death and evil.

Matt and Dwayne spoke several minutes with Flip before heading to the detectives to see if they could garner more information. The detectives could add little to what Flip told them and were waiting for Lydia to recover. They were hopeful once she awakened she could answer the many questions surrounding the deadly attack.

Matt and Dwayne made a series of phone calls to various FBI personnel. When they returned, Flip was gone from the waiting room and the two set out to find him. After a few minutes of inquiring with various hospital staff, they identified Lydia's room in the intensive care unit. They badged their way past the normal roadblocks to ICU and entered the room quietly.

Flip sat by her side, holding her hand, offering prayers for her recovery. The light from the hallway and the medical equipment hooked up to

Lydia monitoring her condition provided the only illumination in the room. The steady hum of one machine and the intermittent beep of another provided the only noise.

Flip looked up and offered a weak smile. He stood and the three walked out to the hallway.

"The doctors say she should fully recover. Both rounds missed vital organs. Apparently the blood from a blow to the face fooled the attackers into believing she would bleed out if the two shots hadn't already killed her. The doctors said it was a miracle she survived. One round bounced around inside but never severed anything important. The other round grazed her scalp."

There was little Matt and Dwayne could say but platitudes and promises. What they could offer was support. Flip was FBI. He was family and by extension so was his wife. They would wait as long as needed.

"Thanks. I really appreciate your concern, but I've got it covered. Just find out who did this," said Flip, a deepening edge to his voice.

"We'll do everything we can. I promise you that," said Matt.

"I'll liaison with LAPD and keep you informed of their progress. Danny Garcia can keep us updated," said Dwayne.

"I don't want liaison," said Flip flushed with anger. "I want results!"

"I understand what you're saying, but LAPD

Homicide is as good as it gets. Let them do their job. We'll offer whatever assistance we can, but we don't want to interfere," said Dwayne.

"Interfere!" shouted Flip. "This is my wife we're talking about, not some hooker working the bus station on Seventh. Matt, what if this was Caitlin? Would you leave this in the hands of the detectives who gave us OJ?"

"Flip, we're going to do everything we can. Trust me," said Matt.

A nurse approached from her station. "If you can't keep your voices down, I'm going to have to ask all of you to leave."

"We're sorry," said Matt as the three returned to the room. The nurse followed to check vitals.

Just as they entered, Lydia stirred. She opened her eyes and started to speak, but Flip spoke first.

"Honey, it's okay. Don't say a word. The doctors say you are going to be fine."

"How's Ben?"

Flip didn't say anything.

The nurse intervened. "Mrs. Mitchell, you really need your rest. You've been through a lot."

"How's Ben?"

Flip just looked at her.

"Oh God, no! Flip, please tell me he's going to be okay."

Flip shook his head and looked away from his wife. In a whisper he said, "He didn't make it."

Tears flowed from her eyes. There was silence for a prolonged moment. Still in pain, she said slowly, "The Mustang broke down, and Ben stopped to help. It was three men. They dumped something a hundred yards or so from our cars. Then they spotted us and attacked. Flip, it was horrible."

"Honey, please not now. We can talk about this in the morning. You really need to rest."

The nurse intervened. "Mrs. Mitchell, I'm sorry. You need to rest. You have a long recovery ahead, and this isn't going to help."

The nurse pulled two syringes from the tray she was holding. She injected fentanyl and a sedative in the IV line. "This will help with the pain and allow you to relax. I think it best you two leave. She really needs her rest."

Dwayne welcomed the opportunity to escape. "We're sorry. Flip, we'll leave you alone. We'll get back to you as soon as we can."

Dwayne turned and walked out. Flip grabbed Matt by the arm just as Matt moved. "Don't let me down."

"Flip, you've got my word."

"Thanks."

Matt nodded with a reassuring look as he left the room.

MATT AND DWAYNE QUICKLY returned to the detectives still standing in the hallway outside the Emergency Room waiting area and told them of Lydia's observations.

The homicide detectives raced out of the building to their unmarked unit. Once they cleared the hospital grounds, the detectives went "code three," lights and siren. Dwayne and Matt trailed the detectives to the Mulholland location.

CHAPTER NINE

The forensic technicians had almost completed combing the area for any clues as to the identity of the attackers. One technician videotaped the location documenting the crime scene. Unlike a TV drama, they didn't find hair fibers lodged between loose gravel, readily apparent with the magical flashlights so popular in prime-time. No mystical DNA testing would be completed during the commercial break. It was just a cumbersome examination of yet another site which became one more L.A. crime stat.

The detectives questioned the technicians, but so far the evidence game of hide-and-seek was a failure. The heavy mist washed away much of the trace evidence.

Based on Lydia's brief remarks, Matt and

Dwayne walked west on the mountain road. The two detectives walked east. Dwayne took the north side and Matt the south. Each carefully examined the road and the ground below. Matt walked slowly, hoping to find any clue along the two-lane road. Although the illumination truck was helpful for the immediate crime scene, it provided minimal light for the ravines along each side of the road. All four were striking out as they inched along Mulholland.

The answer came about one hundred yards from the scene. Matt spotted loose gravel on the pavement, an obvious sign of a recent disturbance. He looked over the edge and spotted a large object at the bottom of a twenty-foot ravine.

"Hey, I may have something," he shouted.

Dwayne and the detectives rushed over as Matt pointed to the object below. A detective hollered at a patrol officer who ran to the scene. The young officer pointed his Streamlight LED flashlight at the object.

"I think that's a body," said Matt.

Rather than climb directly down the side of the hill, disturbing any potential evidence, the four men walked about twenty yards further and began making their way down the slope. As they moved closer to the object, it became apparent. The situation went from bleak to dismal. The body of a dead girl, her clothes soaked from the rain and her hair matted, lay in the muddy underbrush.

The crime scene just got bigger and the stakes larger. Whoever did this doubled-down with the murder of the minister on the road above.

CHAPTER TEN

Himmler's ankle was badly broken and required surgery, all at taxpayer's expense even though he was a fleeing felon at the time it happened. One of the bones severed an artery and several nerves. The emergency room physician called in a specialist, an orthopedic surgeon, who wanted to operate immediately to avoid permanent damage to the foot. Himmler whined throughout the x-rays and examination. When the word *surgery* was used, he cried like a baby, threatening to sue the FBI, the hospital, the doctors, even the city for failing to maintain the alleys. A little Himmler went a long way, and his actions evoked no sympathy.

Upon completion of the surgery, Himmler was moved to a private room where he would remain under guard until he could be transferred to the prison ward at Terminal Island Federal Prison in Long Beach. Two probationary agents were called in from a solid sleep to perform the guard duties. One agent was stationed outside the room and one inside. They were permitted to change off at any time, but an agent had to remain in the room at all times. Himmler's left hand was shackled to the bed, but with the leg elevated and several pins protruding from the thigh-high brace, it was doubtful Himmler would get very far should he decide to tempt fate a second time and flee.

DANNY GARCIA AND STEVE Barnett headed over to Himmler's rented house in Van Nuys. The two-bedroom, one-bath stucco was badly in need of repairs. Grass may have grown on the front lawn at one time, but a car on cement blocks stunted the growth of everything but weeds. *Better Homes and Gardens* had no plans of making his residence the cover of next month's issue. Himmler was that perfect white-trash neighbor every responsible homeowner craves!

Because the house was a suspected meth lab, FBI agents from the Evidence Response Team, known as ERT, were called to conduct the search. Dressed in protective jumpsuits with self-contained breathing devices, the specially trained agents cleared potentially contaminated venues. A drunk might mistake the team for alien invaders. Three members of the unit worked quickly and efficiently to dismantle the makeshift lab while others conducted a search of the premises. Danny and Steve remained outside drinking more caffeine than they should in the middle of the night.

When Dwayne and Matt arrived on the scene, the search was winding down. They briefed Danny and Steve on the situation with Flip Mitchell's wife, the dead minister, and the deceased girl at the bottom of the ravine. Danny promised to coordinate with the homicide detectives and keep the FBI updated.

"You guys can go if you want," said Dwayne, "Matt and I can finish up. ERT is doing the collection. We can book it in the morning."

Steve and Danny didn't have to be told twice and cleared out before Dwayne changed his mind.

"We'll both be in early to help with the paper," said Danny.

"Speak for yourself, Sergeant. I'll be in when I get in," said Steve with a faint smile.

"Get there when you can. There will be plenty of paper waiting when you arrive," said Dwayne as the two headed to their cars.

"Dwayne, there's a twenty-four-hour doughnut shop a couple blocks north of here. I'm gonna grab some coffee. You want some?" asked Matt.

"Yeah, black."

Matt returned within ten minutes and handed a cup to his supervisor who responded with a subdued "Thanks."

There was an extended silence, and Matt sensed the tension. He assumed he knew the reason and after a few minutes said, "You can't blame Flip for being upset back at the hospital."

"Maybe," said Dwayne taking a sip of the coffee. "But we have no jurisdiction in a murder investigation, and my squad certainly has no investigative right to interfere with LAPD. This is best left to the powers above my pay grade to work it out with homicide. I'm not even Flip's supervisor. He didn't need to jump on my case and start making demands of me."

"Dwayne, that was anger and frustration talking. That wasn't Flip. He's a great guy. Let him cool down. Let's see what Danny can get for us, and if asked, we'll drop everything to help out the cops. He's family and we need to be there for him. Don't judge him based on a conversation in the ER."

"You almost sound like a humanitarian."

"I get soft at 3:00 a.m.," said Matt.

The alien invaders made their way out of the stucco dump site carrying several boxes of evidence.

Jennifer Spencer headed up the ERT unit. "Pretty basic lab. Nothing we haven't seen before. Just your everyday, high school chemistry set . . . jugs, bottles, rubber tubing, Pyrex dishes, cheesecloth, and a propane cylinder."

"I'm always amazed how these guys can barely function in society yet can process a complicated formula into a money machine," said Matt.

"Come on, Matt. Even you can follow directions when you want to," said Jennifer. "It's not that difficult. Just follow the recipe. Of course, if you make a mistake, it can mean death rather than indigestion, but that's all part of the cost of doing business."

Jennifer paused briefly. "Did your boy have a girlfriend?"

"Never talked about one," said Matt.

"We found a closet full of women's clothes," said Jennifer.

"Probably a cross dresser," said Matt trying to get a laugh with weak 3:00 a.m. humor.

Matt signed off on the evidence sheet and took possession of the boxes. He thanked Jennifer and her team for their help and promised to try to call them out at a decent hour the next time.

She smiled. "One day closer to retirement."

IT WAS ALMOST 4:00 a.m. when Matt arrived home. Even though he owed it to Caitlin to shower before climbing into bed, he was too exhausted. He brushed his teeth and stripped off his clothes.

She stirred as he pulled back the covers. "I love you," she said without opening her eyes.

"I love you too."

"How'd it go?"

"Not very well."

She sat up in bed as Matt took a couple of minutes to fill her in on the activities of the evening. Before she allowed Matt to sleep, she grabbed his hands and prayed for Lydia and her family. She promised to look in on the family and offered to take personal days from her teaching assignment if Flip needed someone to watch the children while he spent time at the hospital. . . . It was just another reason Matt Hogan loved the most important person in his life.

CHAPTER ELEVEN

Almost every high-ranking law enforcement administrator in Los Angeles relished his fifteen minutes of fame. L.A. was a media Mecca. Enough exposure meant a cushy six-figure studio security job in retirement, so the wise administrators exploited every opportunity. This morning was a moment for such exploitation even if the circumstances required the event.

The press conference was being held on the steps of City Hall on North Spring Street. It was the perfect photo op, and everyone in attendance knew it. The powerful image of City Hall, a landmark, was depicted on every Los Angeles Police Department badge and was used as a frequent reference when Hollywood wanted to identify downtown L.A.

Today was one of those mornings when even the smog cooperated. All the local news channels were represented. Their microphones were precariously attached to the podium with the call signs clearly visible for the TV audience—free advertising—as if any viewer really cared.

The city's mayor was politically ambitious and constantly sought accolades from the Hollywood media. As he straightened his tie, he stepped to the microphone and began the press conference.

"Ladies and gentlemen, I have asked the chief of police, the chief of detectives, the captain of the Robbery Homicide Division, and representatives from the community to join me. I am deeply saddened to report, last night Mulholland Drive became the scene of the latest violence to plague this great city. The Reverend Benjamin Hobbs of the Baldwin Hills Evangelical Community Church and a member of the Los Angeles Police Commission was murdered, the victim of a brutal beating and subsequent shooting. A second victim survived and witnessed the attack. We are asking for the public's help in identifying another apparent victim of this attack."

An aid to the mayor began circulating photos of the deceased girl. She had no identification on her person and her fingerprints were not on file. The coroner's office cleaned up the body and took a photo of the corpse; the autopsy was scheduled for later in the day. Detectives surmised she might be another Hollywood throwaway and were combing their records for any clue as to her identity.

BOBBY HIMMLER WAS SECURED to the hospital bed, his left hand cuffed to the rail. He was on a pain medication drip and used every opportunity to empty the IV. At the slightest hint of pain, Himmler hit the button, enjoying the pain and the subsequent relief, all at no cost to him.

Dawn Platt, a shapely twenty-something bottle-blonde pushed the cart in front of the door to the hospital room. As she removed the food tray from the table next to his bed, she looked at the patient. *Bobby Himmler.* Since she had been told by her supervisor federal agents were stationed inside and outside the room, she wasn't about to reintroduce herself to her one-time cocaine connection. She spied the left hand cuffed to the rail and smiled. *Guess he won't be slingin' for awhile.* With a tray of dirty dishes in her hand, she walked out without saying a word.

The television monitor lodged in the upper right-hand corner of his room was on, the volume turned up, but only Himmler was paying attention. The FBI agent providing security was engrossed in the latest Vince Flynn novel. When the photo of the unidentified teen flashed on the screen and within seconds the mayor mentioned a reward offered by the city council, a broad smile ran across Himmler's face as he contemplated his "get-out-of-jail-free" card.

"Get me Matt!" he shouted to the probationary agent sitting near the door.

"What?" said the agent startled at Himmler's outburst.

"You heard me, get me Matt or whatever that guy's name is who busted me last night. I want him here now."

"I don't know if that's possible."

"Hey dude, anything's possible. I want that guy here with his supervisor right now, or you'll be guarding J. Edgar's tomb for the rest of your career."

Even handcuffed to a hospital bed, Himmler decided he was now in the driver's seat; he may have been right.

CHAPTER TWELVE

In spite of the fact neither had more than a few hours' sleep, Matt and Dwayne reported on time to the newly built Joint Terrorism Task Force off-site. Located in the San Fernando Valley, the off-site was concealed within an industrial complex, and no one outside official government channels knew the really important work being conducted in this secret location. Every precaution was taken to protect the windowless building from physical as well as electronic intrusion. The interior walls were coated with a newly developed substance deflecting every known surveillance device. Even an attempt to record within the building resulted in the conversations being scrambled unless the appropriate equipment was used. It was state of the art, but that didn't necessarily mean cases were solved any quicker. The members of Dwayne's JTTF squad were street-savvy agents more comfortable with traditional investigative techniques than the devices so cherished by those in the "secret squirrel division," as the criminal agents referred to those who worked foreign counterintelligence. Still it was nice to have all the assets available for the "war on terror." Despite what some politicians might posture, it was more than a bumper sticker slogan to those who worked it.

Matt began the burdensome paperwork requirements from Himmler's arrest. Maybe the old West had it right. In a simpler time the sheriff merely buried the bad guys and avoided the reports. Matt finished the FD-302 of the meeting and subsequent arrest and was preparing the affidavit for the criminal complaint he would be filing later in the afternoon. Himmler was in custody and by law had to see a federal magistrate within twenty-four hours. None of this TV garbage where they hide the criminal in lock-up for several days. The Feds required the hearing and failure to do so not only called for the release of the suspect but opened everyone affiliated with the arrest to a civil lawsuit. Matt wasn't about to subject his condo, car, and personal savings to some attorney seeking damages because Bobby Himmler's precious civil rights were violated.

Steve Barnett agreed to book the evidence, download the recording devices, and see that the crystal meth was processed at the DEA lab. Steve conducted a field test on the substance Matt seized from Himmler, and it was sufficient quality to warrant a successful prosecution. Ironically, under the federal statutes, quantity is much more important than quality. A nearly pure sample of a controlled substance which can be stepped on multiple times carries the same punishment as a weak 1 percent sample of the solution. Himmler's meth wasn't the highest quality, and had Matt been a real street dealer, he may have never gone back for a second helping, but it tested positive for the prohibitive substance, and that's all that mattered for prosecution purposes. Matt enjoyed comparing street-level dealers to Caitlin's cooking. Even when she followed a recipe, he never got the same meal twice.

Dwayne was busy preparing a written briefing for Pamela Clinton, the special agent in charge of the Terrorism Division of the Los Angeles Field Office of the FBI. Known to everyone as the Queen Mother, at least behind her back, she demanded to be updated daily by the supervisors under her command. At least with Himmler's arrest, Dwayne had something to write. Terrorism investigations were not always the fast-breaking type cases a kidnapping or extortion might be. Days may go by with little or no progress and it might take the creative writing skills of a best-selling fiction author to make something out of nothing. As Dwayne was putting his prose to paper, the phone rang.

"Dwayne Washington," he answered and then listened. "Calm down. Okay, we'll be there. Tell him to take a Prozac, and we'll come over as soon as we can."

Just as Dwayne hung up the phone, Matt walked into his office.

"Your BFF is making demands already," said Dwayne.

"My best friend?" asked Matt tossing a copy of the FD-302 in Dwayne's in-basket.

"Himmler is demanding to see us right now, claims it's important."

"Think his morphine drip is about to dry up?" said Matt.

"Not sure but let's head over to the hospital and see what he's got."

As the two walked to the parking lot, Steve Barnett was pulling in.

"I got everything booked and shipped off to the DEA lab," said Steve.

"Thanks," said Matt.

"You guys going to lunch?"

"No, the hospital."

"Can I go with you? I wanted to stop in and see Lydia. Flip and I used to work banks together when anyone in this town cared about bank robberies."

"You're welcome to come, but this isn't a social call," said Dwayne.

"Himmler's whining. He claims he has something important. Probably hard evidence proving your unprovoked assault on his ankle last night in the ambulance," said Matt.

"Maybe I'll just pop my head in his room and wish him well."

The three headed to the hospital with Dwayne driving.

CHAPTER THIRTEEN

Dawn Platt stepped into the restroom hoping Mickey would soon return her call. She looked in the full-length mirror, checking herself before she returned to her hospital duties. She looked good and she knew it. In her mind she always looked good, maybe a little too much makeup, but the men she hung with didn't seem to mind.

The prison psychiatrist called her a narcissist, but what did he know. Her problem wasn't her looks; it was her attraction to the wrong men. She was drawn to the outlaw types—the wilder, the better. She never knew her father. He left months before she was born, but her mother described him as a biker. Her mother said little else about this knight of the open road who ran once responsibility became a reality. Dawn's attraction to the "wild bunch" may have been her attempt to find a man like dear old dad, whoever or wherever he was. She just knew bad men and particularly one bad man, Mickey Donovan, really moved her.

Her employment at the hospital was not of her choosing. Her parole officer made the arrangement. Each day Dawn worked her way through every hospital room on the two floors for which she had responsibility. It was the same thing for each eight-hour shift: deliver the food trays and pick up the food trays. Simple, precise, and boring, but failure to fulfill her duties meant a loss of freedom.

When she reached the end of the hall, she felt her cell phone vibrate. She stepped into the stairwell and pulled the phone from her pocket.

Personal calls during work hours were a strict no-no. It wasn't that the job was so great but she was on a work-release program. If she got fired, her parole would be revoked, and she'd be back at Chowchilla, the Central California Women's Facility. It may not have been as bad as the men's prisons at Pelican Bay or Corcoran, but CCWF was not where she wanted to be.

"Hey, baby, guess who's here?"

"You at the hospital?" asked Mickey.

"Yeah."

"I need something."

"But guess who is here?"

"I'm not into games. I need you to get me something."

"Mickey, don't ask me to get any drugs again. They keep that all pretty locked up."

"No stupid, I need some information. They brought in some woman last night who got shot on Mulholland. A preacher who was with her got killed. See what you can find out about that."

"I'll try. But you'll never guess who's here?"

"Who?"

"Bobby Himmler. The Feds are guarding him. He's got a busted ankle with all kinds of pins sticking out. It looks real bad, but Mr. Sunshine is on a drip so he's not feeling any pain."

"How long has he been there?"

"I don't know. I was off the last two days."

"Can you find out when the Feds got him and what he did?"

"I don't know. I can ask. Not sure anyone will tell me."

"Pull the chart. The medical files might have something."

"You're asking a lot, baby. I have to be careful. If I screw up here, I'll end up back in prison."

"Hey, Nike it!"

"Huh?" asked a confused Dawn.

"Just do it!"

"Okay, I'll try. I better go. I love you."

Mickey didn't respond.

"I said I love you."

"Yeah, baby, whatever, just get me the info."

It was not the response she was hoping to hear.

Dawn left the cart parked in the hallway and retreated to the outdoor patio where smoking was allowed. She reached into her pocket, pulled out the pack of Marlboro Lights, and removed a cigarette. Her mind was still on the conversation with Mickey Donovan.

She loved Mickey but wasn't certain he would ever commit. Dawn thought about what she brought to the table . . . a great body. But it was accompanied by a felony rap sheet and at least, for now, a minimum-wage job to satisfy the conditions of her release. The only real skills she thought she had were in bed. She wasn't quite a high-line hooker working the Beverly Hills escort trade, but she made decent money in the downtown luxury bars. She never told her biker boyfriend how she supported herself. He probably suspected but cared so little he never inquired.

Mickey was bad, but he was also a "bad actor" as he liked to joke. He had his SAG card and appeared in a couple of biker movies which went straight to DVD. He hoped someday to make it in Hollywood, but his bad-boy good looks would only take him so far. If he had any talent, he might have a shot, but usually his lines were limited to dropping a few f-bombs in crowd scenes.

Dawn, however, believed in him and thought if he devoted more time to acting and less time to acting the stooge for Boris Gregorian he could succeed. She was ready to commit, even settle down and marry. She loved Mickey, maybe the first man she ever loved. She slept with hundreds but always for money. With Mickey it was love. How could she ever convince him? She had to give him more than a good time. She had to be there when he needed her, and now he needed her. He gave her a mission. Maybe if she got the information, Mickey would see how much she really loved him. She was ready to risk a trip back to prison just to accommodate the man she loved.

In her mind she rehearsed the plan. After finishing the cigarette and tamping it out in the metal ashtray, she unbuttoned the top two buttons on her blouse and returned to the hallway.

CHAPTER FOURTEEN

Dawn headed toward Himmler's room pushing the cart loaded with dirty trays. She stopped in front of the newly minted FBI agent guarding the door. "Can I get you and your partner some food? We have extra meals we're just going to throw away. There's no sense letting it go to waste."

"I think we're okay," said the probationary agent trying to act official but appreciating interest from the blonde.

"Seems like a waste of food. I tasted today's lunch. It's pretty good. The food really isn't that bad for hospital food. Let me get you something."

"No, we're fine."

"Why not ask your partner? He may want something. Wait, I've got a better idea, why not just let me bring you two trays? My dad used to be a cop. I know you don't get paid much so I'd hate for you to pass up a freebie."

She gave him a seductive smile when she said "freebie," tilting her head in such a way no man would question her intent.

"Well . . ."

"You guys detectives with North Hollywood?"

"No, FBI."

She purposely bent over to rearrange some trays on the lower shelves of the cart. She knew exactly what she was doing, and even if the rookie agent had a clue as to her motives, he appreciated the move. She was good.

"FBI, wow!" She said as she slowly rose, still bent at the waist. "My dad always wanted to be an FBI agent. He said you guys were the best and the smartest. It must be really cool to be a Fed. You have to be so proud. Not everyone can be an FBI agent. So this guy in the bed isn't some ordinary crook, huh? He must be big time. I didn't pay much attention when I went in to get his tray. He didn't look like some mob boss or anything. He's not a terrorist, is he? I know you guys work those terrorism cases, the really important stuff."

"No, he's just a drug dealer who got caught last night."

"Last night? I guess they were pretty busy here last night."

"Yeah, that's what I heard. They just called me in for this."

"You must be SWAT or something if they've got you watching a prisoner. Was this guy with that woman who got shot? That was horrible. It was all over the news. Some preacher got killed too. Was this all part of the same case?"

"No, that was something different."

"I can't believe somebody would kill a minister." Then pointing upward, "You're messing with the man upstairs when you do something like that, know what I'm saying?"

"Yeah, God can't be too happy."

"I should say not. The woman's in this hospital too, you know."

"Yeah," said the agent, not realizing he was being played.

"Are the two cases related?"

"No, she's the wife of an FBI agent," said the agent enjoying the attention and the exchange.

"No way, really? The woman who was with the minister is an FBI agent's wife?"

"Yes."

"I'd hate to be the guy who pulled that trigger. You're messing with the big boys now. You're messing with the G-men," she smiled. "I saw *Public Enemy*. That was a good movie. So do you have any idea who shot the woman?"

"We're not really sure."

"I hope you find the guy who did it. So what happened to this guy's leg in here? Looks like it must be pretty painful. I know the Feds aren't real bad like the local cops. You don't beat guys up. You didn't beat him up did you? My dad said you were the best. Always fair."

"No, we didn't beat him up. He broke his ankle running from an undercover deal."

"A drug deal?"

"Yeah."

Dawn started laughing. "No fooling?"

The agent nodded.

"Anybody should know you can't run from the Feds. Good job. Anybody who deals drugs needs to go away for a long time. Thanks for keeping us safe. Let me go get you guys two meals, and I'll try to find some extra desserts. You deserve it for getting scum like that off the street. That's some dangerous work. Glad it was him who got hurt and not one of you guys."

CHAPTER FIFTEEN

Matt, Dwayne, and Steve arrived at the hospital in short order and parked near the entrance in a "law enforcement only" section of the lot. Dwayne hung his microphone over the rearview mirror and threw an FBI Supervisor placard in the windshield.

"I need one of those for my personal car," said Matt. "I always seem to run out of quarters when I park on the street."

"Ever hear 'rank has its privilege'?" asked Dwayne.

"You mean I'd have to attend all those supervisory committee meetings just to get free parking?"

"You got it, big guy," answered Dwayne.

"Forgetaboutit," said Matt, doing his best Tony Soprano imitation.

As they approached, the automatic doors to the hospital entrance opened as if welcoming royalty to the medical establishment. "Bet the Queen Mother wishes she could install these in her office," said Steve.

"I think it's in next year's budget," said Matt.

In the squad bay they were known as "Christmas help," high ranking administrators who cared little about the mission or the people, only their advancement. They came and went with increasing frequency as soon as openings at headquarters or the larger offices became available. Unfortunately for the agents in Los Angeles, SAC Pamela Clinton, the Queen Mother, stayed well beyond the holiday rush. She was as by-the-book as anyone in the Bureau. She attempted to preside over her minions with an iron fist, but most of the street agents ignored her directives and managed to solve cases in spite of her obstacle-laden policies. She micromanaged even the minutia. Her finger-prints were all over every operation until it went south; then somehow she miraculously managed to extricate herself from a paper trail leading to her office. Fortunately for her, democracy had no place inside the FBI. She had no shot at an elected position. She irritated nearly everyone in and out of the Bureau. Her management theory was to avoid confrontation, follow all regulations, and take no risks. It served her well. Why mess with success? She was number two in the pecking order of the second largest field office in the FBI. Her meteoric rise within the Bureau was legendary. A slot at headquarters awaited, and every agent in L.A. hoped to expedite the next promotion.

"Did you tell her about last night?" asked Matt turning to Dwayne.

"Not yet. She's in Santa Barbara at some conference and isn't scheduled back until later this afternoon."

"Don't you read her all-agent e-mails?" said Steve.

Matt snapped his fingers. "You're absolutely right. I forgot all about that. I even marked it in my day planner. Funny how something as important as her travel schedule slipped my mind."

"You might want to check with Caitlin, but from everything I read, Christianity is supposed to include a more compassionate spirit," said Dwayne.

"She's mentioned it a couple of times. It just doesn't seem to be taking."

They walked past the information desk and headed toward the elevators. Dwayne pressed the elevator button, the doors opened, and the three entered, making their way toward the fourth floor.

"Hard to believe we're housing an FBI agent's wife and pond scum in the same medical facility," said Steve.

Dwayne nodded. "I need to check with the doctor and see if we can't get Himmler transferred to Terminal Island or at least to County. These nurses shouldn't have to put up with him."

"Oh, but he is a child of God, a holy creation," said Matt with a smile.

"Maybe Caitlin is wearing you down," said Dwayne.

As they exited the elevator, Dwayne said, "Let's check in with the nurses first."

"Why, they got a cute one working the day shift?" asked Steve.

"Not that I know of. I just want to get the 4-1-1 on our patient before I have to spend the rest of the afternoon with Hitler's love child."

To the surprise of all three and especially Steve, the shift nurse looked like Lucy Liu, a real live *Charlie's Angel*. Steve gave Matt an impish grin and decided it was important to spend extra time learning all about the medical prognosis of Himmler. Dwayne and Matt listened politely as Steve conjured up questions. Finally, with Matt giving him the practiced death stare he perfected for his undercover assignments, Steve took the hint. He started to excuse himself but then looked at Matt and with a command voice said, "You guys check on our prisoner. I'll finish up here."

Steve continued to feign interest in all things medical.

CHAPTER SIXTEEN

As they walked to Himmler's room, a smiling Dwayne Washington said, "Wow! Nurses who look like that almost make a prolonged hospital stay worthwhile. We might have to keep Himmler here a lot longer than I originally planned."

The probationary agent seated outside Himmler's room recognized Dwayne and jumped to a semi-rigid attention when the two approached. Matt stifled a laugh.

"Good afternoon, Mr. Washington," said the young agent.

"Good afternoon," said Dwayne cautiously. "How long you been out of the academy?"

"Three weeks, sir."

"What'd you do before you came in?"

"Law school, sir. I came in right after I graduated."

"Well, call me Dwayne and save the sirs for the ADIC when you're really in trouble. When that time comes, and it will if you're doing your job, ask this guy. He's on OPR's Favorite Hits list. His personnel file is multivolume. This is Matt Hogan, and he's actually a case study at Quantico's management training program," said Dwayne as he extended his hand.

"I'm Gavin James."

"Welcome to the FBI and Los Angeles, Gavin. But relax, it's a long ride to retirement. I understand our boy's been asking for us."

"Yes, sir, he has."

Matt also shook hands and followed Dwayne into Himmler's room. A second agent was sitting in a chair next to the window. Before the agents could say anything, Himmler said, "It's about time. Man, I'm gonna make you guys heroes."

Dwayne looked at the young agent who said, "He's been whining ever since the noon news came on. Claims he's going to get the reward the city council is offering."

"That's right," said Himmler. "I got all the answers."

Dwayne turned to the probationary agent. "Matt and I will handle this. Why don't you guys go grab some lunch. I'll get you on your cell phone when we're ready to leave."

"Sounds great. Thanks," said the agent as he left the room.

"Get out your notebooks; I'm ready to spill my guts . . . if the price is right," said Himmler pausing then asking, "Matt, is that your real name?"

"Yeah, it's Matt."

"Well, Matt, you did a great job. You fooled me. I thought you were one of us. It is a pleasure to be fooled by a professional. Couple times the cops tried to run somebody in on me and I smelled it," said Himmler.

"So I passed the smell test."

"Yeah, you did," said Himmler smiling.

"I guess that's a compliment," said Matt nodding his head slightly, a smirk beginning to erupt on his face.

"Oh yeah, I mean it. You were good."

"Thanks."

Dwayne interrupted, "If we could get beyond the accolades. You got something for us?"

Himmler lit up like a Christmas tree. "That I do, that I do. Saw the news. Saw the mayor right there on the noon news." Himmler pointed to his

TV. "Saw him say they were offering some big reward for information, how'd he say 'leading to the arrest and conviction' of the people responsible for a killing last night of some minister and an unidentified girl. Something also about a witness still alive. I figured that makes what I got important to you guys."

Dwayne said nothing.

"Get to the point, Bobby," said Matt.

"I know the girl."

"What girl?"

"The one they showed on the news."

"And do you have a name for this girl?"

"She goes by Crystal but her real name's Annika."

Dwayne gave Himmler a noncommittal look waiting for an answer.

"Annika what?" asked Matt.

"I don't have a last name. She worked on the Boulevard."

"You mean a hooker?"

"Not really a walker. She was a stripper at the Russian Veil, Boris Gregorian's spot."

"And you know this how?" said Matt.

"My cousin and I hang out there all the time, bikers and bad guys dropping a lot of coin in the back room. Cheap beer and dirty women, know what I mean? Most of them girls are Russian, maybe Ukrainian. They all come from those commie countries over there. It's a pretty sophisticated setup."

"Sophisticated, that's a big word, Bobby," said Matt.

Himmler smiled, "It may be a big word, but I know it means big bucks for me. Where do I sign up for my prize money?"

"You're jumping some major hurdles," said Matt. "It's a long way to payday if that's all you've got."

"Really?" said Himmler almost incredulous his information didn't rate city council's largess. The smile drained from his face, and his demeanor changed in an instant.

"You didn't really believe this is all you have to do to collect?" asked Matt.

Himmler was quiet for a few seconds. He furrowed his brow and then said, "She's not the first to die."

CHAPTER SEVENTEEN

Although Matt and Dwayne were listening to Bobby Himmler, he now had their full attention.

"What do you mean she's not the first?" asked Dwayne.

"She's not the first girl to bite it. Rumors have it several have been off'd when they crossed Boris or his crew."

"Boris has a crew?"

"Yeah, my cousin Jesse's done some things with him."

"What kind of things?" asked Matt still hovering over the reclined Himmler so there was no mistaking who maintained the power position.

"You know, things . . . runnin' girls, weapons, drugs, anything, man. If you're looking for a piece, Boris is the man to see. He's like a jack of all crime."

Matt laughed, "I like that . . . so Boris moves guns?"

"About six months ago, Boris got Jesse a whole crate of AK-47s and a box of handguns. At least I think they were 47s. They might have been something else. I'm not into guns like Jesse is. They looked like those things I see them Arabs pumping over their heads when they're burning the American flag. I do know they were like mint condition fresh off the assembly line."

"What kind of handguns?" asked Dwayne.

"Some kind of autos, short, not real long. It could easily hide in a pocket."

"You mean like a Saturday night special?"

"No, these were well built. Not some cheap thing you get off Alvarado from the Mexicans. I picked up one Jesse had and looked at it. It was about six inches long. It was pretty nice. I think Jesse said they were made in Russia. I almost asked Jesse for one but then changed my mind."

"Does Jesse still have them?"

"I think he's got one or two of the 47s. He sold most of them to some guys with the MS-13. They said they were shippin' 'em down south to Salvador or Guatemala. That's where their homies are. Jesse made a chunk of folding money on that deal."

"What about the autos?"

"He may have some. I really don't know. I'm not into guns. You should know that, Matt. I didn't have one last night. I know throwing a gun into the mix causes more problems than it's worth. If it's a rip, I figure give 'em the drugs. I can always make another batch. If it's the cops, it means more years. I've got priors. The gun means another count and amps it up on sentencing. I'm innocent of that charge."

"Right, Bobby, you're innocent," said Matt with about as much veracity as a criminal defense attorney at a press conference.

"So how'd you know Annika or Crystal?"

"I dropped a lot of coin on her one evening, like multiple lap dances. She was something else, just beautiful and a really good dancer."

Matt laughed out loud.

"What?" said Himmler.

"A really good dancer, you mean like the Bolshoi Ballet?"

"The what? . . . No, not ballet. You mean you've never had a lap dance? She was good, and

I do mean very good. So I sprang for the whole enchilada. Know what I'm saying?"

"Yeah, Bobby. I think Dwayne and I are following this love story."

"That's when she told me her real name was Annika. She said I couldn't tell anyone, especially Boris. He didn't want the girls telling too much about their selves, especially their real names."

"You got any more? Where she was from? How long she had been here? How'd she get to the States?" asked Matt.

"If I wanted some geography lesson, I would've watched the Travel Channel. I had other things on my mind. But Annika's her real name. I'm sure of it. That's gotta be worth something."

"Why do you think Boris had anything to do with her death?"

"Man, things just happen to people who hang around Boris, especially people who cross him. Annika wanted out. She told me that and even asked me if I could help her."

"And did you help her?"

"No, what was I gonna do, fly her back to Russia in my private jet? I told Jesse she was looking to leave."

"Why would you do that?"

"Cause Jesse's got all kinds of connections. I figured he'd know someone who could help.

Listen, I liked her. I figured if I could help I wouldn't have to pay the next time, know what I'm saying?"

"And did Jesse help?"

"No, the next thing I know she shows up on the news."

"So this just happened."

"Yeah, just the other night. That's why I figured Boris is behind it. I don't have nothing specific. But like I said she ain't the first who worked there to disappear."

"Maybe they just moved on," said Dwayne.

"Yeah, maybe so," said Bobby but without much conviction, defeat falling across his face.

Dwayne sensed Bobby was already regretting the attempt to bargain his way out of prison. Dwayne hesitated but only for an instant. "Can you get us in?"

"Sure, pay the cover charge and go through the front door."

"You know what we mean."

"You mean make an intro?" asked Himmler.

"Yeah," said Dwayne.

"I don't know. That's a rough crowd. Matt could just walk in and see what it's all about."

"But you know it's more than that. It could take months for me to catch on. You can make it happen a lot sooner," said Matt.

"Besides, the crowd at the Russian Veil can't be any rougher than the old gang in prison.

Which by the way will be a life stint; this is your third strike," said Dwayne.

There was a prolonged silence. Himmler knew the consequences of this latest arrest. He knew if the DA or the Feds pressed he was looking at life.

Matt was skilled at working the silence and with perfect timing said, "Why go to the pen when you can send a friend."

Himmler broke out into a big grin. "Yeah, I can make the intro. Kind of a shame this sap minister's death is my get-out-of-jail-free card. Nobody'd care if it was just the girl."

"Yeah, it's a real shame, Bobby," said Matt.

"And I can still get the money?"

"Apples and oranges, my friend. Agree to intro me, and you get out of jail. Find the killers and you get the money."

Himmler started to raise his left hand. The handcuffs clanged against the metal bed railing. "When do these come off?"

"Once we know you can put this together," said Dwayne.

"I'm eHarmoney.com," said a grinning Bobby Himmler.

Just then Dawn Platt walked in with two food trays. "Excuse me, you see the guy sitting out here? I told him I'd get him and his partner meals. He's not around."

Dwayne said, "They went to lunch. Thanks for

bringing the meals but they're covered now. You can take them back."

"Wait," said Bobby.

Dawn hesitated, afraid he recognized her.

"Leave one of them for me. I just got my appetite back."

She smiled, left a tray, and walked out of the room.

Bobby tucked a paper napkin into his hospital gown, lifted the cover on the plate, and grabbed at the fish sandwich removing the top half of the bun. He searched around the plate.

"Do you see any mayonnaise?" he asked.

"Yeah," said Matt pointing to a small packet off to the side of the plate.

Bobby took the pickle and tomato off the fish. Holding it up he said, "You guys want these?"

Both Matt and Dwayne shook their heads, as much in disgust as a negative response to his question.

Bobby picked up the mayo packet, ripped it open with his teeth, and spread it on the fish. Replacing the top half of the bun, he grabbed the sandwich with his free hand and took a bite. He began chewing with his mouth open, juices and mayo running down the corners of his mouth. Himmler wasn't exactly that perfect dinner companion, but it looked as though Matt may have found a date for the next big dance.

Matt shook his head in disbelief.

"What?" said Bobby, food spitting past his lips.

"Who knows you got popped last night?" asked Matt.

"Nobody. I didn't make any calls. Your Gestapo guards saw to that."

"What about the product? Was that yours, or did you pick it up off the street?" asked Matt.

"Shouldn't you be reading me my rights or something?"

"Not if you're looking to go home before the sun sets," said Matt.

"Okay. I cooked it myself. Nobody even knows I was dealing with you. My old lady knows I was doing something late, but she didn't know who or when."

"Your old lady? I thought you were in love with Annika," said Matt.

It was Bobby's turn to smile. "Now we're talking apples and oranges."

"Is this other significant other gonna wonder where you are?" asked Matt.

"Hey, it's not like we're married. We got what you might call an open relationship. She works the streets, and she lets me seek the company of others when the mood strikes."

"Sounds like the perfect yin and yang match," said Matt dripping with sarcasm. Matt then looked at Dwayne. "What do you think?"

"I think I can sell it to the bosses."

CHAPTER EIGHTEEN

When Matt and Dwayne stopped at the nurses station, Steve was still working it with Lucy Liu.

"Boss, we need to go," said Matt in a businesslike manner mustering more respect than he often showed real administrators.

"Thanks, men. Were you able to get those issues resolved?" said Steve.

"Yes, sir. It was just like you predicted. As usual you were spot-on. I don't know how you do it each and every time. I guess that's why they put you in charge," said Matt gushing with admiration.

Steve nodded with authority as he handed the nurse his business card and took her phone number.

As they entered the elevators, Matt said to Steve, "The director would be proud of how you are reaching out to our community."

"Protect and serve," said Steve.

"That's LAPD. Our motto is Fidelity, Bravery, Integrity," said Matt.

Dwayne added, "With an emphasis on integrity."

"Whatever," said Steve.

The three exited the elevator on the second floor and headed toward ICU. The waiting room outside the intensive care unit was crowded with concerned family members of the patients behind the double doors. They were hoping for miracles. Some were praying, others crying, still others sleeping. All exhausted from the vigil.

Flip Mitchell wasn't among those waiting. The doors to the unit were secured, and only a limited number of visitors were allowed admission. Steve picked up the phone to call the nurses station.

Matt and Dwayne walked over to the window away from the families and looked out across the parking lot.

Matt said, "This is one place I don't want to spend much time."

"Yeah, hard to live without hope. Glad I worship a God of miracles."

Matt nodded but was ready to change the conversation. "Did you catch Bobby's comment that during the press conference they mentioned a witness?"

"Yeah, I'm not sure that was the wisest move. I'll check on it when we get back to the office."

"Someone might be looking to eliminate witnesses."

Dwayne nodded then said, "Is there any doubt in your mind Boris is connected to all this?"

Matt shook his head. "No, maybe if one person

threw Annika into the ravine, it might have been the next generation of the Hillside Strangler, but three goons in a pickup sound more like biker bar clientele. The fact Lydia wasn't raped makes it sound more like a contract dump than a drunken frat party train wreck."

"Most frat boys or perverts aren't packing either."

"Dwayne, it's too much of a coincidence Annika dies after telling Bobby she wants out and Bobby tells Jesse, the same Jesse who bought automatic weapons from Boris, the owner of the strip club where she worked."

"I'm not a big believer in coincidence."

"Caitlin says it's God being anonymous," said Matt nodding with assurance. "We need to take a hard look at the Russian Veil if we're going to solve who's behind a double homicide and the attack on Flip's wife."

Steve joined the two. "Lydia is asleep. The nurse said Flip went to LAX to pick up her mother who is flying in from Nashville to take care of the kids."

"Did the nurse say how Lydia was doing?" asked Dwayne as the three walked to the elevator.

"She gave me the patient confidentiality speech, but when I said I was the acting assistant special agent in charge of the terrorism division at the FBI and Flip worked for me, she said

Lydia is doing better and should be out of ICU by the end of the week."

"You do realize it's a federal crime to impersonate an FBI administrator?" asked Dwayne.

"Really? Who ever brags about being a bureaucrat?" responded Steve.

"Yeah, Dwayne, Steve's right. It's tough to even get free drinks at a bar when you say you're a Bureau hump. They only comp street agents."

"It shouldn't be a crime to dumb down your law enforcement credentials," said Steve with a look of innocence Dwayne almost believed.

CHAPTER NINETEEN

As Matt and Dwayne were walking to Jason Barnes's office, Matt said, "If I can get him alone, I know I can convince him. He understands the Marine Corps brotherhood. Flip's still in the Reserves. He did a combat tour in Iraq during the initial run up to Baghdad. The boss will approve it just because of that bond."

"You guys and your oorah. How many Marines are in this office?" said Dwayne.

"Enough to make a difference," said Matt with a confident smile. "We need to beat Clinton in there. Give me five minutes, and I can sell the undercover operation."

Kathryn Wilson was the gatekeeper to the office of Jason Barnes, the assistant director in charge, the man who ran the Los Angeles Field Office of the FBI. The always neatly dressed lady with shoulder-length gray hair guarded the ADIC's office like a pit bull with pups. No one crossed the threshold of Jason Barnes's doorway without her permission, and no one dared challenge her resolve to protect her boss. At sixty-three she was nearing retirement but enjoyed every day being privy to some of the nation's most secret investigations. Although never a street agent, she believed herself to be as much a part of the team as any investigator. In reality she was. She was a respected member of the FBI family, loved by many but feared by more.

"Well, if it isn't Frick and Frack," said Kathryn as Matt and Dwayne entered the large waiting room outside the ADIC's office. "I assume you've come to seek permission to impose mischief on society."

Matt smiled. "Something like that."

"He's expecting us," said Dwayne.

She laughed.

"What?" asked Matt.

"I wondered why Clinton came running in here. She must have heard you were in route."

"Nuts," said Matt.

"Your five minutes just got cut in half," said Dwayne.

Kathryn nodded toward the door, giving her approval for the two to proceed. She turned serious as Matt and Dwayne were about to enter the office. "Any word on Flip's wife?"

"We just came from the hospital. She's still in ICU. We didn't get to see her, but I just got off the phone with Flip. She's doing better," said Matt. "The doctors say she will fully recover from the wounds. It's just a matter of time. Fortunately none of the rounds struck a vital organ. At this point it's more emotional and psychological than physical."

Kathryn shook her head slowly. "Poor girl, I guess in our line of work we should never be shocked by man's inhumanity. We see it more than most, but how terrible to observe evil right in front of your eyes."

Both nodded in agreement.

Matt wasn't desensitized to violence and evil. He lived with it every day. It became a part of him, the part he didn't want the outside world to see. Caitlin was his tether to a parallel universe, and their relationship was his reward for surviving another day.

SPECIAL AGENT IN CHARGE Pamela Clinton remained seated, but Jason Barnes rose as Matt and Dwayne entered his office.

"Gentlemen," said the assistant director in charge.

"You don't really mean that do you, boss?" said Matt.

"No," said Jason Barnes. "It's one of those polite tools they teach us at ADIC school. Try to make the agent feel like a gentleman, and maybe he'll act like one."

"I guess in theory it makes sense."

Pamela Clinton gave Matt one of her frequent glares which conveyed her thoughts: *How dare you speak to an ADIC with such informality.* Clinton possessed a huge ego and wore it well. She and Matt were like fire and ice, a battle of personalities; he had one, she didn't.

"Good afternoon, Pamela," said Matt with the hint of smirk hoping to goad her before the meeting even began.

Dwayne and Pamela exchanged pleasantries, but she ignored Matt. A slight Matt noticed causing a smile on his less than cherub face as he sat in the chair to the left of the ADIC's desk.

Dwayne provided a detailed briefing on the investigation to date and laid out the undercover scenario using Bobby Himmler as an informant who could introduce Matt into Himmler's circle of friends.

The ADIC listened intently, his eyes revealing nothing.

"You think you can pull it off?" asked Jason Barnes.

"You mean playing a racist with my wannabe

neo-Nazi informant and getting paid to drop an occasional racial slur at convenient times? Not a problem," said Matt.

Pamela Clinton glared, and Matt knew he was succeeding at irritating the Queen Mother. "Maybe you should be reminded every word you utter will be recorded. We don't need a Mark Furman–OJ situation in this division."

Matt wouldn't give Clinton the satisfaction of directly responding to her comment. He looked at the ADIC, "Don't worry, I'll shut off the tape before I drop the n-word."

Dwayne just shook his head as Clinton let out a disgusted moan. She had a unique way of inserting herself into every issue until it came time to be decisive. Then her silence was deafening.

"Hey, I've been at this long enough to know what I can get away with. I'll talk like my grandmother is gonna be on the jury."

"I thought she died two months ago, or at least that's what you said when you wanted the afternoon off," said Dwayne trying to defuse the budding tension.

"Oh yeah, that's right," said a smiling Matt Hogan. "She did, but her spirit still haunts me so I'll watch my mouth."

Pamela Clinton brushed a hair behind her ear and said, "I'm not so sure this should be worked out of my division. We have no proof Himmler has any neo-Nazi connections. He has not been on any intelligence briefing crossing my desk. I see no domestic terrorism allegations. This is a drug investigation more suited for the DEA or our organized crime division."

"You didn't have a problem signing off on the buy the other night," said Matt.

"That's because that piece of fiction you prepared assured me you would get Himmler to admit his involvement in neo-Nazi activities. As I understand it, he made no such admissions during the buy."

Matt gathered himself, took a breath, and answered in a calm tone, "No, but last night he ran, and just now in the hospital, he told us his cousin Jesse is buying weapons from Boris Gregorian and selling them to MS-13."

"Then I suggest we pass this off to ATF or again to our organized crime division."

Matt shook his head in disbelief. The two locked horns with increasing frequency, and Matt acknowledged he seldom tried to stay above the fray, but this wasn't an argument over some administrative directive from headquarters. It wasn't in his character to back down from bureaucrats for whom he had little if any respect. The rage loomed but he maintained control. His voice intensified, this side of anger. "Pamela, Flip Mitchell's wife was shot twice by the same people who killed a prominent African-American minister who also happened to be a member of the Los Angeles Police Commission. These same shooters dumped the body of a Ukrainian girl we now believe to be working an international prostitution ring, in all likelihood smuggled into this country, maybe even against her will. All of this ties into a man we believe to be supplying weapons, directly or indirectly, to MS-13, a group as dangerous as any terrorism organization we have in this country. And your only response is to pass this off to another agency."

Clinton leaned back in her chair, crossed her legs, and folded her hands on her lap. "I think you summed it up quite well. Nothing you said requires my division to work the case. I haven't heard any allegations of foreign or domestic terrorism. But I have heard gangs, organized crime, prostitution, guns, and drugs. Thanks for making my case."

Matt started to say something, but Jason Barnes held up his hand. "Enough. Pamela, you make sense. Your arguments are noted, and thank you for pointing out the administrative issues."

She smiled, nodding.

"But . . ."

Pamela Clinton's smile faded, and the nodding stopped, her glare now aimed at the ADIC.

"The most important thing Matt said was Flip Mitchell's wife. This is a family issue. We will not farm it out to another agency. Matt is in your division. He brought this case to you. You opened it based on his memo, however craftily written. We aren't passing it to another division. Matt will work it off Dwayne's squad. You will manage it, and we will move to resolve the matter. Dwayne, do you have an issue with what I've said?"

"No boss. I'm onboard."

"Good. Let's move expeditiously on this," said Jason Barnes. "I can get the approvals through headquarters. This is family we're talking about. I want this city to know you don't attack an FBI agent's wife, even if you don't know it, and expect to walk away. I want these guys. So do it right and do it quickly."

"Got it, boss," said Dwayne.

"Pamela, I'll expect you to give me daily updates on this and give these two all the support they need," said the ADIC in the command voice he developed while in the Marines Corps.

She merely nodded in agreement without saying another word.

With that the boss rose from behind his desk, and everyone knew the meeting was over. *Semper Fi.*

CHAPTER TWENTY

Matt spent the rest of the afternoon completing the paperwork for the Himmler buy. Since it looked like Bobby was getting a walk, Matt stopped working on the complaint affidavit even though it was almost complete. He contacted Abby Briones, an FBI analyst assigned to the JTTF. Abby could perform miracles with a computer when it came to discovering information on the Internet: criminal records, credit and property reports, LEXUS/NEXUS, offshore accounts. If the information was somewhere in cyberspace, she could retrieve it. Matt ordered up profiles on Boris, Jesse, and just to be safe, Bobby.

Before heading home, Matt made a quick stop at the hospital; a new set of probationary agents guarded Himmler. He spoke to the agent outside the room. "How's our patient?"

"He's quiet now. I think the morphine drip kicked in. He may be asleep."

"Sorry to ruin it for you, but I need him to sign some papers."

The young agent shrugged his shoulders. He had hallway duty, so even if Matt awakened Himmler, it wouldn't impact the assignment, more suited to a sixth grader monitoring hall passes at the local elementary school.

Matt walked into the darkened room and nodded to the other agent who smiled.

Matt whispered, "I hate to do this to you, but I have to wake him."

Matt took two steps to the bed, grabbed the railing, gently shook it, and whispered in Himmler's ear, "Earthquake."

Himmler jumped and, when he attempted to sit up in bed, was thrown back down because his hand was cuffed to the railing.

"Oh, my leg, my leg!" he screamed, exaggerating any actual pain.

"Shut up. I need you to sign some papers."

Himmler moaned and reached for the morphine drip. "I'm not signing nothing."

"You want to go home?"

"Yeah."

"Then you sign the papers. Otherwise we file tomorrow. You go into the system, and your value to us is zilch. I need you to sign a waiver of your right to a magistrate hearing. Normally we have the hearing within twenty-four hours. By you waiving it, we can keep you here for a couple of days, and then when the doctor releases you, you get to go home."

"The doctor says I may be able to go home tomorrow or the day after."

"Great. Sign the paper, and you're out of here when the doc says so."

"And what if I don't? Maybe I want my constitutional rights. Maybe I want an attorney to review all of this before I sign anything."

Matt looked at the probationary agent and shook his head. "I bet they didn't teach you about guys like this at the academy. See, Bobby here is now a judicial genius. But it didn't come easy. Oh, he knew his alphabet, just not in order. Then he got educated. He was schooled at the Legal Institute of San Quentin where he trained for what was it, Bobby, four years?"

"Five and it was Pelican Bay."

"So after five years of sitting at the feet of some of the finest jailhouse lawyers our penal system detains, Bobby thinks he can play me."

Matt pulled out a second document, the incomplete multipage affidavit with Himmler's name in the caption. It was a complaint, charging him with three counts of manufacturing, possessing, and distributing a controlled substance in violation of 21 USC 841. Matt handed both documents to Himmler.

"Sign the one page and walk; otherwise keep the paperback version of my next book detailing your final days as a free man. If I have to file the affidavit, they will be pumping daylight into you for the next three decades, you understand. On this issue I'm pro-choice and it's your choice. I'm like those late night infomercials, Bobby. . . .

This is a limited-time offer. The clock is ticking . . . tick, tick, tick."

Matt flashed a smile that faded as fast as it appeared. Then he handed Himmler a pen. Bobby hesitated but only for an instant. He signed the waiver and handed both documents back to Matt.

"Wise choice. These guys will let me know when you get released. Then we start to work."

CHAPTER TWENTY-ONE

It had been a week since Bobby Himmler's buy-bust. He'd been out of the hospital for three days, was on crutches, and wearing a thigh-high brace.

He fumbled trying to maneuver his leg out of the cab of the pickup and dropped a crutch as he pulled the pair from behind the front seat. Matt, the lackluster humanitarian, wasn't exactly racing around from the driver's side to assist the handicapped informant. When Himmler finally exited the truck, the two headed to the entrance of the Chinese Gardens, a restaurant located on Roscoe Boulevard in the heart of Los Angeles' San Fernando Valley.

As they were about to enter, Matt spied a large health department "B" in the window near the door.

"B?" said Matt with apparent disgust. "You set this up in a B restaurant? What's the matter with you? We're on the government dime here. At least make sure the health department gives it an A rating for crying out loud. You're talking open lesions on the cooks and cockroach infestation. This is dangerous enough without adding ptomaine poisoning to my worries."

Bobby stammered with a response, "Bu, bu, but this is where he wanted to meet."

Matt cracked a smile at the clearly frustrated meth dealer.

"Are you just jerking my chain?"

"Maybe a little," said Matt. "It's better than a C."

They walked in the front door and headed to an empty booth near the back. Matt grabbed the seat facing the door. "I always get the Wild Bill Hickok seat."

"Huh?"

"The seat so my back's to the wall and I see everything that's going on. I never want my back to the action. That's my first rule. I get the best seat in the house. So don't ever leave me hanging if we're with the targets. I'll cover your back and mine, not the other way around, got it?"

"Got it, Kemo Sabe," said Bobby with a nervous laugh.

"That was the Lone Ranger, but don't forget or I might just put a silver bullet in one of your vital organs . . . and now I'm not jerking your chain."

Bobby understood the directive as they both sat.

Matt slid across the vinyl seat, positioning himself in the middle of the bench. Thank goodness for the near-matching duct tape; otherwise the seat would have clearly visible holes. Add another restaurant to Matt's list of undercover eateries to avoid. He and Caitlin would not be dining here any time soon to celebrate a special occasion.

"You slide all the way over. I want him next to you not me."

"But I don't have much room with this brace and the crutches."

"Give me the crutches," said Matt, conveying the notion Bobby Himmler clearly lacked problem-solving skills. "I'll put them against the wall."

Himmler knocked over the salt and pepper shakers as he lifted the crutches over the table, his hands shaking.

"Would you relax. Everything is going to be fine."

Matt looked around the crowded restaurant. Apparently the patrons weren't scared off by the B rating, and a cheap all-you-can-eat lunchtime buffet beats cleanliness for most of the blue-collar consumers. The walls were papered with red foil and Asian designs. Matt assumed most of the customers were from the industrial complex two blocks south of the restaurant. Knowing the San Fernando Valley was the porn capital of the world and several studios were housed in the complex, he also assumed some of these patrons were taking time away from their idea of art. Matt could only guess how proud the Founding Fathers must be, knowing the First Amendment protects such creativity and filth.

"We'll wait until your cousin shows up before we grab some food," said Matt.

Bobby's left leg, the one not housed in metal, twittered with the speed of a hummingbird seeking nectar, pounding at the bottom of the table.

"Would you relax."

"What if he doesn't buy the act?" asked Bobby.

"Then you go to jail. So unless you always twitch, I'd stop it before he arrives and concentrate on selling your cousin on the game plan we concocted."

Bobby was staring straight through Matt.

"I said, relax. You've been here before."

"I've never been a snitch before."

"No, but I'm not a cop, at least not today. You've introduced one bad guy to another. That's all we're doing."

Himmler wiped the sweat from his forehead. "But what if my cousin knows you?"

"Why would he know me? I've never arrested

him. I'm sure he didn't catch my appearance on *The View* last week."

"What? *The View*? That's his favorite show!"

"Bobby, relax. I've never been on *The View*. You told me yesterday your neo-Nazi cousin never misses the show. Still can't figure that one out."

"Two words," said Bobby.

"And they are?"

"Elisabeth Hasselbeck."

"She's hot. That makes sense," said Matt.

Jesse Himmler entered the restaurant and looked around, seeking his cousin.

"I think he just arrived," said Matt.

Bobby took a quick, deep breath and turned around.

"Jesse, over here."

Jesse strode toward the back booth and gave his cousin a big embrace as Bobby awkwardly rose from the booth.

"Hey, bro, thanks for meeting with me," said Bobby.

"You get the license number of the truck that ran you over? What'd you do to your leg?"

"I broke it playing b-ball the other night."

"You, on a basketball court? Yeah, right."

"No, seriously man, Matt was there. He saw the whole thing." Bobby pointed to Matt. "This is Matt."

Matt extended his hand and noted the strength in Jesse's grip.

Matt smiled. "Seriously, LeBron here was going for a layup when some little Triad gangbanger chopped him off at the knees."

"Jesse, you shoulda seen Matt. He knocked that kid clear across the pavement. Guy thought he was Bruce Lee, and Matt made him cry."

"I didn't make him cry. . . . He chose to cry," said Matt with a wicked grin.

Jesse let out a belly laugh. "Thanks for looking out for Bobby. Never could take care of his self."

Bobby was embarrassed and gave a polite but nervous laugh.

Jesse said, "This one of your cellies from upstate?"

"No, Jesse, Matt's helping me with my business."

"Which business is that?"

Matt intervened. "I decided to throw a little cash into Bobby's painting business and keep his PO off his butt."

"Jesse, Matt's making me look legit to the parole officer."

"You gonna help him paint my mother's house?" said Jesse.

Matt smiled at the 6'3" 280-pound behemoth seated across from him. "That wasn't part of my business plan, but I don't like to argue with somebody who looks like he once played defensive end for the Raiders."

"So how you gonna paint my mom's house with a busted-up leg?"

"The doctor said I won't be laid up long. I promise I'll get to it as soon as I can."

"Where'd you guys meet?" asked Jesse.

"Through AA," said Bobby a little too quickly.

"Since when did you get sober?" asked Jesse.

"I've been clean twelve days now."

"You a drunk?" said Jesse looking at Matt.

Matt had to think quickly. AA wasn't part of the scenario. How was he supposed to hang out at a bar and not drink? Matt said, "My old man was a drunk. I'm willing to help anyone who wants to go clean and sober, but I'm not toting tea in the flask."

Jesse laughed again, turning to Bobby. "Does that mean we won't be seeing you over at Boris's place?"

"Jesse, I'm sober. I'm not nuts."

"Good. You were always fun as a drunk. Hope you ain't changed." Jesse asked Matt, "So are you like Bobby's sponsor?"

"No, just a friend who wants to do everything in my power to keep him clean," said Matt.

"Just make sure he paints my mother's house in something other than gunmetal gray, which is the only color he was allowed to use when he was at Pelican Bay."

"But gray is such a neutral color. It goes with everything," said Matt with a smile.

"Just not my mother's house," said Jesse. "She's been sick, and a fresh coat of paint will cheer her up."

"I'll do a great job, Jesse. I promise," said Bobby.

Jesse nodded as if the response was rhetorical. Matt was certain no one ever did anything other than their best when it involved Jesse Himmler.

"So, Matt, besides investing in my cousin, what else you got going?" asked Jesse.

Matt moved into his cover speech and lowered his voice, "I own some real estate around L.A. I've got a warehouse a few miles from here. Spend most of my time over there. Every once in awhile I'll pick up a truckload of overstock or remainders and move it for a buck or two. It all adds up. It's just a matter of market timing."

Jesse laughed. "Overstock? If you're a friend of Bobby's, then your overstock is someone else's crime report."

All three laughed now.

Matt said, "Yeah, I pick up some bargains every once in awhile. Manage to move them out under the cover of darkness and pocket a profit."

"I'll keep that in mind."

Matt and Jesse got up and headed toward the buffet. Matt said, "I'll bring you a plate. Anything you don't like?"

Jesse interrupted, "He was in prison. He'll eat anything."

CHAPTER TWENTY-TWO

Matt looked out at the waves as they came crashing ashore. The white foam glistened beneath the lights illuminating the shoreline. The restaurant at Paradise Cove in Malibu was one of his favorites.

"What are you thinking?" asked Caitlin.

Matt took another bite of his blackened ahi tuna as he looked back at Caitlin. Their eyes met. He let the flavors linger in his mouth and then said softly, "I'm glad you've got such bad eyes."

"What's that supposed to mean?"

"I'll never understand what you ever saw in me. I can only attribute it to bad eyesight."

"You are such a romantic. You always know how and when to say the sweetest things. Honey, you were the first man I dated who had a real job, a regular paycheck, and a guaranteed pension. What's not to like?"

"Now who's being romantic?" said Matt.

A Pacific storm forced the waves to crash on the shore, breaking in rapid succession. The protection of the restaurant's plate-glass window provided a perfect dinner setting.

"So what's up?" asked Caitlin.

"What do you mean?"

"Matt, your undercover shtick never works with me. The fanciest place you ever take me is Chipotle's and then only with a coupon. You never take me anywhere with cloth napkins unless there's an angle. So what's the angle? I'm assuming it's not divorce or bankruptcy. It must be a new undercover assignment. So spit it out. Let's get it over with so I can at least try to enjoy the rest of dinner."

"For an elementary schoolteacher, you're pretty street-smart."

"You think you survive a Los Angeles School District second-grade classroom merely on the training you receive at some teacher college, get real, Cowboy. Now quit stalling."

"Okay, you win. I had a successful meeting this afternoon with a white supremacist. Looks like it could go somewhere so we're going to take a run."

Matt saw a look of concern overtake her face. Her countenance went from a carefree dinner date to a worried spouse.

Caitlin took several bites of food before she responded. "Well, at least promise me you'll take a shower every morning."

"I wish you understood."

She put down her fork and reached across the table to take his hand. "I keep hoping someday you'll announce you've taken a desk and I need to start ironing a white, button-down, collared shirt every night."

Matt laughed. "You do believe in miracles, don't you?"

"It just always seems so dangerous. Couldn't you find some quaint little stock manipulation scheme at an AARP convention?"

Matt smiled. "Not much of a thrill targeting octogenarians. Besides, you've seen my investment skills. We're living in a condo because I thought gold would never rise above $475 an ounce."

"Does this have anything to do with Flip Mitchell's wife?"

"We think so. We hope so anyway."

"Well, if it's family, then I guess you have my blessing, but I'm serious, can't you find an assignment a little less dangerous? I'm ready to try again. I want to start a family, but it scares me to think about children as long as Jack Bauer here keeps wanting to tempt fate. Why can't you put on a coat and tie like every other agent in the office?"

"Not much fun in that."

"But, Matt, I really do worry. It just seems like with each assignment you take on more risk."

"Maybe I'm an adrenaline junky, and I keep chasing the dragon."

She released his hand. "I'm serious. You're not the one lying home in bed every night praying

God will continue to wrap his protective arms around you. You aren't on your knees every morning asking for my peace and your protection. I love you, Matt, and I want us to grow old together. I wish you would have taken the supervisor slot they offered last year. I guess I just don't understand this insatiable desire to play a real-life James Bond."

Matt took a sip of his Pellegrino and looked out toward the ocean. He was gathering his thoughts as he turned back to Caitlin. "You ever sweat?"

"What?"

"I don't mean perspire. I mean sweat."

Caitlin tilted her head and gave him an inquisitive look.

"You ever have adrenaline dripping from your pores? Sometimes when I'm on my way to meet somebody I know to be truly dangerous, I begin to sweat. I actually tingle and maybe even shake. I can feel the adrenaline pulsating through my body. It's nerves. It's fear, but it's a rush. It means I'm hitting on all cylinders, and it means I'm taking it to the edge. There is absolutely no comparable thrill."

Caitlin reached back across the table and touched his hand. She may never completely understand, but she appreciated his sharing his most intimate thoughts. Then a huge smile overtook her face. "What about on our wedding night?"

106

CHAPTER TWENTY-THREE

Within hours of Dawn Platt's telephone call at the hospital with Mickey Donovan, the bad-boy biker was stopped on his motorcycle for a moving traffic violation. The young LAPD patrol officer who pulled him over ran the usual routine check before approaching the vehicle. The 10-29 came back "Warrants on File." Donovan's infractions were minor, but the multiple "failures to appear" on previous traffic tickets made him a guest of the county until Dawn could post bail.

The Denny's restaurant on Sunset Boulevard just off the Hollywood freeway was open twenty-four hours. The clientele reflected the working demographics. The noontime diners were from the studios, even an occasional executive. After midnight the roaches came out, the night crawlers who roamed the poor side of Tinseltown.

It was late and Dawn Platt was seated in a booth on the east side of the restaurant away from the other customers. From inside the restaurant she could hear the roar of the Harley as it pulled into the parking lot. Dawn turned and peered out the window as she watched Mickey

Donovan dismount and walk to the front entrance.

Denny's was convenient. It was close to the methadone clinic on Hollywood Boulevard where she received treatment. Mickey knew the location. A message from either saying, "Meet me at Denny's" meant only one spot.

She jumped up as soon as Mickey approached the table and threw her arms around him. The square-jawed biker had movie-star good looks but the morals of a twice-convicted felon.

"I'm so glad you're out," said Dawn as she gave him a kiss.

"Thanks for coming up with the money, but what took you so long? A few lousy tickets and you'd think they arrested Al Capone."

"I'm sorry, baby. I did some things I didn't want to do, but I got the money. I even missed two days of work. I called in sick. I just hope my PO bought it."

"Well, I'm out. That's all that matters."

"I got the information you needed," she said.

"Let me have it," said Mickey.

"It was the FBI who brought Bobby in. He got ripped on a drug deal. He busted his ankle pretty bad trying to run."

"He always was an idiot and a loser."

"He's not in the hospital anymore. I checked last night."

"Where is he?"

"I don't know. I called the county jail, and I called down to Terminal Island. Nobody's heard of him. Did I do good calling around trying to find him?"

"Yeah, you did good. I bet he's working off a beef. He's probably on the Feds' payroll by now. What about the woman? Did you find out about her?"

"I think it's the right one. She was brought in the same night as Bobby with two gunshot wounds. She's still in the hospital. I peeked in the room last night, and it looked like someone did a number on her face."

"That's her."

"Her husband is an FBI agent."

"What?"

"Yeah, I was talking to the agent guarding Bobby, and he said she was married to an FBI agent."

"Are you sure? How many other gunshot victims did you have that night?"

"I don't know, Mickey. I just deliver food trays. I'm not the admissions counselor."

"Don't get smart with me!"

"I'm sorry, Mickey, let's get out of here. Let's get married and go someplace else. I talked to a producer the other day."

Mickey interrupted, "Where'd you meet a producer?"

"He was downtown at the Hilton."

"So why were you at the Hilton? Forget it, what did he say?"

"He said Hollywood is moving out of state. Too many taxes and a lot of incentives in other places like North Carolina, New Mexico, even Detroit. I know you could get work there. I'm tired of all this. We're both gonna keep slippin' if we stay here. Please, Mickey. My PO would let me leave. He'd be glad to get rid of me. Save the state a few bucks. What do you say?"

"Would you just shut up? I'm not going anywhere. If you want to go someplace else, then go. I'm not leaving. I got stuff going here. I can make money with Boris. L.A. is a gold mine as far as I'm concerned, and this is the only place to be if you want to make it in Hollywood. If you don't like our arrangement, then leave, but don't be talking marriage or even hooking up."

Dawn broke down and cried, tears flowing down her face. "Dump Boris. He's no good for you. He's no good for us."

Mickey stormed out of the restaurant without saying another word.

CHAPTER TWENTY-FOUR

Matt heard the car pull up in the parking lot. He looked out through the tinted office windows and walked to the rusted metal door, unlocking the double deadbolt. He welcomed Jason Barnes and Pamela Clinton as they entered the rundown warehouse.

"You didn't have to dress up on my account," said Matt as he ushered in the two FBI administrators. Both looked out of place in their business attire as Matt was comfortably dressed in faded blue jeans and a worn sweatshirt. "Welcome to my humble abode."

"So this is what I have been signing off on for the past three months, just so you can hang out here," said Barnes as he surveyed the scene.

"I need to use the ladies room," said Pamela Clinton, not even offering a hand or a smile. She headed for an open door, obviously housing bathroom facilities.

Matt almost let her walk in and close the door but thought better of it and said, "Wait a sec." He walked over to his desk and grabbed a roll of toilet paper. Tossing it to her, he said, "You might need this."

She bobbled the throw and chased the roll as it bounced across the floor.

"You can't keep a roll in the restroom?" asked Pamela.

"It's just another way to screw with the clientele. I like to watch them scramble after they finish their business and realize they don't have sufficient paper to complete the task. Tends to humble even the most hardened," said Matt.

"You are disgusting."

Matt spotted Jason Barnes out of the corner of his eye and thought he saw the slightest twinge of a smile.

"Dwayne should be here any minute. He called just before you two showed up. Want to see the setup?" offered Matt.

"Yeah, give me the nickel tour," said Barnes.

Matt proceeded to show him the office, pointing out three hidden cameras, secreted in the ceiling, as well as a hidden compartment where guns were stored should extra firepower ever be needed. The small reception area was dark as was the hallway leading to the warehouse.

The ADIC followed Matt as they explored the warehouse, an area large enough to accompany most of the contraband any criminal wanted to store. Matt pointed out the loading dock, the infra-red cameras, and the alarm system.

"Not bad. I've seen more sophistication in some of our intelligence and terrorism off-sites, but this fits the bill. Where do you store the monitoring equipment?" said Jason Barnes.

They returned to the hallway, and Matt pointed to a beat-up filing cabinet extending from the floor to the ceiling, next to the restroom. He flipped the center light switch three times, and the cabinet slid to the left revealing a room large enough to house two people but crammed with audio- and video-recording equipment.

"Now that's more like it. That's the kind of 007 sophistication I was hoping to find."

The toilet flushed as Matt closed the opening to the monitoring room by flipping the light switch once. He watched Pamela storm from the bathroom, shaking her hands. "You're out of paper towels," she said.

"That's because you haven't signed our latest requisition. It's been sitting on your desk since last Tuesday. Wipe 'em on your pants, that's what we do most of the time anyway."

Matt saw her eyes piercing through him with a look signaling her intention to get even for embarrassing her in front of the ADIC.

Just then the door opened, and Dwayne Washington walked in. "Hey boss, Pamela, sorry I got held up."

Pamela was still shaking her hands dry.

"Out of paper towels again?" asked Dwayne.

"Yep," said Matt, "I offered to let her wipe 'em off on my pants leg, but she demurred, as the lawyers like to say."

Jason Barnes stifled a laugh as they walked into Matt's office.

Matt decided it might be best to play the proper host. "You guys want something to drink? I just put on a pot of coffee. We've got diet and regular Pepsi. Anything?"

No one responded.

"Guys, I'm trying to be polite. You have to work with me. Come on Pamela, I want to make up for the paper towels."

Dwayne said, "I think we better get down to business. I'm sure the boss has other meetings today."

"This is important. I'll make the time. I'm interested in your plan," said Jason Barnes.

Matt interrupted, "Drinks? I'm getting something."

Matt stood up and headed for the refrigerator.

"Sure, Matt. I'll take a Diet Pepsi."

"You got it, boss. Anyone else?"

"I'd like coffee," said Pamela. "Cream and two sugars."

"Okay and, Dwayne, I know you want a diet."

The ADIC's cell phone rang, and he answered, stepping out into the hallway. He returned a few minutes later. "Sorry, I needed to take that. Headquarters was checking on Lydia's condition."

Matt served everyone as Dwayne pulled out pictures from his briefcase. "This is Jesse

Himmler, the cousin of our informant Bobby Himmler. Every law enforcement intelligence unit in L.A. County says Jesse is the real deal. In any other situation Jesse would be a worthy target. I guess you could call him a registered independent. He doesn't fly the colors of any outlaw biker group or wear the flag of a neo-Nazi organization, but he runs guns and drugs. He did time in Lompoc on a weapons charge and hung with the Aryan Brotherhood when he was in. He's sold guns to the Monguls and MS-13. Yet according to a sheriff's department source, he's moved stolen motorcycles for the Hell's Angels and smuggled speed into prison for the Mexican Mafia."

"So he's covering all the bases," said the ADIC.

Dwayne nodded and continued, "He appears to be respected by all. But our real interest is his association with Boris Gregorian, the owner of the Russian Veil."

Dwayne passed out surveillance photos taken of the front of the bar over the weekend.

"Based on what Bobby Himmler told us, Boris seems to be at least indirectly tied to the attack on Lydia Mitchell. Jesse is one of Gregorian's closest non-Russian associates."

Dwayne then pulled out a surveillance picture of Gregorian and showed it to Barnes and Clinton.

"He looks like one of Vince McMahon's aging

superstars, kind of a fat Russian Hulk Hogan," said Barnes.

"Yeah, he's a big boy. We're carrying him at 6'4" 300 pounds," said Dwayne.

"That was his playing weight a few years ago. I think he's gone a little soft since then so we might want to tack on another twenty or thirty pounds," added Matt.

"Without the shirt he's pretty tatted up," said Dwayne who pulled out another photo showing him at the beach in a bathing suit.

Matt shook his head. "This is borderline obscenity. How can anyone say a picture of a fat guy in a Speedo has any redeeming social value? Where's the Supreme Court when you need them? Surely, the ACLU wouldn't defend this on First Amendment grounds?"

Dwayne looked at Matt who was trying to goad Pamela Clinton into a comment. Rumors circulating recently in the bullpen have her dating a rather large-boned, corpulent attorney. Someone saw them walking hand in hand on the beach below The Chart House in Malibu. She wasn't taking the bait.

"Are you done?" said Dwayne.

Matt waved his arm as if to say, "Continue."

"What do we know about him?" asked Barnes.

"He was a Russian military officer before the breakup of the Soviet Union. CIA claims he was with the Twelfth Department."

"What's that?" asked Pamela.

"Nuclear weapons," said Barnes.

"He came here legally in the early nineties. From all we can tell, he's a gangster capitalist, but we don't have any proof," said Dwayne.

"Anything more?"

"None of the alphabet agencies report anything on him."

"But has anyone targeted him?"

Dwayne nodded. "ATF had an informant into him a couple of years ago, but before they were able to introduce an undercover, the informant disappeared."

Matt interrupted, "No one knows if he went south or took a dirt nap. One day he missed a meeting with his case agent and that was that. Based on what Bobby said, people who cross Boris don't hang around to tell their stories."

Dwayne added, "He's off the grid. His rap sheet is clean. No arrests. He's had some minor liquor violations at the bar but all civil in nature, nothing criminal."

"Can you get to him?" asked Barnes, examining the pictures again.

"We think so. Matt had a very productive meeting with Jesse Himmler, and Bobby's still onboard. They both hang out at the Veil. We need to work our way up to Gregorian. If we are patient and luck breaks our way, we could get there."

Barnes looked concerned even though he knew it was often a circuitous path to success. "That seems like a long shot. First you have to convince Jesse Himmler you're for real. Then you have to convince him to introduce you to Gregorian and hope he believes you. How does that get us close to solving the murders and the attack on Lydia?"

"That's what I've been trying to say since this started," said Pamela.

Matt ignored her, not even looking in her direction when he spoke. "We didn't burn the warehouse with our operation last month so it's still good to go. I'm going to open it up to Jesse and let him know it's available for whatever he might need. Bobby says he's always looking for places to store his swag overnight and . . ."

"What is swag? We can't help him facilitate a drug transaction. If we store narcotics, we have to seize them," interrupted Pamela.

Matt looked at her with incredulity, realizing how little time she spent on the street. Before he could take a swing at the hanging curveball, Jason Barnes offered an explanation. "Swag is an old mob term, an acronym for 'stolen without a gun.' It just means stolen goods."

Matt went on. "I'll leave it up to him. We'll give him the opening and see where it leads."

"We can't let him in here alone. That's a security violation, and we can't record without you being present. That's a Title III violation," said Pamela.

"I know the law. I have no intention of giving him the keys to the kingdom so he can sneak around the warehouse. Every recording will be consensual, and I'll be the consenting party. If I'm not in the room, we won't activate the recording equipment or listen in. We won't be violating Congress's precious wiretap provisions," said Matt.

"It's not precious. It's called the Constitution, and you *will* do everything according to the law and FBI regulations," said Pamela, placing particular emphasis on the word *will*.

The ADIC intervened, "I'm sure Matt has no intention of violating anyone's constitutional rights. I want this guy, and I want it done right. Matt, you have my blessing, as if you ever asked for it. You sound as though you're on the right track. I was hopeful the train was moving a little faster, but at least it's moving in the right direction."

"Then it's settled," said Dwayne. "As soon as practical, we'll try to get Jesse in here and see where it leads."

CHAPTER TWENTY-FIVE

Two days later Bobby Himmler sat in the kitchen of his tiny two-bedroom rental in Van Nuys, a section of Los Angeles in the San Fernando Valley. A realtor might say the house was decorated in earth tones. A maid would say the dingy white walls hadn't been cleaned in two decades. The home was built in the early fifties, and the last repair may have been during Eisenhower's second term. The structure did little to enhance property values in the area, but with neighbors like meth-cooker Bobby Himmler, why worry about real estate's bottom line. If the neighbors really cared, they would have called the cops.

The FBI did a number when they searched his place. Himmler didn't worry so much about the overturned furniture or the contents of the dresser drawers tossed on the bed, what he wanted was his lab back. He was afraid to ask Matt so he went about checking with friends, frequenting head shops in the Valley, and visiting enough drugstores no one would suspect he was back in business.

Tiffany walked in from the living room. Vaulted might be a better term to describe her actions. She was on her third day without sleep and hadn't eaten since Sunday. Food did not sustain her; drugs did. Tiffany was a high-dose, chronic, methamphetamine abuser. "Speed freak" accurately described her. When she was loaded, she bounced higher than the forged checks she often cashed.

Bobby looked at the former cheerleader turned anorexic working girl. What he saw was nothing like the photo in her high school yearbook. Just a few years earlier this 5'6" blonde was attractive enough to be a princess on the court of her senior prom. A smile that once melted a father's heart now revealed a severe case of "meth mouth"— rotten teeth, painful sores, cracked lips. Her gaunt appearance and poor hygiene had no photogenic value other than a "Just Say No" public-service announcement. But Bobby knew he was no cinch for next month's *Muscle and Fitness* centerfold. They wasted their youth and their lives. The music was still playing for the slow-death dance they began the day they discovered an artificial panacea to contentment. Only a miracle could save either.

Before meth Tiffany used cocaine, but the high lasted only twenty or thirty minutes. The first time she smoked crystal methamphetamine, the euphoric feeling remained for twelve hours. She was hooked on the mega-adrenaline rush and never looked back. Now she had no higher priority than determining when and how she would fill her glass pipe. When the translucent rocklike substances melted, vaporized, and were inhaled, Tiffany was taken to another dimension.

"Baby, how's it coming?" she asked.

"Still a ways off."

"I could use a little pop to keep me on top," said Tiffany flashing a desperate grin.

Bobby tinkered with the three-neck flask as the ephedrine-based product cooled. He successfully cooked "ice" many times, but the volatile nature of the chemicals used to manufacture one more nightmare in the world of designer drugs made each batch a potential fireball. The heavily marred kitchen table had all the elements for today's recipe: red phosphorous, hydrochloric acid, anhydrous ammonia, drain cleaner, battery acid, lye, lantern fuel, and antifreeze. This mom-and-pop operation kept Tiffany supplied and Bobby employed.

"Baby, you are so smart. You cut a great deal with the Feds. I can't believe you got a pass, a complete walk. You shoulda been a lawyer. I don't know what I'd do if you got locked up." Then rubbing her hands through his greasy, long brown hair, she said, "You're my baby."

"I bought me an insurance policy. We're golden. They ain't touching me as long as they think I can give them Jesse and Boris."

"How much longer . . ."

The screen door exploded as Mickey Donovan burst in from the backyard, a 9 mm automatic at his side.

Tiffany screamed.

Donovan pointed the gun at her, angled gangster style, parallel to the floor, his face the image of death. "Shut up!" Then looking at Himmler, he said, "It took me a couple of days to find you, puke."

"Mickey, what are you doing?"

The acting may have been bad, like some second-rate movie, but it was all too real. Mickey Donovan was singular in purpose, his eyes fixed on the target: Bobby Himmler.

"You're nothing but filth. Cheese eaters need to be exterminated."

Tiffany screamed again.

"I said shut up!" Donovan fired one shot dropping the former cheerleader.

Bobby attempted to jump to his feet but in doing so his leg, still in the brace, knocked over the table where he was seated. Before he could mount an offensive, a massive explosion ripped through the kitchen, too late for a strategic afterthought.

MATT WAS ENJOYING THE late afternoon sun as he sat at the outdoor table of the West Los Angeles coffee shop. He was drinking a Diet Dr. Pepper and perusing the sports section of the *Los*

Angeles Times. He looked up to see Dwayne pull into the parking lot.

The supervisor hopped out of his Ford Fusion. "Sorry I'm late. Had to sign off on some last-minute reports needing to get out this afternoon," said Dwayne.

"Darn, you mean I missed completing another survey for headquarters. How will they ever function without my input?"

"Sometimes those reports serve a purpose."

"You know the FBI put the 'bureau' in bureaucracy."

"Why don't you catch me up with the investigation, and maybe some other day you can wax eloquently about your disdain for my superiors."

The waitress approached and Dwayne ordered coffee, high-octane, no-frills black.

"So is anything set up?" asked Dwayne.

"I talked to Bobby last night. He said Jesse liked me and the three of us are getting together tomorrow night. I told Bobby to suggest we meet at the Russian Veil. That at least gets me in there with a couple of credible guys."

"Sounds like a good start."

"Stealth or speed? You usually can't have both. Obviously each case is different, but I always find when I look back I could have pushed harder and faster. I know the boss is looking for answers so I want to give him all the ammunition he needs as quickly as possible."

"Your call." Dwayne's Blackberry vibrated as it sat on the table next to his coffee. He read the message. "We've got a problem."

"What?"

"Your dinner plans tomorrow night may have just been canceled. Bobby Himmler's place blew up. Fire and police are on the scene. I better get over there," said Dwayne.

"Was he in it?"

"I don't know, Matt. The text didn't say."

"I'll meet you there."

"No," said Dwayne without hesitation. "Not until we sort things out. Who knows who or what will show up? It's too dangerous. I'll call you as soon as I have anything."

Dwayne ran to his car. Matt sat stunned questioning whether he somehow overplayed his hand and Bobby's cooperation was discovered.

CHAPTER TWENTY-SIX

Later that evening, as Matt pulled into the parking lot of the industrial park housing the undercover warehouse, he noted the lot was empty except for two forty-foot shipping containers at the north end. The employees of the five other businesses in the complex went home hours earlier. He often preferred the cover of darkness, and the well-lit parking lot might expose the urgent meeting Dwayne called with the ADIC and SAC. Matt phoned each of the participants and instructed them to pull around back to the alley entrance and he would let them park inside the warehouse. Matt would do the same. Too many cars in the lot at this hour might arouse suspicion even if only from the patrol officers covering the warehouse district. His call with Dwayne was brief, but the news wasn't good. The operation may have ended before it got started.

He exited the car, unlocked the back door, and turned to the blue metal box to deactivate the alarm. He punched in the code "3-2-4-0-0-7," his private joke since "3-2-4" were the numbers corresponding to F-B-I on the telephone digital pad. Returning to the large warehouse door, he yanked on the chain, pulling it hand over hand as the door slowly rose to a height of about six feet. He secured the chain locking the overhead door in place. *Surely a world-class undercover agent deserves a warehouse with an electric garage door opener.* He returned to his car, pulled into the warehouse, turned off the headlights, and waited in the dark for the others.

As soon as everyone parked inside, Matt closed the garage door and turned on the lights to the warehouse. The four gathered around Dwayne's car as he laid out crime scene photos on the hood of the Ford Fusion.

"We've got three dead," said Dwayne.

"Three?" said Matt.

"Two males and one female. The female has a round in her head, possibly a 9 mm. They found a Makarov in the ashes so at this point we assume that was the murder weapon."

"Bobby said his cousin bought a box of handguns as well as the AK-47s. In all likelihood the handguns would have been Makarovs since they're Russian made," added Matt looking over the photos.

"We'll have to wait for the autopsy to determine the caliber."

"But only one shot, not three?" asked the ADIC, Jason Barnes.

"Yes, just the female. The other two must have died in the explosion."

Jason Barnes examined each picture carefully before he passed them to his SAC. "Do we have positive ID on the victims?"

"Well, Himmler was easy. He had pins in his leg. They still haven't identified the other two. We know Bobby had a girlfriend so she might be the gunshot victim."

Pamela Clinton asked, "So who was the shooter?"

"It's a little hard to tell from the crime scene. Both the male bodies were practically on top of the weapon. Each was within arm's length of the gun."

"It wouldn't make sense for it to be Bobby. He wasn't into guns. We didn't find one on the search the other night, and I doubt if he picked one up since his release from the hospital," said Matt.

"Unless he got scared. He knew he was on our payroll. Maybe he believed he needed some firepower in case the word got out. Informants do stupid things," said the ADIC.

"So do scared people," said Dwayne.

"That's a good point. He may have figured being on board he could get away with carrying if he got caught. It just seems out of character. He was nervous the other day at the meeting with Jesse but not to the point of arming himself. I think he would have given me a clue if he was thinking about picking up some protection. What caused the fire?" said Matt.

"The fire marshal has an idea, but it may be days before he can give us a definitive answer," said Dwayne who picked up one of the photos. "Look at this from the kitchen." He pointed to some beakers on the floor.

Matt shook his head, "He was cooking."

"What?" said Pamela.

"The initial guess from the fire inspector is a meth lab explosion," said Dwayne.

Jason Barnes interrupted, "I've had enough

with all the speculation. I don't work off guesses when I have an undercover involved."

"I understand, boss," said Dwayne. "But it's just too early to tell. Everything points to an explosion and not from a faulty furnace."

"A bullet in a body is no accident," said Pamela.

"No one is calling it an accident," said Dwayne.

"Three people blown up with one already dead from a gunshot isn't an accident. I think the explosion may have been an accident, but I'm concerned about the shooting. If it wasn't Bobby, then it was this other man. I need to know why the female was killed, and does this have anything to do with what we have in the works," said the ADIC.

"I agree we need answers before we go forward. Should we get ERT involved?" asked Pamela Clinton.

Dwayne jumped in quickly to that suggestion. "It would make no sense to bring in the FBI. We have no plausible investigative jurisdiction. We would ordinarily have no interest in a meth lab explosion so it might alert the wrong people if we show up in blue FBI windbreakers and start nosing around the crime scene."

"But if we're shutting down the undercover operation, it would make good liaison for us to offer up our evidence recovery people," said Pamela.

"Who said anything about shutting down the operation?" said Matt with a little too much force.

"Well if Jesse Himmler didn't buy your act, maybe they suspected Bobby was cooperating and you were a Fed," added Pamela.

Like a nuclear blast, Matt mushroomed. "That's the result you'd like, isn't it? FBI, fix blame instantly, and on a brick agent if you can. Maybe we can get OPR involved before the clock strikes midnight, Cinderella."

"Matt!" said Dwayne.

Every street agent knew Clinton's propensity to call the Office of Professional Responsibility in D.C. at the slightest hint of controversy. It was one more reason the rank and file wanted to vote her off the island.

"Let's get back to the business at hand," said the ADIC. "I think we better step away for awhile until we can make a determination as to the cause of this."

Still angry but more subdued, Matt said, "Boss, with all due respect, I think that's the wrong decision. Just like they taught us in the Marines, you run to the sound of gunfire."

Pamela interrupted, "That's the dumbest thing I've ever heard."

"No, he may have a point. Go on Matt," said the ADIC.

"I need to take them on, a full frontal attack. If

I pull back now, we've lost the edge, and I may never recover my credibility. If this was a professional hit gone bad, it was amateur hour. This could have been a disgruntled customer wanting a refund and not willing to seek redress in small claims court. Bobby never won the tweeker congeniality award. He had lots of enemies. Even if this was a hit, it may have nothing to do with me. No one knows he was cooperating except us. No charges were ever brought. No publicity."

Now it was Dwayne's turn to interrupt, "Maybe Bobby was strapped and it was a rip. He killed the female, and before he got off a second shot, the place went up."

Matt didn't buy the theory, but he appreciated Dwayne's coming to his support. "Look, let's do it this way. We will cover the funeral anyway. Put some extra firepower in the surveillance van; I'll show up and see what kind of reception I get. If Jesse walks away, then we know where we stand. He's not going to have me killed at a funeral. If I get the biker embrace, then we continue to march."

Pamela Clinton shook her head. "I recommend we discontinue all undercover ops until we have a definitive answer as to the cause of the blast and what happened inside that house. It's just too dangerous, and we are exposing ourselves to bureaucratic second-guessing and potential lawsuits if something happens before we have all the answers."

Now it was Matt's turn to shake his head as he looked directly at Jason Barnes. "If we wait for the completed investigation, Bobby Himmler's corpse will be calcified and last year's news. We don't have the luxury of time."

Barnes thought for a few seconds. "Okay, here's the compromise. Stay away until the funeral. I don't want you reaching out to Jesse or going near the house. We'll see how you are received and make our next move based on their lead."

"I can live with that," said Matt.

"You're gonna have to," commanded the ADIC.

"I just want to go on the record as opposing any more undercover meetings until the cause of the explosion is resolved," said Clinton.

"We knew your vote before the meeting began," said Matt.

"Matt, that's enough," said Dwayne.

CHAPTER TWENTY-SEVEN

It was a calculated risk but one he was willing to take. It wasn't the first time he'd be among the Sodomites and sinners. He was all too ready to plunge again into the darkness.

"I'm about a minute away," said Matt barely audible over the transmitter he was wearing. Dwayne and three other agents inside the surveillance van could monitor everything Matt said and heard while at Bobby Himmler's funeral. A second van was stationed at the opposite end of the cemetery with four more armed agents ready to pounce if necessary.

Those listening over the wire could hear "Jailhouse Rock" blasting in the background. "Does he ever get serious?" said Dwayne to no one in particular.

An outdoor service was planned, and as Matt pulled slowly into the small cemetery, he observed about fifty people gathering near the hillside grave site. Matt had some comfort knowing Dwayne had his back if this thing went south and, if it did, it would all be on tape.

Cameras, video, and stills inside the van were rolling and clicking.

Matt exited his car and looked up to see soft white clouds, making it another perfect Southern California day. *Another day in paradise. What a great day for a funeral. And I get to hang out with a bunch of smelly bikers and racists bemoaning society's loss of another Nobel laureate drug dealer.*

Matt cleaned up for the service. He wasn't quite formal, more like business casual mourning, but his black dress slacks, a black tee, and a black sports coat far exceeded the long-haired cretins in jeans and cutoffs. *How about a little decorum for crying out loud? The guy is dead.*

He scanned the crowd and quickly spotted Bobby's cousin, Jesse. Matt wasn't armed. It was too dangerous under the circumstances, but if the time came, he had no desire to go toe-to-toe with any of Boris's crew. *Just shoot 'em and let OPR sort it out!*

Matt didn't want to be obvious, but before he had a choice, Jesse, appropriately dressed in a dark suit and stoic in expression, saw him. The moment of truth was near.

Jesse quickly made his way over to Matt, who took a deep breath. Seconds would determine the next phase of the investigation.

Jesse grabbed Matt and gave him a bear hug. With tears streaming down his cheeks, Jesse said, "Thanks for coming, dude. I know how much you meant to my cousin, and I appreciate you being here. He was a screwup, but he was like a brother to me, and I lost someone special when he died."

The hug lasted longer than normal, and Matt kept expecting Jesse to run his hands up and down Matt's back, seeking to detect a recording device or weapon, but the lingering hug was apparently the gesture of a truly grieving man.

Matt wasn't used to behemoths expressing such

emotions so either he was not suspected of being an undercover agent or Jesse Himmler was an Academy Award–winning actor. Matt offered an appropriate response to Jesse's grief, and eventually Jesse relaxed his massive arms. Matt caught his breath and tried hard to hide his shock.

Boris Gregorian and a dark-haired, attractive, twenty-something female were walking toward Jesse.

Matt was hoping the surveillance cameras were clicking at NASCAR speed.

"Jesse," said Boris.

Jesse turned and gave another equally long and soulful hug to the former Russian intelligence agent, thanking him for coming to the funeral. The female awkwardly stood there chomping on her gum, looking around at those in attendance, and giving Matt a brief, forced smile.

Jesse released his hug and grabbed Matt by the elbow. "Boris, I want you to meet Matt. He was a good friend of my cousin and tried to get Bobby straight. He's the one I was telling you about who helped finance Bobby's business."

Matt and Boris shook hands, and Boris introduced his date as Sasha. Not being a devotee, Matt assumed Boris's escort may have a promising career in the world of adult entertainment.

A hush fell upon the crowd when the minister began speaking.

• • •

FOLLOWING THE SERVICE, MATT stood with Jesse, Boris, and Sasha on the blacktop drive and chatted as bikers and dopers left, offering condolences to Bobby's mother. As they passed, several said something to Jesse. Matt had no idea Jesse and Bobby were so close, but apparently everyone at the funeral knew of the tight relationship. At least a half-dozen who passed mentioned they would see Boris and Jesse at the club that evening.

The FBI managed to bury the reports of the crime scene, and the only thing leaked to the press was that three people died in a fire in a Van Nuys home. Any media who cared speculated it may have been a methamphetamine laboratory explosion, but there was no follow up. The three victims may have had value to someone but certainly not many. There was no clamoring for the truth.

"The paper said three died in the fire. Did you ever hear what happened?" asked Matt.

"Matt, I don't want to hurt you . . ."

Matt tensed. Was this the part where he was in for a beating?

"I know how hard you worked to get him straight, but apparently Bobby was cooking and the lab exploded," said Jesse.

"Oh, no," said Matt feigning surprise. "I thought he turned it around."

"I'm not sure he was using. You may have helped him stay sober. I just think he was trying to make a buck. Bobby was good at chemistry. He could cook with the best of them. He just couldn't stay away from tasting his product. If he started cooking again, it was only a matter of time before he started dipping. He wasn't strong, Matt. That's why he needed someone like you."

"And the other two, what about them?"

"Tiffany was his girlfriend. She lived there. When I first met her, she was beautiful, but she fell fast once she got wired full time. Bobby used to be so proud to walk her around. He called her his 'arm candy.' But then they both started smoking and never climbed out of the pipe."

"What about the other guy?"

"That was Mickey Donovan. We all know him." Boris nodded.

"Mickey may have been the customer, but if he was, he was more of a wholesaler than a retailer. I'm not even sure he used," said Jesse looking to Boris.

"I never knew him to use, and if I found out he did, he would have never worked for me. I don't need those types around me. They can't be trusted—a businessman, yes, a user, no. They get caught, and they make up all kinds of stories to avoid the American gulags. It doesn't take much to break a user. They don't think straight once the supply is cut off."

"Listen, Jesse, I'm really sorry about Bobby. I thought maybe I could keep him straight. Obviously I was wrong. I should have watched him more carefully. I almost feel at fault. I should have realized with the broken leg he would have too much time to think and start coming up with ways to supplement his income since the painting business was on hold. Maybe had I loaned him money to tide him over until the leg healed, it would have made a difference. He was a proud man. He never asked."

Matt's eyes started to water; he could cry on cue when the director demanded.

Jesse put his arm around Matt's shoulder. *I hope they are getting pictures of this. Say "cheese."*

"This was not your fault, bro. You tried to help. Bobby slipped. There is plenty of blame to go around, but most of it falls on him. He was weak. It cost him his life."

Matt reached over to shake hands. "I better get going. It sounds as though you have lots to do this evening mourning the loss of your cousin. I will let you do that. It was nice meeting you. Sorry it didn't work out."

Jesse grabbed Matt. "Hey, no, we want you to come to the club tonight. Bobby would want you there. This ain't over, bro. I told you the other day we might be able to do some business. I wasn't talking about painting. This isn't the time to talk about it, but in a few days I'd like to get together."

"I'd love to honor Bobby. Where are you meeting?"

"We're having a wake at my place, the Russian Veil," said Boris.

"The Russian Veil?" Matt repeated the words slowly as if exploring his subconscious.

"It's on Ventura Boulevard."

"Yeah, I know the place. I've never been in but I've driven past."

"We'll start gathering after nine in the back. Tell them at the door you're my guest," said Boris.

Several more people exited shaking hands with Bobby's mother. Matt could see the disdain Boris had for the attendees. Both Boris and Sasha were dressed in Beverly Hills chic. Even though much of Matt's everyday wardrobe consisted of Costco warehouse bargains, Matt was semiformal compared to most. Boris shook his head as the Unwashed masses left the funeral. "These guys give the white race a bad name."

CHAPTER TWENTY-EIGHT

Matt headed straight to the kitchen, his nose following the smells of dinner.

"Hey, babe."

He kissed Caitlin who was bringing in the tri-tip she just removed from the grill. Showing him the meat, she asked, "Is this too rare?"

"Baby, you know I always want my beef rare but

"Cowboy, sometimes you can almost be disgusting," said Caitlin as she leaned over and stole a second kiss.

"At least you said 'almost.' I guess that means I haven't crossed the threshold of common decency yet."

Matt began setting the table.

"Speaking of decency, how was the funeral?"

She put the broccoli on the table.

"I have a feeling I will finally get this whole salvation issue figured out, and then when I get to heaven, God's going to stick me in the section housing dirty bikers."

Caitlin opened the refrigerator and pulled out the salad she made earlier. "They'll be washed clean once they get to heaven."

"I'm not sure these guys will bathe even when

God calls. I think I spent the afternoon with a lot of prodigal sons who wasted their inheritances and still aren't ready to run home to Pops."

Caitlin held up two bottles of salad dressing. Matt pointed to the Newman's Light Balsamic Vinaigrette.

"Just remember the father welcomed his son with open arms not a closed fist."

"It might be easier to welcome these guys with a loaded automatic."

"Jesus ate with sinners."

"Would he hang out at the Russian Veil?"

"He's there. He may not be too happy, but he's there just asking for a relationship."

"I'm glad to know he's there. Maybe I'll run into him tonight. I have to go back."

Disappointment overtook her smile. "Matt, why?"

"I've been invited to a wake for the departed."

"There's a reason why sex is rare," Caitlin said sitting down at the table. "You pray."

"That almost sounds like it's my punishment for working late again tonight."

"I CAN'T TAKE A chance," said Matt talking on his cell phone with Dwayne. Matt was heading east on Ventura Boulevard toward the Russian Veil. "I have no idea what these guys are going to do. I've learned the hard way the experienced pros are tough to predict, and Boris is no

141

amateur. I may have to strip just to walk into the place. As soon as I'm comfortable, I'll strap on a wire, but until then you'll have to trust me."

"It's your call. I was just asking the question. But you were wired at the funeral. Will that cause a problem not being wired now?"

"I understand your concern. I talked it over with Patti Weiss at the U.S. Attorney's office, and she didn't have a problem since this is the first meeting at the club. She just wanted me to document it in the 302 why I wasn't wired. I can cover it on paper."

"Just hope we don't miss a smoking gun," said Dwayne.

"If we do, I'll have to get them to shoot again."

CHAPTER TWENTY-NINE

Matt parked on the street and walked to the rear of the club as Boris instructed. Most patrons entered from the front, but a wake in Bobby's honor was being held in the back room. The invitation-only ceremony would be Matt's first opportunity to view Boris and Jesse on home turf.

A man with a Budweiser tumor sat on a bar stool at the back door. Matt didn't recognize him from the funeral, but to Matt all trailer trash looked alike. "Yeah?"

"I was a friend of Bobby's. Boris invited me tonight."

"Down the hall and to the left."

"Thanks."

"To the left. Not the right. Make sure you go to the left."

Matt kept walking. "Is that my military left or the other one?"

"Huh?"

He entered the darkened hallway, sizing up the environment quickly. It was second nature. Every time he entered a new venue, he sought the exits, the escapes, the covers, and the concealments. He had walked down too many "dark alleys" not to make the effort to ensure his safety.

As he turned left, it was readily apparent he wasn't attending a sedated ceremony honoring the dead. A glance around the room confirmed his belief why first cousins should never marry. Those in attendance appeared to be short on brains and long on brawn. The chatter was rapid and fervent. Even before he began to hone in on specific conversations, he could pick up bits and pieces and realized the thirty or so in attendance were not happy-go-lucky members of a local humanitarian outreach organization. The room was an incubator for hate.

Matt was outside the wire in the enemy's lair. For most it would be a pucker-factor moment;

for Matt it was his element. He lived for these incursions beyond the comfort of a bureaucrat's desk, always ready with an alternative truth.

Jesse spotted Matt and made his way to him. Extending his hand, Jesse greeted Matt like a close confidant. He gave Matt a quick handshake and then a hug. Matt hoped the others were watching this gesture of recognition because it might help solidify Matt's bona fides within the group.

There was no subtle pat down or search, not a hint of suspicion. He could have worn a wire, but in this noise he wouldn't get much of a recording. It had never happened, but he feared the day when he's caught wearing a wire in some noisy venue where there was no evidentiary value to the meeting, just overcautious prosecutors and bureaucrats seeking to protect themselves from allegations of misconduct. Screw the undercover. We need to save our jobs. *Focus.*

Jesse ushered Matt past a few people almost shoving them out of the way as the two headed for the bar. Jesse drew two cold ones from the tap and handed one to Matt.

"To a new brother," said Jesse as the two touched glasses.

"To an old brother who is no longer with us, God rest his soul," said Matt.

Jesse started to talk but then saw someone

across the room. "Excuse me a minute, Matt. I need to settle something. Not sure he should even be here." Jesse took off leaving Matt standing alone.

Before Matt could take a drink, he was bumped from behind and fell forward spilling most of the beer on the floor. "What the . . ."

"Sorry, man," said a 5'6", 250-pound, shaved-head, human fireplug who stumbled reaching for another drink.

Matt eyed the poster child for white-trash week at federal lockup. His arms may have been bigger than Matt's thighs. Matt faced off against much bigger men but had no desire to challenge this sequoia tree stump standing before him.

"Just trying to get another beer. You new here?" asked the stump.

"Yeah, I'm a friend of Jesse's. This is my first time. Bobby and I were friends. I was helping him with his painting business and a few other things he had going."

Stump, who was half in the bag, looked Matt up and down. "Are you with the Northern Virginia Human Relations Council?"

"Huh?" said Matt.

Stump's eyes were glazed over. "Where's your green armband?"

Matt was still confused.

Stump glared. "The name's Andrew."

"Sorry Andy, not quite following you."

"I said Andrew. Just call me Andrew MacDonald. You still don't have a clue, do you?"

"Afraid you got me, pal," said Matt.

"You ever do time?"

"Nope," said Matt, "but I take it you didn't get those tats at *Miami Ink*."

Andrew's look signaled contempt, and he walked away without saying another word.

There was a commotion in the back of the room. Matt turned in time to see Jesse pick up a guy and literally throw him out of the room. Even over the noise of the crowd, you could hear the patron as he landed against the wall in the hallway. Matt leaned up against the bar and saw no one come to the aid of tonight's first contestant in the human log-toss competition.

When Jesse returned, Matt sought an explanation.

"I get off on pain, theirs not mine."

Matt offered a confused look.

"He was Bobby's main supplier of ephedrine. He smuggles it up from Mexico. I know he was behind Bobby getting back in the business."

"Does he have a name?"

Jesse jumped on the question. "Why, you plan on going into business?"

Focus. Matt asked a stupid question. Stupid questions get you killed. In his undercover role it made no sense for him to have any interest in Bobby's drug dealings. Even in this case it didn't matter. *You're not investigating an ephedrine connection.* He needed a quick recovery.

"No, but Bobby said some guy who traveled back and forth to Mexico might be able to hook me up with Dianabol. I thought maybe this was the guy."

"Did he give you a name?"

"Yeah but I can't recall, maybe Dwayne something."

"This guy's not named Dwayne. You're not into body building. Why are you asking about Dianabol?"

"A buddy was asking me about it."

"Well, you don't want to deal with this guy. The crap he slings is veterinary grade, and even that is underdosed. I can hook you up if you're interested."

"Yeah, maybe later."

Matt breathed a barely audible sigh of relief. *Focus.* He and Jesse said little but leaned against the bar and looked out across the room. Women marched in and out throughout the evening, their dress more suitable for beach volleyball, but no one complained. Most were beautiful or at least seemed to be in the dimly lit back room.

A few people came up and offered words about the deceased. Soon a crowd gathered. To hear most tell it, Bobby sounded like multiple episodes on *America's Dumbest Crooks.*

There was a speeding ticket late one night in

Long Beach, a high-speed chase ending in a crash just as he was about to get on the freeway going the wrong direction. No one was hurt. When the cops dragged him out of the car, his explanation was straightforward. Some guy stole his hashish, and he was trying to catch him. Bobby's salvation on that one was a news copter recording the chase and a policeman being a bit too free with his nightstick as he coaxed Himmler from the car. The principals agreed to let bygones be bygones, and the incident went away. The bar crowd hoisted a beer to Bobby.

Then there was Halloween a few years back. Dressed up like Superman, he burglarized bedrooms as the owners were passing out candy at the front door to the kids of his confederates. They hit the gated communities in northwest San Fernando Valley and made a killing: jewelry, coin collections, even a flat screen TV. At one point the parents made the kids change costumes and revisit a house so Bobby could go back for a second helping. Another beer for the deceased!

Or the time he carjacked a neighbor's Volkswagen because he was late for a court appearance in Van Nuys. What made it especially humorous to the now drunk crowd, Bobby couldn't drive a stick. He learned in route grinding gears across the Valley. Jesse laughed the loudest on that story because Jesse ended up replacing the transmission and paying off the lady not to file charges. Lift your glasses to Bobby Himmler!

Matt could add a colorful story that might be worth a laugh but decided not to contribute the truth behind a tweeked-out runner and the broken ankle. And of course there is always the one about the exploding meth lab. Yeah, Bobby Himmler was a million laughs. He'll be missed.

As Matt learned that evening, Himmler may have been good for a felony a day. Check next year's crime stats; if the numbers are down, thank Bobby Himmler.

CHAPTER THIRTY

Even though Dwayne had a desk at the new JTTF off-site in the Valley, he spent hours each week at the FBI's main office in Westwood, the upscale Los Angeles community UCLA calls home. Matt and Dwayne sat on the empty patio of a Westwood coffee shop just a few blocks from the Federal Building. Matt reasoned not many Russian Veil patrons would be traipsing around L.A.'s coveted Westside so the relatively open meeting with Dwayne was safe.

Both were drinking iced tea, and Matt had one leg up on a third chair at the table explaining his

encounter the previous night with the 5'6"
sequoia stump.

"Andrew MacDonald?" said Dwayne.

"Yes."

"Green armbands?"

"Yes."

"The Northern Virginia Human Relations
Council, you don't have a clue, do you?" asked
Dwayne.

"What are you talking about?"

"I'm black and I know about it."

"About what?"

"*The Turner Diaries*. It's a novel written by
William Pierce, the leader of the National
Alliance. He used the pen name Andrew
MacDonald. The book is about the overthrow of
the government and ultimately the extermination
of all Jews and minorities. The Order was an
organization in the early eighties named after the
group in the book. They murdered Alan Berg, a
radio talk show host in Denver. Timothy
McVeigh had a copy of the book in his
possession when he was arrested. I guess you
could say it's required reading for all right-wing
nut jobs," said Dwayne.

"Maybe I should have done my homework.
Can I borrow your copy?" said Matt with a
smile.

"You think it's fatal?"

"They didn't pounce, and I walked out of there

in one piece. I'll talk to Jesse. See if he brings it up. Maybe I can rehabilitate myself through him. I'm a criminal businessman not some fringe-type lunatic. I'll play it off that way. But I'm guessing Andrew MacDonald isn't Stump's real name. I'm not sure he can read, let alone write."

THE NEXT DAY MATT followed up on Jesse's signal to call him, and Jesse seemed open on the phone. The two set up a meeting for a late lunch.

Matt pulled into the back parking lot of the Chinese Gardens, the restaurant where he first met Bobby Himmler's cousin.

Matt walked in, held up two fingers, and took a seat in the rear.

The waitress did a slight bow and in broken English asked Matt if he wanted a drink. He ordered iced tea, and she quickly responded with a tall, presumably clean glass of sweet, lemon iced tea.

Matt watched the front door as he sipped on the sweet tea. Jesse seemed friendly enough on the phone, and Matt assumed if his cover were blown Jesse would have picked a less public place for a confrontation. Still the fear of exposure permeates the thinking of every undercover agent. The feeling nags at your inner core and never completely dissipates no matter how experienced or how familiar you are with the respective targets. But Matt knew if that inner fear ever left it might be time to quit because without it you lose your edge. Fear brings focus. Careless confidence can mean death.

Within a few minutes Jesse showed up and spotted Matt. He said something to the waitress as he walked in and joined Matt in the back.

Jesse greeted Matt with a hug, but Matt could feel Jesse's hand run down his back. He was checking for a wire or maybe a weapon. *Too many B-movies Jesse, I don't carry there anymore.*

"So what's the deal with you and your cousin?" asked Matt laughing. "White racists and the only place you want to meet is some Chinese restaurant that occasionally gets clearance from the health department."

Jesse smiled as the waitress brought his drink. Jesse held up his glass. "Best sweet, lemon iced tea in the Valley."

"That's what Bobby told me too."

"So what do you think?" asked Jesse.

"About the tea?"

"No, about the other night."

"Some decent-looking women, that's for sure, but this is L.A.; beautiful women are everywhere."

"What about Boris and the guys?"

"Felt somewhat like an outcast. I think a few of your friends are sporting felony records."

Jesse laughed. "An indictment is not a

conviction, and I'm sure everyone who spent time away has been rehabbed."

Matt laughed as well. "I'm not sure they were all rehabilitated."

Jesse then came around to Stump. "Just a warning. Andy is a cautious man. He fears infiltration and is suspicious of all strangers. I'm not exactly sure what happened, but you didn't pass the test."

Matt explained the encounter without explaining he now understood *The Turner Diaries* reference.

Jesse gave a hearty laugh. "Andy pulls that Andrew MacDonald crap on everyone. Some people read the Bible in prison. Andy memorized *The Turner Diaries*. He thinks everyone who isn't familiar with the book can't be trusted and must be a cop. Andy is a true believer and one man you want on your side. He was the weight-lifting champ of Lompoc when he did a nickel on a gun-running charge."

"I guess if I was a cop, they would have made me read the book before they sent me in," said Matt.

"Makes sense to me. I'll clear it up with Andy. Don't worry."

Jesse took another long gulp of his tea as the waitress waited to refill his glass. Matt wanted Jesse to take the lead and sipped on his drink as well.

Jesse started to rise. "You ready to eat?"

The two headed to the buffet line where Jesse far exceeded the owner's expectations of consumption per customer. Jesse piled it on. He took the "all you can eat" advertising as a challenge. Matt moved through the line rather quickly and was seated when Jesse approached. The biker placed his plate on the table and returned for a second plate, filling it with every entrée he missed on the first trip.

As Jesse sat down to begin, Matt asked, "Did your doctor say you aren't getting enough MSG and cholesterol?"

Jesse merely smiled as he stuffed his face with everything Chinese. They ate in silence. Every effort at conversation was ignored by Himmler.

After devouring the food, Jesse foraged on a third trip through the line. Then he announced he was ready to discuss business. Before he asked a question, he belched without apology, and the strong smell of garlic lingered through Matt's answer.

"Yes, you can rent out a piece of the warehouse, assuming I have room. I move a lot of stuff in and out depending on what becomes available. Call me when you need it, and we'll see where we stand."

That was the only question Jesse asked, and he left, leaving Matt with the check. It could have been handled with a phone call. On the positive side Matt had an undercover meeting, he didn't die, and the cost of the lunch was picked up by the government. *Little victories make a winning strategy.*

CHAPTER THIRTY-ONE

After the meeting with Jesse, Matt went to the warehouse. He had some trash he wanted to deposit in the wastebaskets to make the place look lived-in and current. It was a delicate balance . . . trashy chic. Every couple of days he did a garbage run.

Just as he punched in the security code, disarming the alarm, his cell phone rang. Matt spied the caller ID.

"What's up?" said Matt as he headed to his office.

"Good news, I guess," said Dwayne.

Matt grabbed a Pepsi from the refrigerator and plopped down at his desk. "The Queen Mother got orders to the Czech Republic."

"No, but the fire marshal finished his investigation, and the coroner's report came back."

"That was quick."

"The ADIC made a couple of calls. He's got more juice than I do."

"So what's the verdict?"

"The three victims as we suspected: Robert Himmler, Michael Donovan, and Tiffany Adams. Himmler and Donovan died from the meth lab explosion. Adams COD, a 9 mm to the head courtesy of the PSM Makarov found at the scene."

"And the shooter?" asked Matt.

"Still not sure. They couldn't pull prints off the gun, and it wasn't registered. But since Tiffany was Bobby's live-in, it makes more sense she was killed by Mickey."

"Unless there was some sort of love triangle no one knew about."

"If that's the case, it doesn't impact our investigation."

Matt ran his fingers through his hair as he leaned back in the chair. There was a long pause.

"Matt, you still there?"

"Yeah, I'm just thinking. Why the gun? It doesn't look like a drug deal gone bad. No one walked away with their life let alone money or drugs. Could Mickey have confronted Bobby over the cooperation issue? But how could he have known?"

"You met with Jesse. Did he have issues with you?"

"Not really. We even discussed using the warehouse. If there are rumors floating around about Bobby's cooperation, they haven't reached Jesse."

"We will keep poking around from our end. I've got Steve Barnett doing a full background on Mickey. As long as you're comfortable, I vote we continue to march. You seem to be solid with Jesse."

"I'm still good to go. I'm glad we didn't avoid the funeral until after the report. Thanks for backing me at the warehouse."

Trying to do his best imitation of Dionne Warwick, Dwayne sang, "That's what friends are for."

"You are so talented. Maybe I can get you a spot on karaoke night at the Russian Veil."

"What's going on there?"

"I'm heading over tonight."

"You gonna wear a wire?"

"Yeah, we won't get much of a recording. It's pretty noisy, but maybe I can sneak off in the corner with somebody. Never can tell when those admissions will come."

"You need cover?"

"No, I'll call you before I go in and after I come out. I've found a cover surveillance team usually causes more concerns than protection. I've been burned a few times. I'm not worried, at least not yet."

"Okay, your call."

"I do have one issue."

"What's that?" asked Dwayne.

"How do I expense the lap dances?"

Dwayne let out a huge laugh.

"No, I'm serious. I'm not sure I can stay in there all night without getting a dance. Bobby said it would be expected. He said the girls will be coming up to me, and I can't put them off all evening. The Queen Mother's never going to approve a straight line item 'lap dance.' How do I handle it?"

"Did you reveal this part of the assignment to Caitlin?"

"She doesn't know and I have no plans of telling her."

"I guess just put it under 'meals and entertainment.' But don't go hog wild on the debauchery."

"I'll be reasonable. Heck, maybe the Queen Mother doesn't even know what a lap dance is?"

"She can't be that stupid!"

"That's a bet I'm willing to take. Maybe I'll try to slip one through on a voucher, and we'll find out," said Matt.

"Just focus your innovative thinking on the task at hand."

CHAPTER THIRTY-TWO

Matt parked on the street and headed east to the Russian Veil. Even from a hundred feet away he could hear the pulsating music. *So much for getting a quality recording.*

A new face stood at the door collecting the cover charge. Matt didn't recognize him from the funeral or the wake and hesitated before reaching into his pocket.

"If you're coming in, it's ten dollars. Otherwise move out of the way," said the doorman with a distinct Eastern European accent and lacking the social skills of a carnival barker.

He was at least 6'5" and weighed somewhere this side of a ton. As if his size wasn't memorable enough, the single eyebrow running across the Cro-Magnon dome made this an unforgettable face. If Matt were choosing sides, Face would be a number one draft pick. Matt handed him the ten dollar cover charge and hoped he did nothing to offend this guy. *Bouncers can be so temperamental.*

A red curtain was the only thing separating the sidewalk from sin, that and Face. Few who entered would leave with their soul intact. Matt was determined not to join the majority.

A crowd greeted the undercover agent as he pushed aside the curtain. The bar was packed two deep. It was a mix of outlaw bikers, blue-collar workers, and Eastern European refugees, probably Russian Mafia wannabes. Two girls were on the stage dancing, still dressed, but the song had just begun. Give it time. Along the far wall Matt spotted a half-dozen girls performing for individual customers, gyrating to the sounds of the music. He was looking for a familiar face. He spied Stump but thought better of engaging him in witty conversation about such classical pieces of literature as *The Turner Diaries*. Eventually Matt saw Jesse at the far end of the bar and elbowed his way through the crowd.

"Yo, you made it," hollered Jesse in an effort to be heard above the noise.

"Is it always this crowded?"

"Once a week Boris has a lap dance happy hour. When he sounds the gong, for one hour all lap dances are ten bucks. It rang about fifteen minutes ago. Give it another forty-five minutes and the place will clear out. These cheap idiots will go home to their wives and girlfriends. You wanna dance?"

"You're not my type," responded Matt with an impish grin.

Jesse looked confused at first then got it. "No, idiot, you want me to set you up with a girl? Some are really talented."

"I can tell. I bet most are classically trained."

"You'd be surprised. You want a beer?"

"Yeah, that sounds better."

Jesse hollered above the noise and was able to command the bartender's attention. He ordered two drafts. Matt noticed Jesse never paid for the drinks.

Each grabbed the frosted handle of a stein and toasted. Following Jesse's lead, Matt turned to watch the on-stage entertainment.

"Boris has quite an operation."

"Nothing slows the cash flow," said Jesse.

"What's your role in all this?"

Jesse didn't hesitate. "I provide the security."

"You mean you're not a paying customer?"

"Rule number one. I never pay for beer."

"What's rule number two?" asked Matt.

"As long as you're my partner, you never pay for beer."

"So now I'm your partner?"

"You were Bobby's partner and that makes you mine. I loved him. He had a rough life, and not too many people could stomach him. You must be a special person to have put up with him . . . or a cop."

Matt smiled. "Yeah, I'm part of a new reality-based TV show *Cops and Strippers*. It's on the Family Channel."

Jesse let out a belly laugh and toasted Matt a second time.

A tall, thin white guy whose bathing habits would rival a deployed combat Marine made his way over and whispered into Jesse's ear.

"Yeah, I'll handle it," said Jesse. "Matt, you meet J. D. Pinney?"

"No."

Jesse introduced the two and instructed them to follow him as he headed to the back of the club.

"Wait here," said Jesse.

Jesse walked into the room without knocking. Matt heard a loud crash and within seconds Jesse was dragging some half-dressed guy by his long hair. Jesse opened the back door and threw the guy ten feet into the parking lot.

"No refunds and I never want to see you back here again."

"Another disgruntled customer?" asked Matt as Matt, J. D., and Jesse stepped out into the parking lot.

"We got time limits. He exceeded his."

"Remind me to wear a watch," said Matt cracking a smile.

Jesse and J. D. both lit up cigarettes. Jesse offered one to Matt, who shook his head and said, "That'll stunt your growth."

"Now you sound like my mother."

The area at their feet was littered with cigarette butts and condom wrappers.

"I take it the back room is for more than just casual conversation?" asked Matt.

Jesse and J. D. smiled but said nothing while blowing streams of smoke toward the sky.

The aroma from the cigarettes was more like dirty socks than fine North Carolina–grown tobacco. "What are you guys smoking?" asked Matt.

"They're free," said Jesse.

"Free of what. Smells like day-old horse crap at the county fair."

"They're counterfeit. Every once in awhile Boris picks up some cases and gets rid of them at a deep discount."

"Even on the cheap I think I'd go genuine."

The two finished their smokes, and Jesse invited Matt back into the club. "Let's go see Boris."

Jesse knocked on the closed door to Boris's office. Then heard, "Come."

Boris's office was large and well decorated. In contrast to the bar, it was clean, almost compulsively clean and orderly. The chairs were black Corinthian leather, the desk solid cherry. Black and white photos of Russia expensively framed adorned the far wall. The near wall had six video monitors. There was coverage of the bar and the main floor. The hallway leading to the back rooms was also monitored. Matt's suspicions of prostitution being a viable part of the business plan were confirmed as he watched a man with one arm draped over a dancer walk

163

into a back room. He was in a hurry and obviously didn't want to exceed his time limit.

"Jesse talked to you about using your warehouse," said Boris.

"That he did," said Matt eye-balling the hub of the operation.

"I'd like to come over and take a look someday soon."

"Anytime. As long as I have room you can rent space. It's secure and discreet. There are cars, trucks, and containers going through the complex all day so any traffic looks routine. It's pretty quiet at night so you have to take that into consideration. The best I can tell, LAPD patrols twice a night. I've stayed late many times waiting for deliveries. I'll see a black-and-white maybe once during the evening and maybe once between midnight and six."

"You've never had a problem?"

"Never. And just so we're clear, I'm not interested in moving drugs through there. Drugs bring too much heat, and those Feds start throwing around the forfeiture statutes. Even if they can't prove anything, they can break up a business in a hurry."

"You have my word. I'm not interested in drugs."

CHAPTER THIRTY-THREE

Matt pulled up to the Westwood coffee shop. Dwayne was waiting on the patio drinking a cup of coffee. As Matt passed the waitress, he ordered and joined Dwayne at the table.

"How'd it go last night?"

"Not bad for the first time."

"Do I need to sign off on a few lap dances?"

"No, I got out of there with my virginity."

Matt explained what he observed inside the club, and both agreed the probable cause was too weak to even begin thinking of planting a microphone in Boris's office or tapping the phones. Then Matt mentioned the counterfeit cigarettes.

"That's interesting. Boris has counterfeits. I guess it makes sense. Based on all our intel, he is into just about everything," said Dwayne.

"We may be able to exploit the cigarette connection."

"How?"

Matt leaned in a little closer. "Last year after we finished up the investigation at World Angel Ministry, I briefed security personnel from Philip Morris, R. J. Reynolds, and JTI. They were interested in the counterfeit cigarette aspect of the case. Apparently they have sued a lot of retail outlets for selling the fakes. They have also cut off distribution of legit cigarettes to those outlets caught selling counterfeits. That seems to have a bigger impact on the illegal sales than enforcement efforts by ATF or the State Franchise Tax Board."

"Makes sense. A fine isn't much of an incentive when the profits are so great, but cutting off a legitimate source of supply might really impact business."

"The guys from JTI said they could give us a good price on cigarettes if we ever needed them as part of a sting."

"What do they distribute in the United States?"

"Their big three are Mild Seven, Export A, and Wave."

"I don't think your biker buddies would be caught dead lighting up a Mild Seven," said Dwayne.

"I know it's not Marlboros or Camels, but Export A is high end. Might class up the club. Besides as cheap as these guys are, I could probably pass off Virginia Slims with the right back story. If I could pick up fifty to a hundred master cases from JTI, I would tell Boris they're stolen, and it might give me an in."

"Sounds like a plan. Go ahead and reach out for them. Let me know if you need anything from me."

"I'll make the call," said Matt.

CHAPTER THIRTY-FOUR

Matt sat on the wooden bench next to the wall. Gallo's Gym was like a second home. He worked out every morning but looked forward to the two or three times a week he could climb into the ring and test his amateur skills with professional boxers possessing world-class efficiency. The bumper-sticker slogans were wrong; violence sometimes is the answer. Although outside the ropes those who follow the rules often lose. The ring taught Matt the skills and discipline to survive the streets.

He still maintained an element of secrecy at the gym. Only the owner, Rock Gallo, a Marine veteran from Korea, knew Matt's real occupation. No one else asked or seemed to care. The gym wasn't a place to socialize. It was home to real boxers with real skills and a real determination to make it in the world inside the ring. It was survival of the fittest. No socialism, no equality, no affirmative action. If you won, you progressed. If you lost too often, you looked for other work. The only thing the other boxers knew about Matt was he was willing to climb into the ring with anyone, could take a beating, and often dish one out. He was respected, and in the gym only that mattered.

As he wrapped his hands, he was watching Fernando Perez, a light heavyweight from Panama. Perez was lighting up the boxing world. He was 15-0 with a half-dozen knockouts. His hands were lightning fast, and he had a powerful right cross capable of turning protruding chins into mush. Matt had been on the wrong end of a few of those right crosses so he understood firsthand the power behind the punch. The lesson was an easy one; keep the hands high and close to the face.

The sounds of the gym were unique: the whine of the ropes, the patter of feet as the boxers danced, the rhythm of speed bags, and the clang of a recently installed bell at three-minute intervals. Matt walked to an empty peanut bag and joined the symphonic overture. He really could make the bag sing, and it was one place his mind seemed to relax. Despite what most administrators and even many street agents believed, undercover work wasn't something gun-toting actors turned on only when the surveillance tapes were rolling. There were no tranquil seas, only crashing surf. Undercover work was a 24/7 mind-set, and it seemed as if every waking hour was spent trying to concoct that next scenario. When Matt was at Gallo's, the UC world was somewhere beyond the walls of a smelly, noisy gym.

Matt worked the speed bag, the heavy bag, skipped rope, did a zillion crunches but never climbed in the ring. Rock was working with Fernando for an upcoming HBO fight in Las Vegas, and all the attention was centered on the Panamanian's preparation. Even though Rock turned eighty earlier in the year, his mind was quick and alert. As far as Matt was concerned, Rock had the most analytical boxing eye of anyone he knew. He could spot an opponent's weakness better than anyone in the game.

Rock climbed out of the ring as Matt was finishing his workout.

"How you doin', kid?" said Rock.

"I'm doing great. How's he doing? You got him ready for next week?"

"He's money in the bank."

"You got the other guy sized up?"

"It won't go three. It amazes me why no one picked up on it yet."

"Oh, here it comes," said Matt. "You found the weakness."

"Yep, I found the weakness, and Fernando is going to exploit it right to a title shot. He may be an under card next week, but by the end of the year, he'll be battling for the belt and headlining an HBO special."

"You're that sure?"

"Matt, you've seen this kid work. You've taken a few standing eight-counts. He's got the fastest hands I've ever seen. Watch the fight next week. Everyone thinks this kid from New Jersey, they call him The Beast, is the next champ. He's already been crowned. Our fight is just supposed to be a warm-up for his title. Well, they're wrong. Atlantic City has the same pattern once he gets into a rhythm; three left jabs, a right cross, and then he drops his left to go to the body leaving the chin wide open. Every time. He starts it late in the second round and always by the third. He's strong, and he gets away with it because no one has been willing to work within his wing span. Fernando's gonna play with him, and then by the third the Great White Hope will be joining the ranks of the once-weres."

"I better get my money down."

"It's safer than t-bills."

"Thanks, Rock," said a smiling Matt. Hollering up to Fernando, Matt said, "Feast on The Beast in Vegas!"

CHAPTER THIRTY-FIVE

'll bring you a carton, but I'm not hauling around a bunch of cases of hot cigarettes in my car," said Matt.

"What kind of salesman doesn't offer free delivery?" said Jesse.

"The kind that's moving stolen merchandise. Why don't you and Boris come over here and take a look at the product. I've got a hundred cases in my warehouse. I'll give you a good price, but I don't plan on keeping them around for long. I've got some Iraqi in San Diego who may be driving up tomorrow. He'll buy the whole lot so if you and your Russian sidekick are interested you better get over here today."

"Let me check with him, and I'll get back to you. Do they have tax stamps?"

"Of course, I'm full service."

"Sounds good."

Matt hung up the phone assuming the ruse worked and Jesse and Boris would be guests at the warehouse before the afternoon was up. The refrigerator was stocked and the snacks were fresh. He threw a day-old paper in the trash just to make it seem as though Matt frequented the place daily. He stirred up the dust but never wanted it to look too clean. It was a warehouse, not Martha Stewart's living room. Being the ever gracious host, Matt even put toilet paper in the john. At least initially he wanted to impress his visitors. He could screw with them later.

In the warehouse at the far wall, Matt stacked one hundred master cases of Export A. Each case had fifty cartons. Matt was trying to concoct a plausible story as to how he obtained the cigarettes. He probably would use the gastronomical approach; whatever gut feeling he had at the time he divulged his scenario would be the correct answer. As long as he kept the story straight, it wouldn't matter to Jesse or Boris. In fact they might not even ask. Besides, why would he even reveal his source? The cigarettes are genuine, the tax stamps real, and the price is well below wholesale. They are going to buy them regardless of the story he tells.

His cell phone rang and he answered, "When you coming over?"

"How'd you know we were coming?" asked Jesse.

"Because Boris strikes me as an extremely smart entrepreneur, and only an idiot or a moral man would pass up this bargain. Boris is neither. When are you coming over?"

"We're leaving now."

Matt walked into the hallway, flipped the middle light switch quickly three times, and the file cabinet slid to the left. He entered the small room, turned on the recording equipment, checked to make sure it was working, and left.

About ten minutes later as he was sitting in his office, sipping a Pepsi, he peered out the window. A black Cadillac Escalade with smoked-out side windows and chrome dubs pulled into the lot. *Why don't you just stencil "mobster mobile" on the side panels?*

Matt let Jesse knock a couple of times before he unlocked the front door.

"Sorry, I was on the phone with my guy in San Diego."

Boris and Jesse entered. The reception area was simple and uninviting. A worn couch and chair, poor lighting, and dust greeted the guests.

"Glad you guys could make it. Come on in my office."

Matt ushered them in and offered them a drink. Seeing Matt had a Pepsi on his desk, Jesse asked for a Pepsi. Boris wanted a Diet.

"So what do you have for me?" asked Boris.

"No small talk. No 'how about them Dodgers?' Come on, Boris. We hardly know each other," said Matt smiling.

"You want me to explain the marginal propensity to consume?" said Boris.

"Matt, Boris is a busy man. I told him you had a great deal on cigarettes. He's interested. That's all you have to know," said Jesse.

Matt continued to smile, an almost wicked smile if you knew the undercover agent. He pulled a package of Export A from the desk drawer and tossed it to Boris. "Fair enough. I've got one hundred master cases, fifty cartons to a case sitting in my warehouse. I'm looking to move them quickly. Make me an offer."

Boris examined the pack and sniffed the outside.

"They're genuine, my friend. Made from the finest reconstituted sheet tobacco, not those dirty socks from North Korea Jesse was smoking the other night."

"You know a lot about cigarettes."

"I read."

"Does each pack have the tax stamp?"

"Like I said, these are genuine all the way. Tax stamps on every pack. I even threw in the Surgeon General's warning label just to impress you."

"How did you come across these?" asked Boris.

"Oh, now we are beyond the traditional price of the product. The name of my source will cost you extra. Just know you won't find a better product at a better price unless somehow your crew is working the same truck stop as my connection."

"Very well. Let's take a look."

The three walked into the warehouse.

"It seems empty. Not a good use of your resources," said Boris.

"It's available when I need it. Right now my suppliers are on hiatus. But that could change with a phone call."

As they walked over to the master cases, Boris asked questions about the warehouse setup. He examined the boxes and within seconds made up his mind. "I am satisfied. Besides, now we know where you live. I know there will be no problems with the transaction or the guarantee."

"As long as your money is green, we won't have a problem. As to a guarantee, the cigarettes are genuine and stolen. That much I can guarantee. Once you take delivery, I have no idea what you or anyone else is talking about, assuming I'm asked."

Now it was Boris's turn to smile. "Let's return to your office and negotiate a fair price."

"My thoughts exactly."

MATT WATCHED THE BLACK Escalade pull from the parking lot and punched in a familiar number on his cell phone. "Elvis has left the building."

"Are you clear?" asked Dwayne.

"Yep, they just left. I made a sale."

"Great. You make a profit?"

"What do you care? I get to pocket the excess, right? They're sending a truck over at five to pick up fifty cases."

"Why didn't you sell him everything?"

"I told him I promised some cases to a guy in San Diego who has helped me in the past. This just makes me more desirable. We bought some major credibility with this. He kept eyeing the warehouse and asked a lot of questions about capacity, security, and access."

"You want me to contact SOG and take them away tonight."

The Special Operations Group, or SOG as it is known in FBI parlance, consists of several six-man surveillance teams. They are professional, discreet, and well respected within the Bureau.

"No, not this time. I don't really care what they do with the cigarettes. I would hate to get burned our first time out."

"Okay, it's your call."

CHAPTER THIRTY-SIX

Although Matt was hoping to get home at a reasonable hour for dinner, he agreed to wait at the warehouse until the truck arrived. He told Boris to have his men there by five, but it was already five thirty and still no truck. Matt picked up the phone and started to punch in Boris's number when he spied a U-Haul pull into the parking lot.

Matt ran outside and directed Stump to the warehouse entrance in the alley.

"Sorry, I'm late," said Stump from the cab of the truck after pulling into the warehouse. It sounded like a genuine apology.

"You're fine. I didn't have much going tonight anyway. Had the game on and was watching it when I saw you pull up. Where's your green armband?" asked Matt.

Stump said nothing but allowed a smile.

Matt pointed to the cases of cigarettes. "Just back the truck over there. We'll get 'em loaded pretty quickly."

Stump maneuvered the vehicle around the warehouse into position and stopped when Matt signaled. As Stump jumped from the cab, Matt opened the rear doors to the truck.

"I expected you to bring some help," said Matt.

"I guess the Bear figured it was only fifty cases and I could load them myself."

"The Bear. I assume that is a term of endearment for Boris."

Stump smiled. "You're using college words on me. Yeah, endearment, as long as that's not some gay thing. It's what I call Boris."

"To his face?"

"Sometimes. He doesn't mind. I just have to smile when I say it."

Stump removed his wife beater T-shirt, and Matt was faced with a human canvas displaying the work of some of California's most prominent prison artisans. Even to an accomplished undercover agent, prison tats were intimidating. Matt didn't view them as a badge of honor like a Silver Star or Purple Heart, more like an advanced degree in criminality, a red-flag warning.

"Who does your work?"

Stump smiled. "The AB."

"All of that done while you were away?"

"Who says I went anywhere?"

Matt laughed out loud. "I may not be up on the latest edition of *The Turner Diaries*, but I'm not stupid. I don't have a hundred cases of stolen cigarettes in my warehouse because the local Boy Scout troop was unable to sell them at their latest fund-raiser. Besides, someone mentioned the other night you were the weightlifting champ at Lompoc. I assume they weren't referring to the city's annual flower festival."

Stump nodded. "I was away for awhile."

Matt and Stump began to load the cases into the truck. They talked as they worked.

"You from Los Angeles originally?" asked Matt.

"I grew up in Sacramento."

"What brought you to L.A.?"

"I met Jesse in Lompoc. He got released before I did and told me about Boris so I settled here."

"How long you been out?"

"A little over a year now."

"Are you still on paper?"

"Yeah, I got a tail."

Stump paused and looked at Matt for a long five seconds. Matt may have overplayed his hand asking about parole. "You seem to know a lot about the system."

"I've never been in, but I've worked with guys who have. Bobby and I were friends. I've worked with others like him. You learn a lot just by listening. If I can help a guy, I will. Of course if he can help me, it's even better."

Stump seemed to relax as he resumed loading cases. Without saying a word, they worked out an arrangement where Stump grabbed the cases from the floor, handed them to Matt who stacked them in the truck.

"So what were you and Bobby into?" asked Stump.

"A little of this and a little of that. Mainly he needed some financial backing to get back on his feet."

"Bobby wasn't the best businessman. About the only thing he could do was cook. Most of that he used or at least Tiffany used. She was chronic. If you were financing his meth operation, I hope you weren't planning to make a profit."

"I was trying to help him with his painting business and make him look legit to his PO. I guess any profit I hoped to make with his sidelines went up in smoke. Bobby never mentioned Mickey to me." Matt took a long breath to make the inquiry seem so casual: "Was he involved? Was I splitting profits with silent partners?"

Stump slowed up long enough to get a better grip on the case of cigarettes. "I can't see Mickey involved with Bobby. Mickey may have bought off him, but they never got along very well.

Especially once Bobby got to using so heavily. Mickey never thought Bobby could be trusted. He figured he was weak."

"Funny, Boris said the same thing about both Bobby and Mickey."

Stump continued grabbing boxes. "I hear these politicians on TV say torture doesn't work. They're wrong. It works. I've watched weak people fold with just a threat."

"So you agree they were weak?"

"Yep."

"Even Mickey?"

Stump nodded. "He was always trying to impress Boris. Boris never paid much attention to him because Mickey had little value, except show. He dogged it whenever he could snatch the opportunity. Mickey was too concerned with looking good for the camera. He wanted to be a movie star. Whenever he got some bit role, he'd invite Boris to the set, but Boris never went. He didn't care about Hollywood. He always said, 'What's so big about actors? They ever really kill anybody but their old ladies?' He didn't believe any of them were real tough guys. Mickey wasn't much of an earner and needed someone to do his heavy lifting. Unless you carry your weight, Boris has no use for you. The only thing Mickey ruled was women. He could party-on all night, and some women liked that; but as far as being a man, it was all beach muscles."

"Why do you think he was at Bobby's?"

"I can tell you it wasn't socializing," said Stump.

"Did Mickey and Tiffany have a thing?"

Stump laughed out loud. "Mickey got a lot of action, some of it pretty good. He didn't need some skank like Tiffany. You ever meet her?"

"No."

"Mickey brought one girl around a month or so ago, Dawn Platt. I think she was on work release over at the hospital. She was hot. I mean sizzling. He had her. He didn't need some filthy street walker carrying who knows what disease. This Dawn could have made some money at the Veil, but Boris only likes those Russian chicas at his place. There wasn't much Mickey had I wanted, but if he was to send me his female table scraps, you wouldn't hear me complaining."

Stump handed the last case to Matt who threw it on top of another case. Matt hopped out of the back and slammed the doors shut. Within a minute Stump was gone.

CHAPTER THIRTY-SEVEN

The Joint Terrorism Task Force off-site was in the west end of the San Fernando Valley. With the UC operation in full swing, Matt wasn't allowed to go to the main office in Westwood, a decision which was fine with him. The JTTF's location was secret and not even known to most FBI agents. Matt could handle all his official correspondence and paperwork from the off-site. The less time he spent in the Westwood office, the less opportunity he had to cross the Queen Mother and bring OPR onboard.

The Office of Professional Responsibility was the FBI's answer to Internal Affairs. Two months ago Matt finished paying off an OPR assessment for a Mercedes he crashed during an undercover assignment several years earlier. OPR opined Matt was "outside the parameters of normal work standards," and an allotment to the U.S. Treasury began. Every two weeks Matt and Caitlin saw a small chunk of every check remain in D.C. to pay for a car Matt didn't own and could never drive again. The ruling didn't really improve Matt's driving prowess or diminish his investigative initiative, but he tried to limit his liability and exposure. He would still keep the world safe for democracy but on his terms even if it meant fudging some Bureau-mandated reports.

Matt ran every morning before heading to the off-site or the warehouse. He had several different runs, but his favorite was a five-miler which took him past the high school. There he would pause long enough to do his twenty pull-ups and continue his run.

The sweat was dripping down his face as he entered the back door of the condominium. Caitlin was at the breakfast table, eating cereal and reading her Bible. He grabbed a carton of orange juice from the refrigerator and took a large gulp.

"Not from the carton, Cowboy. Get a glass."

"Why?"

"Because I might want to serve orange juice to our friends sometime."

"You mean your friends. I think all my friends are locked up."

"Maybe you should work on your interpersonal skills."

"I have interpersonal skills. I just have a basic mistrust of humanity."

"That's a tough way to go through life."

"Tell me about it," said Matt as he headed down the hallway. "But at least it keeps me alive on the street. Maybe once I retire I'll quit playing Judas and betraying everyone I meet."

Caitlin cocked her head and watched her hero retreat to the bedroom. She worried about the impact a lifetime of working undercover was having on the man she loved.

MATT QUICKLY DRESSED AND headed to the Valley. His first stop was Flip and Lydia Mitchell's home.

The Mitchells' home was a typical San

Fernando Valley ranch home: stucco, shake roof, tiny yard, and huge house payments. They lived in the neighborhood called Northridge, made famous by the earthquake of 1994. Cracks in the retaining wall were the only evidence remaining of the massive quake.

They sat on the back patio where the California sunshine warmed the morning air. Lydia was recovering from her injuries. Most of the bruising was gone and all of the swelling subsided, but scars on her face from the cuts and gashes remained.

"The hardest part was telling the kids and seeing their reactions every morning. Maddie, our five-year-old, hasn't slept in her bed since that night. She's so afraid the men are going to come back. We kept her home from school the first few days, but she seems to be doing a little better."

"Have you heard anything from LAPD?" asked Matt.

"Nothing," said Flip, "How about you? Have you seen any reports?"

Matt shook his head. "I'm working on a special project and haven't had a chance to speak to anyone. I'm sure Dwayne has been in contact."

"You undercover?"

"Let's just say I'm working on a special project."

"Does it involve Lydia's attackers?"

Matt avoided answering and asked, "What can you tell me about that night?"

Flip understood the meaning behind Matt's avoidance of the question. With a slight smile he nodded.

Lydia repeated the story she told the police, which wasn't much. "I do seem to be remembering a few more details. There were three of them. I recall the driver was short and powerful. He was built like a tank and fast. He was quick out of the truck. I'm pretty sure it was a Dodge Ram like Flip's surveillance vehicle. I'm not sure of the color. It was dark. The other two were bigger. One was muscular. The other was thin. The thin guy may have had a beard. They were all white. But that's about it. It all happened so quickly."

"Does that help?" asked Flip.

"Flip, it all helps. But make sure you tell LAPD. They need to know, and it needs to come from Lydia. And I would prefer you not tell anyone I was here or at least asking questions. Dwayne is insistent we not interfere with the investigation. We'll support them any way we can but not take a direct hand that might taint a prosecution with the appearance of over-reaching."

"I understand. I'll call the detective. They've been good, just not quick with the results," said Flip as he took another sip of coffee.

"You know how that goes. They can only go where the evidence leads them." Matt paused then asked, "You back to work yet?"

"The office has been great about carrying me. I'll probably head back out to SOG next week sometime."

Matt got up to leave. "I better get going. I'll stop back in a few days. Let me know if you need anything."

CHAPTER THIRTY-EIGHT

Los Angeles might be the ethnic-diversity capital of the world, and Caitlin's second-grade class reflected a cross section of the city's culture. Her students were black, white, brown, and yellow, represented seven nations and four world religions. It was early in the school year, and Caitlin had not met all the parents. The first parent-teacher conference was still two weeks away. So far she encountered few problems, and the year was shaping up nicely, at least as nicely as can be expected for any public school in the Los Angeles Unified School District.

One student made an immediate impression. Michael Hughes was tall for his age but maybe the most polite student she ever had. He was neat and unfailingly helpful. His desk was immaculate, and every response was studded with a "yes ma'am" or "no ma'am." Michael was also the self-appointed enforcer in the classroom. So far he never abused his role so Caitlin allowed him free rein when it came to chastising miscreants on the playground. Caitlin noticed even one of her glances to a student for inappropriate conduct resulted in a Michael Hughes tune-up during the next break. He wasn't a bully, just the class disciplinarian. Since slashes in the school budget resulted in cutbacks in classroom aides, Michael's assistance was welcome. Caitlin just kept a close eye to make sure he didn't exceed his implied authority.

The warm afternoon sun felt good, and Caitlin enjoyed the opportunity to stand in its radiant heat as she assumed her post and monitored recess. After teaching for nearly a decade, she had learned to almost tune out the noise as the children ran and screamed at fifteen minute intervals. She looked engaged but her mind was elsewhere. Suddenly her senses were on high alert. She heard something startling her out of her recess trance.

Someone used the word *kike*. She bristled at the epithet. As she surveyed the playground, she realized the words came from the mouth of Michael Hughes. Michael was sticking his finger into the chest of Isaiah Goldman. Isaiah, a third-grader in Mrs. Stanton's class, had been on the wrong end of several reprimands early in the school year. He enjoyed teasing the girls, but there was no call for this type of language. Caitlin was shocked a second-grader used the term and questioned whether he understood the meaning but knew she needed to intervene immediately.

She hustled over to where Michael had Isaiah cornered against the building, preventing an escape from the enforcer's wrath.

"Boys, what seems to be the problem?"

Isaiah was in tears.

"He was making fun of Angela. He called her fat and made her cry. I warned him yesterday, but he did it again today," said Michael.

"Isaiah, I'll talk with you later. For now go sit on the bench. I need to speak with Michael."

Isaiah was only too eager to escape the immediate scolding and raced over to the picnic table.

"Michael, I appreciate your sticking up for Angela, but I was very disappointed to hear you call Isaiah a name."

"You mean kike?"

"Yes, Michael that's not a nice word, and we shouldn't use it. It is not acceptable speech. Where did you ever hear it?"

Caitlin had never disciplined Michael, and he fought back the tears.

"J. D. says it. He calls our neighbor one."

"Who is J. D.?"

"My mom's husband."

"Do you know what the word means?"

He shook his head.

"It makes fun of someone because his parents are Jewish. It would be like me calling you a bad name because of the color of your skin or hair or eyes. Even though your stepfather may have used it, I'm sure your mother would be disappointed if she knew you were speaking like this on the playground."

The life drained from his brown eyes. A tear tracked his cheek. "Please don't tell my mom. She'll tell J. D. I'll get a beating if he knows I got in trouble at school."

"Let's make sure it never happens again."

"I'm sorry, Mrs. Hogan. I'll never use that word again."

"I think you owe Isaiah an apology."

"But he called Angela a name."

"I know, and he's going to apologize to her as well."

Caitlin marched Michael over to the bench, and the apologies began.

CHAPTER THIRTY-NINE

Matt walked past Face, the 6'5" bouncer maintaining his post at the entrance to the Russian Veil. Being Jesse's friend at least saved the FBI the cover charge. *It's not what you know; it's who you know.* The place was crowded with blue-collar laborers and unemployed bikers, a typical Friday night crowd. Two women were dancing on stage, and each of the side tables was taken by a customer and his lap-dance companion. Matt knew he could avoid an issue with lap-dance expenditures this evening because Jesse invited him to the private room where a dozen or so would be watching an HBO boxing pay-for-view event.

Boris passed the word Matt was to be treated with utmost respect, not quite family but a close friend. The cigarettes brought Matt the credibility he hoped. Beers were on the house, and should Matt choose, he received "employee discount pricing" on all lap dances. Matt was never quite sure how much that was and so far had not taken advantage of this special benefit.

Matt entered the back room without knocking. It wasn't even close to the Playboy mansion or something out of *Cribs* but could best be described as biker chic. A huge flat-screen TV was on the far wall, and neon-lighted signs of every domestic beer adorned the side walls. Comfortable black leather seats were scattered throughout the room. The "No Smoking" sign could barely be seen through the haze of genuine Export A smoke compliments of Matt's contact at JTI.

As soon as Matt walked in, Boris approached with a cold beer. They touched glasses in a toast to nothing but Friday night and then talked about nothing of significance. Jesse soon joined in the drinking and the conversation. As the evening was taking shape, Matt pulled from inside his jacket four Gurkha Centurians.

Boris's eyes brightened, and his huge hand gripped the six-inch jewel. Holding it to his nose, he said, "They call these the Rolls Royce of cigars. You have exquisite tastes, my friend."

"If the fights fall my way tonight, I'll be able to afford my exquisite tastes."

The pay-for-view boxing card from Caesars began at 6:00 p.m. Three twelve-round bouts were on the card, the feature fight being the WBC Super Middleweight title. Matt's interest, however, was in the first fight of the evening. Fernando Perez, the Panamanian light heavyweight from Rock Gallo's gym was going up against Blain Wright, a powerful Aryan with a well-deserved prison record. Most boxing experts believed Wright would be wearing the green WBC championship belt by the end of the year. He was the Great White Hope, even if that hope had a felony conviction. Tonight's fight was a foregone conclusion as far as the Russian Veil customers were concerned. Wright was blood, even if he wasn't related to the rabble in the back room. He was white and he would win. His undefeated twenty-win record, sixteen by knockout, made him the betting public's favorite as well.

Wright was skilled, there was no doubt, but promoters yearned for a white boxing champion in any weight class. Matt wasn't eager to climb into the ring with the Russian Veil's HBO favorite, but he knew some of the fights were milk runs. Fighters long past their prime took the bouts needing a payday just to cover everyday living expenses. The bouts were lopsided, and the public was cheated of a real fight. It certainly wasn't fixed, but anyone with boxing sense knew the outcome before the opening bell. Tonight might be Blain Wright's first true test in the ring.

No one sat once the TV came on. The excitement inside the back room was genuine. No one was even drunk . . . yet.

When Fernando Perez walked from his dressing room to the ring, Jesse's boys cursed and shouted racial slurs as if Perez could hear them through the big screen. Matt kept quiet but smiled, pumping his fist in the air as if championing the cause for racial superiority. Rock Gallo held the ropes as Fernando entered the ring. When Rock helped him with his robe, Fernando, a naturalized American citizen, was wearing red, white, and blue shorts, honoring his adopted country. That further infuriated the bikers, and more curses colored the smoke-filled room.

Blain Wright then entered the TV picture, and spontaneous cheers arose from the back room. Matt smiled, high-fived, and chest thumped the others. He hadn't seen this much excitement since the state basketball playoffs in his senior year of high school. With the inside scoop from Rock, Matt assumed the cheering would subside by the middle of the third round. Blain entered the ring and removed his robe. His back and left arm was a canvas of prison artwork. Anyone with street sense knew the ink was not the product of a local strip-mall tattoo parlor, nor was the boxer from the finest finishing schools of the Eastern establishment.

Michael Buffer made the introductions and with his trademark call let the words roll from his tongue, "Let's get ready to rumble!" The crowd went wild, both in Vegas and at the Russian Veil.

The referee brought the two fighters to the center of the ring and gave the obligatory instructions neither heard. They touched gloves and returned to their respective corners. Within seconds the bell rang, and they got it on.

Both fighters came out throwing punches. Most light heavyweights size up an opponent, dance around the ring for a few rounds, and attempt to pace themselves for a twelve-rounder. Not these two. It was a slugfest from Jump Street.

Blain Wright took control early, throwing more punches than Fernando, landing some solid jabs. Matt always said the longest three minutes of your life are in the ring, and Matt agonized with every punch Fernando absorbed. It was difficult to tell how many of Blain's punches were effective. Fernando's quickness may have spared him a lot of damage. He slipped many of Blain's jabs, but a few managed to find the mark. The bell to end the first round came just as Fernando was starting to find a comfort level in the ring.

The cameras followed Fernando to his corner. Rock threw out the stool and began toweling off his young fighter. The cornerman treated a small cut above the right eye as Rock provided advice in Spanish. When the crowd at the Russian Veil heard the instructions in Spanish, more curses were hurled at the television. "This is America! Speak English!" Followed by laughter. The bell rang and the second round began.

Blain again took charge, proving he may deserve an undefeated record. He cut the ring in half and started pouring on a jab-cross combination. Fernando countered with some quick jabs, but Blain was winning the second round. With fifteen seconds left in the round, Fernando went down while backpedaling from a combination. The referee ruled it a slip, but as soon as Fernando went down, Matt, lost in the moment, hollered, "Get up!"

Twelve sets of eyes immediately turned to Matt. *Focus.* These weren't ordinary glares but pure hatred piercing him. The bell rang ending the second round.

Forgetting any newly formed friendship because of Bobby, Jesse was the first to pounce. "Who are you hollering for?"

Stump followed in rapid succession, "You cheering for some spic?"

Jesse yelled, "Go hang out in Boyle Heights with your greasy burrito buds! We don't need your kind in here."

The taunts came from all sides as everyone joined in but then jackals always attack when the victim is down. Matt was trapped in a goldfish bowl visible from all sides.

Before Boris could intervene, Matt responded convincingly, "I got five Benjamins that say this fight goes four rounds. I can't have this wetback from Panama take a dive before the fourth!"

Everybody laughed including Jesse and Stump. Maybe he staved off death one more time. *Be the hunter, not the hunted. Focus!*

"But I'll tell you one thing, this Great White Hope better protect his chin. He drops his left every time he goes to the body. This kid draped in the flag may be illegal, but he's got the fastest hands I've seen in awhile. He's gonna slip one in, and that undefeated record is going the way of the Pontiac."

The bell rang. The third round began. Blain stormed to the center of the ring, threw two jabs, and backed off. He then stepped forward, threw three quick left jabs, followed by a right cross, dropped his left hand to go to the body, and before he made the shot, Fernando nailed him. The Panamanian snapped a lightning fast right cross to the chin, and an undefeated Blain Wright folded like Sunday's paper. The referee could have counted for the rest of the evening, but the Great White Hope was headed for the recycle bin.

Those same twelve sets of eyes, three minutes ago shooting arrows at Matt, now looked to him in admiration. He called the shot for all to hear.

Matt threw down his beer in disgust, glass splattering on the floor. "It had to go to the fourth for me to collect! I'm outta here." He goose-stepped out the door; inside he was laughing hysterically.

• • •

WHEN MATT ARRIVED HOME, Caitlin was sitting in the dimly lit living room watching a movie on the Lifetime channel.

He easily recognized the network, kissed Caitlin, and headed to the kitchen to grab a soda from the refrigerator. "I always get worried when you watch these movies because it's usually some wife who manages to kill her husband and get away with it."

"I married you. I don't need Hollywood to teach me the techniques for the perfect crime. How was your night out with the boys?"

"I scored a few points. How was your day?"

Caitlin explained the situation with Michael Hughes.

Matt took a sip of his Pepsi then said, "You would think as a society we would have advanced beyond racial hatred and stereotyping."

Caitlin laughed.

"What?"

"This is coming from my husband who wants to charge people for DWA, driving while Asian."

"You know what I mean," said Matt. "When you instill that garbage in a child, it is so difficult to erase. People can change, but that type of lunacy is tough to combat. Look at those news clips on FOX when Palestinian kids are chanting death to America and playing out hatred like it's some parlor game. How are you going to handle this?"

"God's love can change any heart. I'm just going to have to watch Michael a little more closely. He's really a great little boy."

"Sounds like he's a next generation neo-Nazi."

"Matt, he's in the second grade."

"My point exactly."

CHAPTER FORTY

Matt arrived at the warehouse an hour before his scheduled appointment with Boris. He ensured the audio and video equipment were in working order and updated the trash to make it look as if he hung out daily at the undercover off-site. Nothing spells conflict for a UC op like a two-month-old newspaper sitting in the trash. Hard to explain why a viable business has cobwebs.

Matt watched Boris pull into the lot and was waiting at the door as Boris walked up the sidewalk. Matt held the door, and without even a greeting Boris marched to the restroom.

"Sortir," said Boris.

"And good afternoon to you as well. It's the door next to the file cabinet," said Matt as he returned to his office.

"I know where it is."

Matt heard the toilet flush, and within seconds Boris entered the office. "Did you wash your hands?"

"Yes," said Boris.

"Liar, I'm out of soap and paper towels," said Matt with a smile.

"What are you, a government health official?"

"No, but I am secret agent sent to penetrate the criminal underworld of former Soviet Union," said Matt with a very poor Russian accent.

Boris laughed.

"What can I do for you, comrade Boris?"

"Is your warehouse empty?"

"It is right now."

"Are you expecting anything in the near future?"

"Not really. I have something coming later in the week, but right now it's clean."

"I may need to store some items in your warehouse for a couple of nights. Not too many questions."

Matt got up and walked over to the refrigerator. "Want a Pepsi or a beer?"

"Give me diet."

"Oh yeah, I forgot the Indian summer swimsuit season is upon us and you need to look strapping in your Speedo."

Matt handed the three-hundred-pound-plus bear a Diet Pepsi. "What do you need to store?"

"Give-ups."

"Give-ups?"

"The small garage behind the Veil can hold most of my swag, but I have a thriving car sales business, and in the next few days I may have an overflow problem."

"You sell cars?"

"I sell cars overseas."

"I didn't know that. But what does *give-up* mean?"

"I take the cars owners no longer want and can't afford. They bring me the car and pay a small disposal fee. I arrange to have the car shipped to Dubai or elsewhere overseas, and then as if a miracle occurs, the car turns out to be stolen. The owner collects on the insurance and is very happy to have money in his pocket and to be out from under the payments."

"But he still has to pay off the loan. Doesn't that hurt his credit when he goes to purchase a new car?"

Boris slouched in his chair as he took a long drink. "Not if the insurance and lease agreements are set up the right way. My people only buy from those dealers who understand the intricacies of auto financing."

"In other words the salespeople and insurance agents are in on it."

After taking another sip of the Diet Pepsi, Boris smiled. "You understand capitalism and the American way."

"How hot are the cars you want to put in my garage?"

"Cold as the beer I serve on Friday night."

"Last Friday I thought the beer was warm."

"You should have complained to the management."

"Not sure it would do any good. I don't think the owner is necessarily consumer friendly. I've seen how he treats customers who overstay their welcome so I'm afraid to say too much about his beer."

"Maybe so, but these cars are cool. The owners don't report them stolen until the vehicles are safely on their way to the Middle East and I give the okay to call the police."

"I don't see a problem. Just make sure it's only your boys who bring the cars over here. I'm not interested in advertising to the world I store give-ups for the Soviet Empire."

"Understood."

"You are a walking advertisement for the entrepreneurial spirit. Keep this up and maybe next year you can make Fortune 500's Top Crook edition."

"America has been very good to me."

"Yeah, I can tell. That's why every chance you get you rub our noses in it."

Boris let out one his deep belly laughs. "You are starting to catch on, Comrade Matt."

Matt walked Boris to the door and slammed shut the double bolts as soon as Boris entered his Escalade and drove off. Matt raced back to the hallway, opened the recording room, and removed the tapes, replacing them with new ones. He prepared the evidence envelopes and started the chain of custody. Once he completed the administrative matters, Matt called Dwayne.

"Boris wants to store cars at the warehouse."

"Cars?"

"Yep, this guy is into some type of insurance fraud where he ships cars the owners don't want to the Middle East. The owners report them stolen and collect on the insurance. This guy is into everything . . . murder, prostitution, guns, insurance fraud."

"There's probably nothing he won't touch as long as the price is right."

"I told him I'd store the cars."

"When is he bringing them over?"

"He didn't give me a date. I assume as soon as he has inventory, maybe tonight."

"Tonight?"

"Yes."

"Matt, why do you do this to me?"

"What?"

"This changes the scope of the undercover operation. I have to run all this past the Queen Mother, the ADIC, and then back to D.C."

"Why do you need to go home? You don't have a social life."

"I used to before I came to L.A. and met you."

"When you run this up the chain, remind them

we aren't actually storing stolen cars. At this point all we are doing is providing overnight parking privileges to the target of our investigation," said Matt.

"I like that. We don't know for certain these morons are going to report the cars stolen or Boris is going to ship them overseas."

"Not at this point."

"Keeping that in mind, maybe I won't have to cancel my evening."

"See, as long as we keep the lines of communication open, we can work through our problems. Since I've got you on the phone and we're expanding our communication skills, where do we stand with getting a wiretap?"

There are two types of court-approved wiretaps at the FBI's disposal. One is under the auspices of the Foreign Intelligence Surveillance Act of 1978. The seven-member FISA Court meets twice a month to approve requests from the intelligence agencies, including the FBI. The purpose of the FISUR, as it is called in the Bureau, is solely to gather intelligence. The requirements for obtaining such an order are less restrictive than the criminal wiretaps issued under Title III authority granted under the Omnibus Crime Control and Safe Streets Act of 1968. Because Boris is not a known foreign intelligence officer, despite his impressive KGB resume and the fact this is a criminal investigation not an intelligence fact-finding mission, the Title III is the only permissible route. Wiretaps are manpower intensive and an administrative nightmare. They are never popular with the troops but loved by administrators who are often graded on the number of wiretaps they manage. One fact remains solid: a good wire gets the desired results . . . evidence resulting in convictions. If the FBI goes the Title III route, it means assigning an agent to write the affidavit and getting a prosecutor in the U. S. Attorney's office onboard.

"I'm not sure the PC is strong enough," said Dwayne.

"That's up to the lawyers to decide how much probable cause we have, but I sure wish we were on Boris's phones and had a bug in the office," said Matt.

"The trouble is this is a Title III not a FISUR."

"I understand. I just think we should be exploring the possibility."

"You're just saying this because you know you won't be working a monitoring shift," said Dwayne with a smile in his voice.

"I know how much headquarters values supervisors who churn out wires, and I'm trying to help you get ahead in the organization."

"So in other words, you've got my back."

"Exactly."

CHAPTER FORTY-ONE

The next day Matt was in the automobile storage business. Boris called ahead, "We're about five out."

"I'll have the garage door open. Drive around back and pull in," said Matt.

Matt heard the engines racing as the cars pulled into the parking lot and raced down the side road before turning into the warehouse. Boris led the way in his black Escalade followed by four cars: three SUVs and a Ford F-250.

Boris was the first to exit the vehicles.

Matt greeted Boris with an extended hand. "Al Gore is going to love you for shipping a lot of carbon footprints overseas."

Boris smiled. "I am only too happy to assist the Yankee consumer in reducing his personal blight on the environment. Maybe I can be the next Green Czar?"

"I smell a spot in the administration for my comrade."

The four drivers exited their vehicles: Stump, Jesse, J. D., and Face. Matt lured the men to a table. He broke open a six-pack of beer and passed out the cold cans. Almost in unison the men popped the tops on the cans and began to drink. Matt situated the table near enough to the cameras to ensure everyone was caught on tape.

MATT WAS ABLE TO get home at a decent hour and was looking forward to spending a relaxing evening at home with his wife. When he arrived, Caitlin was walking out the door.

"Where are you going?"

"I've got parent-teacher conferences tonight and tomorrow night. I told you this morning."

"I don't think so."

"Cowboy, I told you, and you said your issues with management stem from the negative reports your parents always received during your parent-teacher conferences."

"Okay, now I remember. What about dinner?"

"I got takeout from Three Amigos. There's a Steak Burrito Supreme on the counter. Stick it in the microwave for thirty seconds, and you'll be fine."

She kissed her memory-deficient husband and headed to school.

Caitlin may have been one of the few teachers who enjoyed parent-teacher conferences. It was an opportunity to meet the parents and gain a better understanding of her students. Like a wise street cop she could size up the parents pretty quickly and often from just one meeting gain valuable insights into how best to work with the student throughout the remaining school year.

The conferences were fifteen minutes, which didn't provide much time to discuss problems in detail but did allow for establishing concerns and setting an appointment to map out appropriate strategies to deal with issues.

The school year had been relatively problem-free. In fact, Caitlin only wanted to discuss issues with three sets of parents. As was her style, she wouldn't immediately bring up the problems but praise the child, pointing out any positives and then bring up the concern. Matt used to tease her claiming she was like the real estate agent who pointed out how the walls of the run-down shack went all the way from the floor to the ceiling. Caitlin could find positives in everyone.

She didn't consider Michael Hughes to be a problem. On the contrary, he was one of her best students, and she appreciated him in her classroom. Yet she was debating whether she needed to address the racial comment he made on the playground two weeks earlier. She was hoping the discussion this evening would lend itself to an opening.

Michael was always clean, but it was obvious the family was not part of the economic aristocracy. His clothing was humble hand-me-downs. Caitlin wasn't quite sure what to expect, but it certainly was not what she encountered as J. D. and his wife Alicia entered the classroom.

A single mother was leaving just as J. D.

walked in with his wife following a few steps behind. J. D. was a little over six feet and slender but with a Budweiser tumor occupying his midsection. His wife-beater T-shirt revealed tattoo artwork covering both arms, his shoulders, and even his neck. His long hair was pulled back in a ponytail, and like the jihadists, he didn't believe in trimming his beard. Alicia was plain but polite. Like her son, she dressed humbly, probably thrift-store bargains. There was a slight discoloration below her right eye, maybe cheap makeup or maybe an aging bruise.

Caitlin swallowed as the introductions began.

"I'm J. D. This here is Alicia. Michael's her kid but I'm here cause I'm interested."

J. D. started to walk around the classroom, eyeing the pictures on the walls and the posted essays.

"Thanks for coming. I'm Caitlin Hogan."

J. D. continued his quick-pace travels between the desks, eventually finding a seat.

"Bet you don't get too many stepparents showing an interest, do you?"

"We get our share, but I appreciate your coming, and I'm sure Michael appreciates your interest."

Caitlin took the lead and spent the next several minutes praising Michael, emphasizing the great qualities he demonstrated day in and day out in the classroom and on the playground.

"Well, you let me know if he ever gets out of line. I'll beat him until he sees straight. I believe in education. I'm not a big fan of public education, too many destructive influences. We need to teach truth. Not watered down with new-age slop from the mud people. We was gonna homeschool him until we heard you was his teacher. We heard good things about you." Pointing to his wife, J. D. added, "Besides, she's too stupid to teach."

"I'm sure your wife would be a fine teacher, but Michael is doing well, and I'm certain this is a great educational environment for him."

"Yeah, well I don't know about no environment, as you call it, but she's stupid and he better learn. He's not getting any points like we're giving these minorities. There's no level playing field for a white man, not is this society. He ain't got a chance. He'd be better off if we spoke Mexican and snuck across the border or painted the map of Jerusalem across his face. Yeah, if he was a Zionist, he'd have it made."

Alicia started to say something, but before she got past "J. D." he ordered her silence. His loud abrupt manner cast a darkening pall over the evening.

"Sir, I agree Michael must do well in school and learn as much as he can in order to compete in the world. But bigotry isn't going to level the playing field."

"You callin' me a bigot?"

"We are each a unique creation of God. I'm saying this country's multicultural heritage makes us stronger as a nation and will make us stronger as individuals once we appreciate its diversity."

"That sounds like liberal doublespeak. You and your husband got kids?"

Caitlin smiled. "Right now I have twenty-two children in my care."

"Huh?"

"And Michael is one of those twenty-two."

"I get it. Maybe I was wrong about you being a good teacher. Maybe I should let dummy here educate her son."

"I hope before you and your wife make such a decision we could sit down and discuss it. I'm afraid we don't have time this evening to really explore the issue. I do believe Michael must learn to get along with people from all walks of life. That's what makes America great, and as soon as Michael understands that, he will be better prepared for what lies beyond this classroom."

J. D. didn't have a comeback. He said a quick good-bye and grabbed his wife as they exited the classroom. It was easy to understand where Michael learned the racial epithet. Caitlin was glad she didn't bring up the playground overhear; the discussion would have fallen on deaf ears.

• • •

WHEN SHE ARRIVED HOME, Matt was camped out in front of the TV watching a classic James Bond movie with Sean Connery.

"Oh great, just what you need, more Bond."

"This is *Dr. No*, a training flick."

"I think you watched too much Bond during your formative years," said Caitlin as she bent over to give him a kiss. Then she asked, "What's 88 mean?"

"You'll have to give me a few more hints."

"What does the number 88 mean?"

"It could be the jersey number of a wide receiver in football."

"It's a tattoo on the neck of one of my parents."

"It means you have a problem. Who is it?"

"What does it mean?"

"The eighth letter in the alphabet is H. The number 88 stands for HH or Heil Hitler. It's a symbol a lot of neo-Nazis wear. Which one of your beloved parents pays tribute to the fallen leader?"

"It's not important." She kissed him again and said, "I'm going to bed."

"Is that an invitation?"

She responded with a seductive smile.

Matt forgot about Bond and followed his idea of the most beautiful woman in the world into the bedroom.

CHAPTER FORTY-TWO

Matt yanked hard on the chain raising the large steel door to the warehouse. Boris called earlier in the day. Stump and J. D. Pinney were picking up twenty more master cases of the Export As. Even if Matt never engaged anyone in criminal conversations at the warehouse, the ruse of the stolen cigarettes enhanced his rep on the street.

Stump pulled in and maneuvered the pickup to the far corner where the cases were stored. In order to maintain credibility, Matt arranged for a forty-foot container to be stored at the warehouse as well. Several years earlier Matt posed as a warehouseman when two Mafia thugs from the East Coast extorted an independent trucking company in Long Beach. Matt confronted the two and recorded their threats on audio- and videotape. He was also on the receiving end of two body shots from the larger of the two Sicilian leg-breakers. Matt swallowed his pride on that venture, but both pleaded guilty and were still enjoying some well-deserved R&R courtesy of the federal penal system. The company owner had been an FBI fan ever since, and when any operation called for a truck, tractor trailer, or container, he was only too happy to oblige. Matt arranged for empty, sealed containers to arrive at the warehouse every few days, making the warehouse look like a viable operation.

Before Stump could turn off the engine, J. D. jumped out of the truck and ran to the restroom.

"Too much coffee?" asked Matt.

"Naw, too much beer last night. He's been going like a racehorse all day," said Stump.

"I think he just wanted an excuse from loading the cases into the back of the truck," said Matt.

"You may be right. He gives lazy a bad name."

Matt and Stump began loading the cigarettes. They were easy to maneuver so even Matt couldn't complain about heavy lifting. It only took the two men a few minutes to complete the task.

"Where's Boris moving these?" asked Matt.

"I don't ask. I'm just supposed to take 'em back to the Veil. He's got his customers. We got more important things to do tonight."

"Like what?"

Before Stump could answer, J. D. returned.

"Good timing, J. D. We just finished loading the truck," said Stump, who then headed for the restroom.

When Stump was out of ear shot, Matt said, "Stump says you got something big going."

"Yeah, Boris got Jesse, Stump, and me on a

mission. We need to teach somebody who got outta line a lesson."

"I don't understand," said Matt trying to be nonchalant but begging for a criminal admission.

"Boris don't take crap off nobody. Somebody tried to extort money from the boss and threatened to go to the cops. You don't ever want to cross Boris. He's real quick to have us teach 'em a lesson."

"Sometimes brute force sends the right message," said Matt with conviction.

"You got that right, and Boris ain't afraid to send a message."

"That makes me feel a lot better. I'm glad to know we're dealing with a careful man."

"He's careful. He wasn't happy with the last dump job we did. We need to do better, or you might find my body at the bottom of some ravine."

Matt laughed, "I guess those kinds of failures make the eleven o'clock news."

"That one did."

"Can I get you a beer or something? I've got plenty in the fridge?" said Matt.

"Yeah, thanks."

Matt returned with three beers and handed one to J. D., who twisted the top. Before Matt could open his, Stump stormed out of the restroom cursing like a deployed sailor, wiping his hands on his pants.

Matt smiled and promised to restock the paper towels.

"Why you washing your hands anyway?" asked J. D.

"Cause I needed to. He's outta toilet paper too."

J. D. and Matt both laughed out loud. Then J. D. said, "Oh, yeah, I should have told you before you went in. I used up all the roll blowing my nose."

"Just open the door. We're outta here," said an angry Stump.

"I'll see you guys over at the Veil. I gotta get my money from Boris," said Matt.

"Hey, why don't you come with us? Help us unload the truck. We'll go do our other job and then head back to the Veil, and we'll party," said J. D.

"Shut up. He's not coming with us," said Stump.

"Yeah, I'll catch up with you, J. D. I still owe you a beer."

J. D. gave Matt an inquisitive look. He had no idea why Matt owed him another beer, but he wasn't going to pass up free booze so he gave the undercover agent a big smile and a thumbs-up.

Matt had no intention of joining them. He had a much more important mission. He hustled over and rolled up the door.

Stump goosed the accelerator, and the tires squealed as the truck pulled from the warehouse.

As soon as Stump and J. D. left, Matt grabbed the tapes from the machines and headed over to the Russian Veil.

On his way Matt called Dwayne but was only successful at getting his voice mail. "You need to listen to today's tapes. J. D. admitted to doing a dump job for Boris. They may be doing a number this evening. J. D. wasn't clear, but I think he, Jesse, and Stump are going to be dancing on somebody's face tonight. What we thought was a simple cigarette run may have turned into a felony. I'm running over to the Veil now to pick up the money for the cigarettes. I'll try to see if I can get any admissions out of Boris and beef up the PC for the affidavit." Matt paused, "Dwayne, we're getting closer."

He then called Caitlin. The answering machine picked up. "Hey, hon. I need to work a little later this evening. I know I promised we'd go out. Let me take care of this, and I'll get home as soon as I can. Sorry. I owe you big time. I love you."

CHAPTER FORTY-THREE

Dmitri arrived in Mexico City two weeks earlier and made his way to Sasabe, a small Mexican border town sixty-five miles south-west of Tucson. It was here he would meet his contact for the next leg of his long journey north.

Run by a shadow network of underground capitalists, Sasabe was no tourist paradise. It was a way station in the route to America, the daily jumping-off point for hundreds seeking the freedom and opportunities the United States offered. The town was dirty and dusty. Its rutted unpaved streets made travel difficult, even for the new pickup trucks parading up and down the main roads. The hot dog vendors with their homemade carts catered to those preparing to make the illegal border crossing through the Sonora desert. Homes and huts converted into smuggling stores featured dark clothes, water bottles, and camouflage backpacks, not for school children and soccer moms but those preparing for the journey on foot. Meth and caffeine pills were as popular as candy bars and packaged food items.

Hotels sprang up in recent years, but most wouldn't make it in the AAA Travel Guide. The modest stucco buildings lacked even modern conveniences. But at three to four dollars a night, Dmitri couldn't expect the Ritz. The hookers worked cheap as well. Smuggling was driving the economic success of this town once known for cattle and bricks imported into the United States.

Dmitri learned enough Spanish to navigate his way through Mexico. Getting a visa into the

United States was a lengthy process, and he had no interest in alerting the U.S. authorities to his presence. The money for the flight to Mexico City and payment to the coyote who would smuggle him across the border were sound investments.

AS MATT EASED TO the curb to park, he saw a dark blue Range Rover Sport pull from the parking lot behind Boris's club. With the tinted windows Matt couldn't be sure of the driver, but the car reminded him of the one driven by Dr. Ubadiah Adel al-Banna or Dr. U as he referred to himself. Dr. U did some volunteer work at World Angel Ministry, Matt's undercover assignment the previous year. They only met once when the doctor delivered boxes of medical samples to the charity. Even then it bothered Matt a Muslim physician was contributing to the efforts of an evangelical medical missionary organization. Visions of his undercover assignment flashed through his mind, a montage of faces raced before him. Matt quickly dismissed the thought. *There are a lot of dark blue Range Rovers in Los Angeles. Focus.* He needed to get his game face on for mobsters, bikers, strippers, and whores.

Matt entered giving Face a fist salute. Matt was one of the boys, now welcomed anytime at L.A.'s low-class den of iniquity. He stopped briefly and pointed to the SUV heading eastbound on Ventura Boulevard, "Do you know who was driving that Range Rover?"

Face looked east. "No, didn't see him." He paused briefly then said, "Boris deals with some Middle Eastern dishrag, probably a rug merchant. He comes here every once in awhile. I think he drives a blue Rover. Maybe that's him."

"Thanks, no big deal," said Matt as he headed past the curtains concealing the stage from the sidewalk.

Cleanliness in the club was not a priority for Boris. The darkness hid the filth both physical and moral. Several bikers were at the bar, and more of the riffraff sat around the stage as two girls performed. Boris spotted Matt within seconds of him entering the bar and made his way to the undercover agent. Boris stopped briefly to talk with one of the patrons and then extended his powerful right hand, greeting Matt.

"Glad to see you, my friend. Stump and J. D. dropped off the cases a few minutes ago. Thank you."

"Boris, I am so glad to help out a fellow entrepreneur in a life of crime."

Boris let out a huge belly laugh and slapped Matt so hard on the back he almost lost his balance.

"Where are those guys? I told J. D. I owed him a beer."

"They are taking care of business."

"Anything I can help you with?" asked Matt.

"It doesn't concern you," said Boris with a bluntness conveying the notion to never revisit the subject. The Russian then clapped a strong hand on Matt's shoulder. "The boys tell me your warehouse has quite a turnover of containers. Every time they go there's a different box."

"I have to earn. I work with a couple of guys who need to move stuff in and out. I don't ask a lot of questions. The less I know the more they pay. I just ask for a bill of lading to cover me in case the Feds ask."

"Do the Feds ever ask?"

"I've never had a problem or even an inquiry. As far as anyone knows, I run a clean shop."

Boris released his grip. "By the end of the week, I may need to rent some space from you."

"Not a problem. Just let me know. Even though I take American Express, cash is the preferred currency."

Again Boris let out a huge laugh. "Yes, those service fees on credit cards can eat into your profits. Do you really take credit cards?"

"Why? You aren't going to pay me with a check or a credit card are you? Jerry Springer tried the check bit with a hooker years ago, and it ruined his political career."

"But it made him a star on your TV."

"There's probably more money in sleaze TV than politics anyway."

"In Russia, as in your country, both pay handsomely. Let's go back to my office. I'll get you the money for the cigarettes."

As the mismatched couple walked past the stage, Boris pointed to a dancer strutting on the walkway as the music began. "She is new. She just arrived this week. She is very good. Would you like to spend some time with her? I can arrange a very private session."

"She's pretty, but she also looks a little young. You aren't recruiting from Russian junior high schools, are you?"

Boris slapped Matt on the back again, causing Matt to fall forward catching himself with a quick step. "She is legal, but I like them to look young. Fulfills a fantasy."

"For you or the customer?"

"If I like it, I know my well-educated and worldly patrons will find pleasure in the performance."

Matt laughed, "Well-educated? I'm the first high school graduate you've had in here since you've opened."

"You may be right. Maybe it's just my fantasy." They continued walking to the office, and as Boris was about to open the door, he said, "Just so you know, all my girls are of age, and I have the paperwork to prove it. Nothing brings the heat faster than underage girls. I don't need the FBI snooping around."

"That's good to know, but I wasn't worried. You're too smart to leave yourself wide open to the Feds asking questions."

Matt glanced up at the monitoring screens in Boris's office. He watched a long-haired customer who tipped the scales just this side of three hundred pounds taking a girl into the room. "Maybe you should charge by the pound."

Boris looked up at the screen and picked up his phone. "Keep an eye on room two. Some whale just walked in with Tatiana. I don't want her hurt."

Boris walked over to the wall and pulled back a large black-and-white photo displayed in a hinged frame. Behind the photo was a wall safe. Using his body to conceal his actions, Boris entered the combination, grabbed the handle, and popped open the door. He removed a white business envelope and tossed it to Matt.

"I counted it. It's all there. But feel free to count it again if you like . . . if you don't trust me."

Matt opened the envelope and spied the cash. "We're fine. I'm invoking the six-four-three-zero-zero rule."

"And what is that?"

"If someone six foot four weighing three hundred pounds tells me all the money is there, I'm not going to argue with him."

Boris nodded without saying a word.

There was a loud knock at the door.

"Come," shouted Boris above the noise from the bar.

Jesse, Stump, and J. D. entered the room. Jesse and Stump betrayed nothing, but J. D. shot Matt a nervous look as he crossed the room. Stump was nursing a large gash on his left arm.

"Didn't your mother tell you not to play with sharp objects?" said Matt, referring to the cut.

Stump said nothing.

Even though Boris just paid for what he thought to be stolen merchandise and thus Matt was a coconspirator in some felony, he waved Matt out so the three could report.

Matt drew a long, slow breath, stood up, and walked out. "Sorry I couldn't stay for the whole play, Mr. Lincoln."

CHAPTER FORTY-FOUR

Matt drove east a few blocks on Ventura Boulevard. His home was west, but he took a different route every time he left the Russian Veil. His routine was no routine: side streets, u-turns, exiting freeways and jumping right back on, never the same route twice. Caution was key. He checked his mirrors often, seeking a tail.

As soon as he was clear of the Veil, he tried Dwayne. Matt's call again went to voice mail.

He turned on the radio and had the music blasting; home was where he quieted his life. Now he was celebrating the rush of another successful meeting. Matt was singing along with Charlie Daniels. "Simple Man" would be his theme song when the Hollywood TV moguls came banging on his door seeking to make their next true-to-life, long-running FBI drama series. He sang it loud, "Panty-waist judges let the drug dealers go." His performance was interrupted by a single yelp from a siren. He looked in the rearview mirror. An LAPD patrol unit lit him up, the red and blue lights flashing.

Matt slammed the steering wheel. He couldn't walk a ticket in his undercover car. He would have to pay, and he doubted the Queen Mother would sign off on a reimbursement. Had he been in a Bureau car, wearing a weapon, and in possession of his badge, he would plead for professional courtesy.

Matt turned down the CD player and pulled over to the curb. He was still too close to Boris's place. Had he been on the other side of town, he might have asked permission to go to his trunk and take out his badge and credentials secreted in a specially built compartment. He rolled down the window. Through his mirror he saw the lone police officer unwind his massive body from the patrol car. *Somewhere a circus is missing a trained grizzly.*

"Good evening, officer."

"License, registration, and proof of insurance."

"Can I ask what I did wrong, officer?"

"License, registration, and proof of insurance."

"Okay, my registration is in the glove compartment. I'll need to reach over and open it."

"So do it."

Matt cautiously reached across the front seat and opened the glove compartment. He removed a small folder containing the registration and proof of insurance and handed the documents to the officer. When the officer took the two pieces of paper, Matt noticed the man's fingers. The left hand had the letters R-A-G-E tattooed on the respective fingers. A partial tattoo could be seen above his wrist, but the rest was hidden by the long-sleeved shirt. The work was pure prison, done with a sewing needle and the ink from a ballpoint pen, San Quentin blue.

"Let me see your license."

Matt opened his wallet and showed it to the officer. The grizzly took the wallet and examined the driver's license. He then returned the wallet.

"Everything's in order."

"Thank you, officer, but why did you pull me over?"

"Your vehicle matched the description of a

recent stolen car, and I just needed to make sure this wasn't the vehicle in question."

"Thanks, officer. Have a good evening."

Matt slowly put the documents back in the glove compartment and stuffed his wallet in his back pocket. He waited for the patrol car to leave before he pulled from the curb. He drove several blocks, went down a side street, circled the block, and eventually made his way to the freeway. As soon as he pulled onto the Ventura Freeway, the 101, he called Dwayne, who picked up on the third ring.

"Did you get my message about J. D.?"

"Yeah, Matt, great work. We're getting a lot closer to solving this thing."

"Listen, I just got rousted by one of Boris's boys."

"What do you mean?"

"I got pulled over by a black-and-white. He claims he thought I might have been driving a stolen car, but he never unstrapped his holster and never asked me to remove my license from my wallet."

"Maybe he was just poorly trained."

"Yeah, maybe in prison. He had prison tats. No, this was a test and I passed."

"Where'd Boris get a patrol car and uniform?"

"Boris has his fingers into everything. He's probably got a contact at one of the studios. The Queen Mother almost blew it."

"How so?"

"I knew she'd never sign off on reimbursing a moving violation, and I almost tried to badge my way out of a ticket."

"Glad your integrity prevailed."

"Heck with integrity. I was just going to pump up my next voucher to cover the cost of the ticket, maybe a ghost meal here or there."

"La, la, la, la . . . I didn't hear that. Listen, something important came up today."

"What?"

"We had a Dawn Platt walk into the complaint desk at Westwood late this afternoon. She works at Valley General."

"Mickey Donovan's girlfriend."

"Yeah, how'd you know?"

"Stump told me. It was in one of my 302s. Check with Steve."

"I will. Anyway she came in and said Mickey asked her to get information about Lydia Mitchell. She thinks Mickey went to Bobby Himmler's to confront him about cooperating. She told Mickey about Bobby being in the hospital and gave him the Mitchell address."

"How'd she get the information?"

"I haven't heard. Steve is going to debrief her tomorrow. He was down at the U.S Attorney's office working on the wiretap affidavit when she walked in and wasn't able to interview her. Apparently she wants to go back to Texas and was hoping to trade the information for a plane ticket. She's cooperating so we should get everything in the morning."

Matt had a second call on his phone. "Hey, this is Boris. I need to take it. But we have to talk. I think the boys may have tuned up someone tonight."

"Okay, we'll talk later."

Matt clicked into the call-waiting feature on his cell phone. "Yeah, Boris, what's up?"

"I need to store something in your warehouse tonight."

"Tonight?" said Matt almost irritated. "Can't it wait until morning?"

"No, I need to store it tonight. We'll get rid of it first thing in the morning."

"Okay, what is it?"

"A car. Stump and Jesse will bring it over."

"Have them meet me there in thirty minutes."

CHAPTER FORTY-FIVE

Matt made his way back to the warehouse and was waiting for Stump and Jesse when they arrived. He had the warehouse door open and they pulled in, each driving separate cars. Stump was driving a Dodge Ram, and Jesse was in a faded red Nissan Sentra with Texas plates. As Stump was maneuvering the pickup around the warehouse to pull out, Jesse parked the car against the west wall.

"I turned around on the freeway to come back here so you could park some beat up rice-burner in the warehouse overnight," said Matt.

Jesse was not in the mood for any of the typical Matt. "Boris needs this done. It's a favor for him. Don't ask questions."

"What's going on?"

"Matt, don't ask questions. Someone will be back tomorrow around ten. Be here."

With that Jesse climbed into the truck and Stump drove off.

Matt watched the pickup leave and remembered Lydia Mitchell's description of the truck on Mulholland the night of the murders. He lowered the warehouse door and was preparing to call Dwayne with this new fact but decided to give the Nissan a quick once-over.

"Hard to believe anyone is still paying on a car this old. What could it be worth to an insurance company? Even if you total it, we're talking less than a grand."

He grabbed his cell phone and called the office. "FBI."

"This is DT7-13. Give me dispatch, please."

"Dispatch."

"Hey, Laura, it's Matt Hogan. I need a 10-28 and a 10-29 on a Texas plate."

In less than a minute Laura Langwell reported

the results. It was getting late, but this newest problem needed resolution immediately. Dinner with Caitlin was off.

"NOW WHAT?" SAID DWAYNE as he answered the phone after reading the caller ID.

"We've got a problem. Stump and Jesse just brought a car to the warehouse. I ran the plate. The registered owner is an Elliot Platt of Houston, Texas. J. D. said Boris was upset with somebody. He must have learned Dawn came to the FBI."

"Is the car still there?"

"Yeah."

"I'll call Steve and we'll be right over."

"I've got more good news. I'm pretty sure there's blood on the driver's seat. Better bring ERT with you, and we need to work fast. I popped the trunk, and it was empty, but we may have a crime scene."

MATT ENSURED FROM THE outside the place looked deserted. He kept the lights off in his office and the shades drawn. The warehouse had no windows so even if a party were happening, only the noise would give it away. Dwayne and Steve arrived within the hour. A short time later Jennifer Spencer and two members of her Evidence Response Team arrived.

"That piece of crap looks like my brother's car," said Jennifer.

"I thought firefighters made good money," said Matt.

"They do, but when you are on marriage number three and both the formers are still on scholarship, the salary can look depressingly small."

Matt briefed everyone. Steve was concerned Dawn Platt may be the latest victim in Boris's ever-expanding criminal conspiracy.

"I better get over to her place."

"See what we have here before you make the run," said Dwayne. "I don't want to show our hand too soon."

The agents closely examined the car without touching it. Jesse left the front window down so Matt pointed out what looked like a bloodstain on the seat. It wasn't bright red, having been exposed to air, but it appeared fresh sitting on top of the fabric. There were no apparent spent rounds in the car so no one would hazard a guess as to the cause of the bleeding, if in fact it was blood. The ERT agents were putting on gloves preparing to process the car.

"Wait guys," said Matt. "We have a problem. In all likelihood this is a crime scene, but you have to process it without making it look like you've been here."

Jennifer shook her head and said, "Matt, you've been watching too much television. The powder residue left from lifting prints doesn't just blow away, and we'll need to rip out the seats to do this correctly."

"We can't let that happen. Boris said the car would be gone first thing in the morning. I can hold him off a little while with an excuse why I can't be here, but it will look suspicious. This obviously is more than an owner give-up. He's going to chop it or destroy it as soon as a yard is available," said Matt.

"Not much to salvage. I think this is meant for the crusher," said Steve.

"In any event the evidence goes out the door as soon as anyone shows up," said Dwayne.

Matt looked at Jennifer. "Can you at least do a presumptive test to determine if this is blood?"

"Sure," said Jennifer. "I can spray Luminol on a portion of the seat. If blood is present, even as little as one part per ten million, we'll get a read."

"Will that affect blood typing or DNA analysis?" asked Dwayne.

"No, it can interfere with some serologic testing, but I won't destroy the entire sample just in case we need more procedures."

Jennifer sprayed a small portion of the seat. Matt flipped off the warehouse lights, and in the darkened room the stains glowed a blue-white.

"You can flip the lights back on, Matt," said Jennifer. "You've got blood."

"I've got an address for Dawn. We should get

over there tonight. It's looking more and more like they found out about her trip to our office and decided to silence her," said Steve.

Dwayne walked around the car again. "But what about the car? This is a crime scene."

Matt rubbed his forehead, pausing before he spoke. "I've got an idea."

"Let's hear it," said Dwayne.

"Jenn, you sure this is like your brother's car?"

"Same make and color. I'm not sure of the year. It's not like Nissan was trying to make a fashion statement every September."

"But it's close enough?" asked Matt.

"Yeah."

Dwayne intervened, "Matt, what are you getting at?"

"Let's call up Jennifer's brother and buy his car. We swap plates on this one. Pour something red on the driver's seat to simulate blood and hope they crush it before anyone checks the VIN."

"How do we pay for it?" asked Dwayne.

"I could phony up a bunch of meal receipts, or we could call the Queen Mother and get permission," said Matt.

Steve repeated the oft-said truism of the Bureau, "It's easier to get forgiveness than permission."

Matt jumped back in, "Let's give him mid–Blue Book, and after the car is crushed, we tell Her Highness."

Dwayne slowly nodded in agreement knowing his career was hanging by a thread.

"Then we're set," said Matt who walked over to the workbench and picked up a screwdriver preparing to remove the Texas plates.

"Do we need to take an oath of silence?" said Steve with a broad smile.

Dwayne was now shaking his head slowly. There was a thin line between initiative and integrity just as there was between stupidity and conviction. He may have crossed both.

Everyone in the garage knew Supervisory Special Agent Dwayne Washington was uncomfortable with the decision he just made, but no street agent would give him quarter.

"Manipulating the bureaucrats is almost as satisfying as locking up criminals," said Matt as he was removing the plates. "I can live with the consequences. I just finished paying off a car OPR said I was at fault for totaling. Caitlin and I are used to being garnished. If need be, we'll just extend the payments."

"We can process this back at our garage," said Jennifer getting back to the business of the Bureau.

"Call your brother," said Matt. "Tell him we're gonna make him an offer he can't refuse. Steve, how close are we to getting up on Boris's phones and a mike in the office?"

"This might put us over the top with the

probable cause. I'll get back down to the U.S. Attorney's office first thing in the morning."

"You better take a run at the address for Dawn Platt," said Matt. "We may have another dead body on our hands." All were in agreement.

CHAPTER FORTY-SIX

The next morning SOG followed J. D., who drove the substituted Nissan from the warehouse to a salvage yard in Pacoima in the northeast San Fernando Valley. J. D. was inside the office less than ten minutes. When he exited, he hopped into the Nissan and drove around back.

Flip Mitchell's Sixties team was conducting the surveillance. When it was reported over the air J. D. drove around back, Flip jumped out of his truck and made his way through the scrub brush until he found a vantage point of the wrecking yard. He watched a machine turn the red Nissan, believed by Boris and his crew to be the crime scene, into recycled waste. No questions asked. No VIN numbers checked. No ownership documents exchanged.

J. D. ran around to the parking lot in front, jumped into Jesse's car, and the two returned to the Russian Veil.

• • •

JENNIFER SPENCER PROCESSED THE Nissan. She was able to lift latent prints from the vehicle tying Stump, Jesse, and J. D. to the car, not a major revelation since the video from the warehouse proved Stump and Jesse delivered the vehicle, but there was still no Dawn Platt. A spent round was found lodged in the backseat. It looked like a 9 mm, but the results from ballistics tests might be weeks away. So far there was no crime. Dawn failed to show up at work, and the parole officer reported this violation, at least allowing her name to go into the system. Steve Barnett set a lead for the Houston FBI office to interview the registered owner and was awaiting the results. Every piece of evidence has a voice, but the judicial choir only sings when all the voices come together. So far no song.

DWAYNE PULLED AN END-AROUND on the Queen Mother and briefed the ADIC, Jason Barnes, on the car swap before telling Pamela Clinton. Barnes was a decisive leader, a skill learned in the Marine Corps, and praised Dwayne's team for its late-night initiative. The euphoria was short-lived when Dwayne returned to his office and found that Clinton bounced Matt's latest voucher. He knew his undercover agent would not take the news well but picked up

236

the cold phone in his office, refusing to postpone the inevitable.

Matt could handle the most dangerous situations. He was great at surviving the worst. He could face down the most hardened criminal without flinching, but his composure vaporized when confronted by administrative directives having no bearing on the prosecutorial outcome of the case.

As expected, the undercover agent exploded when he got the news. "What!"

"She kicked back the voucher. The cigars are a no-go."

"You have got to be kidding me!"

"Nope," said Dwayne. "Under her reading of the guidelines, cigars are a gift. Before a gift can be expended, you need ADIC and headquarters approval."

"That's not right. I've done it before!" screamed Matt.

"Not with her as the SAC."

"Then call it meals and entertainment," countered Matt.

"That won't work because the receipt is dated on a day other than when the meeting occurred. All meals and entertainment expenses can only be reimbursed on those days in which an actual meeting occurs."

"Then I'll phony up a 302 and say I had a meeting."

"It won't work. You can't backdate a computer entry. She'll check, and that's all the ammo she'll need to post your fanny in Death Valley. Eat the expense and be a less gracious guest in the future."

"This is amazing."

"I'll need a check for the cigars," said Dwayne.

"You'll get it. Just don't look at next month's voucher too closely."

"Matt, it's not worth it."

"Yeah, well she didn't risk her life with a bunch of neo-Nazi bikers, and now I have to skip a mortgage payment to pay for a box of Gurkha Centurions. Dwayne, she's never been on the other side of the wire. She's never even been in the green zone. I'm selling a lie while she sits behind a desk all day and watches White-Out dry."

Dwayne tugged at his collar as Matt's tirade continued. Dwayne let him vent. It was more than cigars. Both Dwayne and Matt knew it.

Finally Matt said, "Tell Her Highness the check is in the mail."

The call abruptly ended. Upset with the Queen Mother's accounting, Matt cancelled a planned meeting with Boris that evening at the Veil and headed home early.

CHAPTER FORTY-SEVEN

Matt took her hand and held it gently, occasionally squeezing it as they walked in silence. A kiss of the warm night winds blew in from the desert, and a dull moon overhead provided more than enough illumination. Safety wasn't an issue. They chose the Thousand Oaks community, a suburb of Los Angeles, because it was annually rated one of America's safest cities. Besides, even on a romantic nighttime stroll with the woman who knew him best, Matt was armed.

"That smile looks good on you," said Matt.

"It's been awhile since we've taken a walk."

"I really am sorry. This case has taken much more time than I anticipated, too many late nights and not enough lunchtime meetings. Maybe I should concentrate on white-collar criminals who want to bribe me over a leisurely brunch in Beverly Hills."

"Don't tease me, Cowboy. That's what I've been trying to tell you. At least with the white-collar criminals you bathe."

"Come on, I've been practicing my best hygiene skills with this assignment."

"Yeah, but you still come home smelling like stale biker and cigarettes."

Matt squeezed her hand. "It's not like I'm hanging out at Bath and Body Works in the mall."

"I understand. When the scene is set in hell, don't expect angels to be singing in the choir."

"Exactly, you do pay attention to me when I tell you about my day."

He leaned over and stole a kiss.

"How are you coming with your Bible reading?" she asked.

"I'm keeping up. I may be a few days behind, but I stash a Bible in the bottom drawer of my desk at the warehouse. When the bad guys are late, I try to catch up."

Caitlin laughed. "The perfect time for reflection, right before some serial killer strolls into your undercover off-site."

Matt smiled. "Yeah, he's strapped with a .40 cal looking to make me an even dozen on his hit list, but at least I die with the Bible opened to 'thou shall not kill.' " He paused, waiting for her to respond, but Caitlin said nothing. "Actually I'm really getting into the Old Testament. That eye-for-an-eye philosophy fits in perfectly with my investigative theories."

"We live on this side of the cross, Cowboy," said Caitlin, shaking her head knowing Matt was trying to get a reaction. "My grandfather used to quote Micah. Maybe you should check him out?"

"Your grandfather? I thought he died."

She playfully hit him. "No, Micah, the Old

Testament prophet. He made it pretty simple; do justice, love kindness, and walk humbly with your God."

"Humility has always been a tough one for me."

"Yeah, I noticed," said Caitlin as she leaned over and kissed him.

"And that kindness bit, you haven't seen who I've been dealing with lately. Not always easy to put on a smiley face, turn the other cheek, and pretend you mean it."

A car passed, lighting the road ahead.

Caitlin released his hand and hooked her arm through his. "I believe in a God of second chances who is seeking a relationship with each one of his unique creations."

"I'll agree he made some unique characters, but he can't be too pleased with the actions of some of his creations I keep running into."

"Matt, I'm sure you must be right. Mankind is far from perfect. The God we worship can forgive anything, but we still have to live with the consequences of our actions. He's willing to erase all our failures and betrayals. It's a matter of what you are willing to live with."

They waited for a pickup truck to pass before they crossed the street.

Caitlin continued, "My God loves me so much he was willing to sacrifice his own Son just to have a relationship with me. Do you understand how special that makes me feel?" She paused, waiting to see if Matt would respond. When he didn't, she continued, "You know someday I really want to have children."

Matt interrupted, "I'm doing my part."

Caitlin laughed, "Not when you work late every night." She paused and with conviction said, "Each time we've been pregnant, I was so happy, but then to lose those babies hurt so much. My soul still aches. I know we will make great parents and will love our baby with all our being, but I also know I can't out love God. He was willing to let his Son die for me. Think about that, Matt. I know you would give your life for me. You would give your life for a friend or an FBI agent or a Marine. But would you give *my* life to save someone you didn't know? Would you willingly sacrifice our child's life for a complete stranger, someone with whom you had no relationship, someone who didn't even know you or denied you or even defiled you? That's what God did when he left Jesus on the cross. I worship a God who willingly gave his Son for me."

They walked in silence as Matt reflected. It was a lot to comprehend. He had so many unsettled thoughts.

"I love you," said Matt.

"I love you too, Cowboy," said Caitlin.

"You wanna go make a baby?"

She squeezed his hand.

"I'll take that as a yes."

CHAPTER FORTY-EIGHT

The morning light was peeking through the office window. Boris was sitting at his desk, reading the newspaper and drinking Russian coffee, when his phone rang. After several rings Boris reached over and removed the phone from the cradle.

"Yes."

"It's Dr. U."

"Good morning."

"I need to stop by and see you."

"Sure. I'm here."

"Good."

"You're the only doctor I know who makes house calls."

"I will be by in about an hour. Have your pants down when I get there, and I will check your prostate."

Boris belched and let out a huge laugh. "I'm looking forward to it."

Dr. U arrived in about forty-five minutes and entered through the back door of the club. He walked into Boris's office and closed the door behind him.

"You made good time," said Boris.

"Traffic wasn't so bad." Dr. U smiled. "Many

infidels must have stayed home from work today."

"What can I do for you?"

"I am in need of a loaded military-type truck and a detonator."

"Loaded with what?"

"Anything that goes boom," said Dr. U continuing to smile. "I have an important mission, and I need your assistance."

"A mission that needs a military truck and a detonator?"

"Yes, can you help me?"

"What are you planning?"

"That is not for you to know. Can you help?"

"For the right price I can get anything. When do you need it?"

"Soon."

"Do I get the truck back?"

"You ask too many questions."

"Your business is your business. But my price depends on whether this is a rental or a purchase."

"Consider it a purchase."

"And the detonator, what is it detonating?"

Dr. U said nothing.

Boris smiled. "That is why you need to purchase the truck. There will not be anything left to return."

"You are beginning to understand. Can you get me a truck?"

"Yes, of course."

"And will the detonator be a problem?"

"The detonator is the easy part, but you will be purchasing my comprehensive explosion package. Unfortunately there is no off season. The price remains high throughout the year."

"Provide me a figure. If it is fair, we will purchase."

"It won't be cheap. A pound of C-4 goes for around $100,000."

"I am aware nothing the Russians sell comes cheaply."

Boris laughed, "Capitalism at work. With sufficient cash I can fulfill almost any need. So your terrorist cells continue despite last year's setback?"

Dr. U's smile disappeared. "I am not a terrorist."

"Right, I keep forgetting. The Wahhabi Islam you preach is a liberation movement creating what the current administration calls man-made disasters in order to bring your enlightened beliefs to the infidel masses. Spare me your mock protests to my insensitivities. I can get all you need."

CHAPTER FORTY-NINE

Oscar Cano was short and thin. His brown leathery skin looked like a baseball glove left in the backyard for weeks, if not months. Cano, no Mexican Harriet Tubman, exploited everyone he smuggled to freedom. He was a coyote and charged the people he escorted across the border. The locals called him a *pollero*, and the illegal immigrants he transported were his *pollos*.

To Cano these people were merely a commodity, pawns in a chess match he played daily with the U.S. Border Patrol. Hundreds of thousands crossed each year, and a growing number of them died in the Sonora Desert.

Leaning up against the faded wooden garage, Cano took another drink from the cold bottle of Corona Extra. The hot sun baked everything in its wake, and at least for the moment Cano found shade. He let out a loud belch as Dmitri cautiously approached.

"I am looking for Oscar Cano."

"Many people seek Oscar Cano. Who are you?"

"I am Dmitri."

"You have found him. I am Oscar Cano."

Dmitri extended his hand but Oscar didn't take

it. Instead he threw the now empty bottle of beer into the brush. It landed on a rock and the glass shattered. "Go inside. We will leave in an hour."

A dozen men and three women were sitting on the dirt floor, all preparing for the trip scheduled to begin at sunset. Each appeared to be Mexican although Dmitri suspected one or two might be from Guatemala. He was the only non-Latin member of the group. "OTM," as the authorities called them—other than Mexican.

Each had a plastic jug of water. Some had small bags but not the suitcases or carry-on luggage you would find at any other transportation center catering to international travelers. Almost everyone was young, early twenties, if that. They appeared healthy, but there was no air of excited anticipation for a new venture. Some had been this route before only to be captured and deported. It was a costly mistake. The U.S. authorities were kind, some might call them helpful, if caught. The Border Patrol and even the Minutemen provided first aid, food, and water; but there was no reimbursement of the fees paid for the coyote's services.

Those who tried this before knew the consequences of even a successful trip: nighttime travel through the desert cold, unbearable heat during the day, hunger, dehydration, broken and bloody feet. It was not a trip for the timid, the infirm, or the weak.

The bigger fear each had was the coyote. His payment came up front and with no guarantee. He might run at the first sign of trouble, abandoning his travelers to fend for themselves. The women also knew of the "rape trees." Scrub brush in the desert where the coyotes hung the panties of the women they sexually assaulted along the way. The trophy trees served as not only a monument to the conquests but a warning to those who failed to cooperate.

CHAPTER FIFTY

Matt parked in the back lot and entered the club through the rear entrance. No more on-street parking, pumping the meter with quarters, and confronting Face at the front door. Matt was in. The stolen cigarettes brought him more credibility than any informant. His storage of the owner give-ups solidified his bona fides. His new status allowed him to park in the rear.

He was past the confidence-building stage of the investigation. He wasn't liked by every patron at the Russian Veil, but Boris put out the word "Matt is okay." That was all anyone needed to know. "You got a problem with me, check with Boris."

As always the music was loud. Matt wore a

wire, but it served little purpose inside the main bar area. No amount of technical support could clean up a tape well enough for a jury to decipher a criminal conversation. The real purpose of recording everything was to prevent the defense from attacking the case by claiming Matt only selectively taped conversations. Defense counsel made their money by reviewing the evidence, looking for holes in the collection of evidence, and attempting to make an issue of even the slightest crack in the government armor. Inevitably, if the recorder failed, that was the conversation the defense claimed Matt threatened the helpless accused, or when their client got religion but Matt talked him out of withdrawing from the conspiracy. It was almost as if every lawyer attended the same church, and they preached from the same sermon notes.

As he walked through the bar, Matt made a habit of looking at the dancers. In reality he was looking through them. Caitlin was prettier, and these certainly weren't the kind of girls he wanted to take home to dear old mom. The women did not hold his interest. The mystery was gone once they took off their clothes. The Victoria's Secret catalog was more alluring, but he couldn't really scan the bar in an obvious attempt to collect notes as to who was present. Guys went to the Russian Veil to watch women not shoot the breeze about an extra-inning baseball game. Matt had to play the role.

He changed his pattern on occasion, but typically he headed to the far end of the bar, ordered a beer, and from the back assessed the crowd. It was always the same bunch of rowdy patrons, the drunk and the desperate.

He was nursing the beer when Stump approached.

"Andrew MacDonald, I presume," said Matt throwing out his hand.

Stump didn't smile at the *Turner Diaries* reference.

"The Bear wants to see you in his office."

"Am I being summoned to the principal's office?"

"He didn't tell me. He just told me to get you."

Stump never cracked a smile, did an about-face, and Matt followed. Stump knocked on the door and waited for Boris to grant permission. After several seconds a loud "come" could be heard over the noise from the bar. Boris was on the phone, and Matt wandered around the office appearing to view the photos on the wall but in reality sizing up locations for the tech team to implant microphones.

When Boris hung up, Matt said, "I've never asked you, but these photos are really great. They look like something Ansel Adams would take."

"I took them."

"Seriously?"

"Yeah, in the old Soviet Union I took many photos as part of my job."

"And what job was that?"

"No need for you to worry. That life is behind me."

"Were you a spy?" Matt knew the answer but mockingly, in a singsong voice said, "Boris was a spy. Boris was a spy."

Stump glowered. "Your warehouse and stolen cigarettes don't buy that much grace. I'd knock off the singing."

Matt realized he pushed it too far. He backed off immediately. "So what business did you want to discuss?"

Boris flicked his hand toward Stump. The meaning was obvious; Stump wasn't welcome during this part of the conversation. Stump took no offense, grabbed a bottle of beer from the refrigerator, and left.

"What, you don't want any witnesses when you kill me?"

"Something like that," said Boris. He tilted his head as if examining Matt, his eyes panning Matt's profile. "What's your problem?"

"I didn't know I had a problem," said Matt lowering himself into a plush chair near Boris's desk.

"Are you not into girls?"

"What's that supposed to mean?"

"Are you a tea-drinker? A goluboy?"

"I have no idea what you're talking about."

"Why don't you bother the girls? You never have a dance. You never ask to take one into the back rooms. Everyone else I bring here can't keep their hands off my girls. Are you into men?"

Matt laughed out loud. "Why don't you borscht eaters just come to the point? No, I'm not into men. My wife doesn't let me date."

Now it was Boris's turn to laugh.

"Most of your girls are beautiful. But I'm betting a few are carrying some commie STD no strain of penicillin can ever cure."

Boris slammed his fist on the desk. "My girls are clean!"

"Whoa, big guy." Matt needed to de-escalate the tension in a hurry. He rose, walked over to the refrigerator, and pulled out two cold bottles of Baltika. He handed one to Boris, and they saluted each other in a mock toast. "Don't take it so personally. This is a community property state. One night of ecstasy could cost me half my net worth. Your girls aren't worth it to me."

"Not even a massage? The girls give a great back rub and will go just as far as you direct."

"Maybe a massage." Matt paused and gulped his beer. "So you called me into the Bat Cave just to inquire into my sexual preference?"

"No, I asked you back here to discuss business.

But before I said anything, I needed to learn a few things."

"So, have I educated you?"

"Yes." Boris took a huge gulp of Baltika and put the bottle on the desk. "My business requires assistance."

"Doesn't every business? What kind of assistance? If you're far enough in debt, maybe you qualify for a federal bailout."

"I don't need a comedian. I need a partner who isn't into handling the merchandise."

"I'll repeat an earlier question. What are you talking about?"

"Matt, all my girls are from the Ukraine. I need someone with no criminal record who can sponsor the girls. You're clean. We could set it up through your business."

"I'm listening."

"We move the girls from Odessa to Turkey . . ."

Matt interrupted, "Turkey?"

"Yeah, the Turks have lax entry requirements. It's easier to move them from Turkey into the U.S. than directly from the Ukraine."

"What do you need from me?"

"We can bring the girls in under H-1C, H-2B, even L visas depending on the business we create. I need a verifiable company for the I-129."

"You are way ahead of me. I have no idea about visas let alone H one whatever you said."

"The H visas are temporary nonagricultural

workers. The L visa is for intracompany transferees. We could set up several businesses. Depending on what we created, we could bring in any number of girls. My people create the paperwork on the other side. I just need someone clean on this end."

"And you think I'm clean?"

"I checked you out. You don't have a record, and your credit is good. On paper you look like the dream American entrepreneur. More importantly, you and your ancestors aren't from Eastern Europe. No ski or 'i-a-n' at the end of your name."

"A reverse racial profiling, hey Boris?"

"Exactly. You're catching on."

"So what's in it for me?"

"Pure profit. No risk."

"There's risk if we get caught."

"Not if you set the company up right. You can argue the documents were counterfeited, the identity stolen. You're a smart guy. You can come up with any number of excuses."

Matt leaned back in the chair and put his hands behind his head. "Sounds pretty intriguing, I might be able to pull it off. Let me think on it. I want to make sure I can set it up so I've got plausible deniability in case immigration people start nosing around."

"Don't take too long. I need to move some more girls in here soon."

CHAPTER FIFTY-ONE

Those inside could hear a vehicle approach. The noise startled the men and women huddled in the dilapidated building. A few men rose as if preparing to flee. Each worried the local authorities or even the federales had discovered the meeting locale and arrest was imminent. Eyes darted toward Dmitri.

The authorities cared little about the smuggling of Mexicans across the border, but other foreign nationals brought interest. Since 9/11, the United States pressured Mexico to halt the transporting of the OTM, the "other than Mexican." Both sides of the aisle in Washington were fearful of alienating the Hispanic vote, but the U.S. and Mexican governments reached an accommodation when it came to at least appearing to stop other nationalities from illegally crossing the border.

Everyone breathed a collective sigh of relief when they heard Oscar Cano talking with the driver; they were still safe.

Cano pulled back the wooden door to the garage, the rusty hinges groaning with the movement as he struggled to get it open. The light from the setting sun crept in as Cano entered.

"Everyone up. Grab your water and food. We leave now," said Cano.

The people rose, anxious to begin the next leg of a journey that for some began weeks ago. For Dmitri the journey began half a world away.

"Vaminos. Rapido."

Dmitri slowly got to his feet. He was older than any other traveler. All of whom spent their lives doing manual labor. His life was as a truck driver. It was not physical. The most labor-intensive work he did was hooking the trailer to the tractor. Usually others unloaded the cargo from the containers. His reason for coming to America differed from the others and was singular in nature.

"How long will the trip across the border be?" asked Dmitri.

"Not long," replied Cano.

"A few hours?"

"Si, a few hours."

The others heard the answer but said nothing. It made no sense to engage the coyote in discussion let alone argue with him. They knew the truth. The trip to Three Points, Arizona, the next stop on the journey, was at least three or four days. Several made the trip before only to be caught and deported. It was no Sunday stroll. The terrain was formidable. There were no safe routes by foot. A decade earlier American authorities concentrated their enforcement efforts on

California and Texas, believing no one would choose to cross the Arizona desert. But as the Border Patrol stepped up efforts, the illegal crossers moved to the desert. Thousands died seeking the freedom and prosperity the United States offered.

Cano led the group behind the garage where the pickup truck parked. The driver got out and removed eight backpacks from the bed of the truck. He gave one to the first eight travelers boarding an old yellow school bus. At least half the windows were broken, and the sides of the bus were covered in graffiti. Most people passing by wouldn't suspect the bus even ran. In America it would be destined for the junkyard, but this was a Mexican border town. The rules were different.

The packs weighed thirty pounds and would be rotated among the travelers. For the women they were difficult to maneuver, but the backpacks were part of the deal. If you wanted to cross, you carried a pack.

The passengers climbed onboard and jostled their way through the narrow aisle, banging the packs on the seats.

"Cuidado, stupido!" shouted Cano from his position outside the door.

Each person took a seat.

Cano boarded. He glared at a young man seated on the bench behind the driver. Cano didn't need to say a word. The young passenger understood and headed to the rear of the bus as Cano took the seat.

The driver turned the ignition, grinding the starter several times. The bus sputtered and coughed as the engine attempted to kick over. With one giant belch the engine fired. The driver put it in gear, and the group headed west beyond the newly constructed twelve-foot border wall.

The sun had set, and just a sliver of the moon was visible in the clear Mexican skies. The stars provided most of the light. The passengers craned their necks to look north where the United States and unknown opportunities awaited.

Several miles outside town the bus stopped, and the passengers exited. The real journey was about to begin. The rest of the trip would be on foot, and no one was guaranteed a successful crossing.

The trip was one the coyote took every time. The route may change depending on Border Patrol sightings, but the group would make its way north through Arizona's Altar Valley. Eighty percent of the valley was government-owned, shared by the state and the Feds. Some Indian reservation. Some managed by the Federal Bureau of Land Management. Heading through the Altar Wash, the southern third was made up of the Buenos Aires Wildlife Refuge. It almost sounded picturesque, a vacation holiday.

But for those making the trip on foot with limited resources and guides who didn't care, the trip could be a death march. Each year the Tucson Section of the U.S. Border Patrol averaged more than 200,000 apprehensions. Those were the lucky ones. The Sonoran Desert was the hottest of the North American deserts. Many died in its heat. Dehydration was the serial killer.

The backpacks weren't food, bedding, or first aid kits for weary travelers. The thirty-pound packs were filled with drugs. This trip it was cocaine. Sometimes it was marijuana, sometimes heroin. These border crossers illegally entering the country were also pushing controlled substances through the pipeline. This was no longer about poor people seeking work in America. It was drugs, crime, and human trafficking via Cocaine Alley.

CHAPTER FIFTY-TWO

I can see all kinds of legal problems," said Dwayne as he sipped his Diet Pepsi.

He and Matt were sitting at an outdoor table of a Westwood café next to Kami's where Matt just had his hair cut. The afternoon sun was beating down on the street as waves of heat floated up from the asphalt. Matt wiped the sweat from his brow as he waited for a couple to pass on the sidewalk.

"That was the first thing I thought of when Boris proposed the plan last night. It's going to take the lawyers months to sort this out back at headquarters. I'm just not sure how I can back out or even delay for more than a week."

He viewed Boris with suspicion and contempt, the same feelings he had for much of headquarters. It was a healthy perspective on both. It kept him safe on the street. Too many times the bad guys had time constraints the Bureau wouldn't acknowledge. The Supreme Court said, "Justice delayed is justice denied." In the shadow world of the undercover agent, decisions delayed wreaked havoc on operational plans.

"Let me run it past the ADIC. If Barnes supports us in theory, maybe he can run interference in D.C. As I see it, the primary issue is actually bringing women into the U.S. Once they are here, we can't send them back if they want to stay. We'll have to coordinate with ICE. Then there's the liability if something happens to the women in route. I'm not sure I can get the approvals in a week."

"They sure make it look a lot easier on TV. It's amazing what they can accomplish during a commercial break."

Dwayne could only smile. "If we are going to

push this, I think we'll need as much information as we can get on the whole operation. Can you talk to one of the girls?"

"I don't know. My lack of interest in his women made me an acceptable business associate." Matt paused. "I'll think of a reason . . . maybe a massage."

"The more ammo I can give the ADIC, the stronger our case will be at headquarters."

"While I'm thinking up a reason for an erotic massage, you think up my story to Caitlin."

"The truth will set you free," said a laughing Dwayne.

"Freedom isn't free, especially in a community property state with no-fault divorce laws."

MATT LEFT WESTWOOD AND headed over the Sepulveda Pass to Gallo's Gym. Maybe if he could get in a good workout, he could relax enough to think of a plausible story for Boris . . . and Caitlin.

He parked on the street, dumped quarters in the meter, and walked down the back alley leading to the gym. No sign marked the entrance. Gallo's wasn't open to the public. In fact, it wasn't open to a lot of boxers. Rock only took those willing to work. As Rock said, "The sick, lame, and lazy need not apply."

He was surprised when he got upstairs to find he was the only boxer at the gym. He and Rock talked for about fifteen minutes. Then Matt put in time on the heavy bag, the speed bag, and the rope. He worked up a sweat in the forty-five minute session but also came away with a story.

CHAPTER FIFTY-THREE

On his way to the Russian Veil, Matt called Caitlin and apologized for another missed dinner. He conveniently forgot to mention his back was hurting and he might need some nonprofessional medical assistance.

He drove east a few miles before turning into the parking lot.

Matt eased his body out of the car and slowly made his way to the rear entrance where he was greeted by Stump, smoking a cigarette.

"Gonna stunt your growth."

Stump uttered an obscenity.

"Boris around?" asked Matt.

"He's in his office."

Matt hobbled over to the office, slightly hunched over, and knocked on the door.

"Come."

Matt opened the door.

"I didn't expect to see you so soon. I thought it would take several days for you to have an answer for me on my business proposition."

"I spoke with my attorney this afternoon. I'm looking into ways to legally set up multiple corporations through an offshore holding company."

"Sounds like it could work. Can this attorney be trusted?"

"He's my attorney, not some guy I saw advertising on TV. He's covered me in the past. He thinks it's a tax shelter so I'm not worried about him. He knows who pays his fees."

"If he becomes a problem, let me know. I'm not afraid to cancel the guy's ticket if he can't provide quality legal protection."

"Thanks, Boris, I'll keep your offer in mind." Matt faked a painful look as he lowered himself into a chair.

"You okay? You look like you're hurting."

"Yeah, I threw my back out. I popped a handful of Celebrex but it's killing me."

"Why not let one of the girls work on it?" offered Boris.

"I need real help."

"No, seriously, my girls can help." He picked up the phone. "Tell Irina to come in."

The ruse worked. It wasn't Matt's idea to handle the merchandise; Boris suggested the massage. With his credibility still intact, he might get a chance to ask questions without arousing suspicion.

There was a knock on the door, and before

Boris could answer, a short, slender blonde with shoulder-length hair walked in. She looked to be a teenager. Even though she was heavily made up, her face had a few tell-tale blemishes. She should have been preparing for the high school homecoming dance, not entertaining men in some low-life bar in Los Angeles.

"Irina, this is Matt. He needs you to work on him."

She smiled but it was not a welcoming smile, more obligatory, the kind a hostess offers at Denny's late into the lunch-hour rush. She turned to the door and began to walk out.

Matt lifted himself out of the chair with an Emmy Award–winning pain performance. "Thanks."

"Get back to me when your lawyer has some answers, but tell him to hurry."

Matt grabbed the door, held it for the young Ukrainian, and allowed Irina to lead the way.

They headed down the long hallway passing several rooms before they came to a partially opened door. Irina opened it and motioned for Matt to enter.

"I give you few minutes to get ready. Take off clothes. Lie facedown on bed. Cover with sheet if want."

Matt was no rookie when it came to massages. He boxed long enough to welcome trained hands rubbing out all kinds of knots; a deep-tissue massage solved a lot of hurts. Matt just wasn't sure Irina knew Swedish massage from Russian erotica.

The room was dark. A single dim lamp provided the only illumination. Matt assumed it was too dark to videotape the activities, unless the Russian installed infrared cameras. *Caitlin would not be real happy with this setup. Death might be preferable.* Water from a desktop fountain trickled in a steady, relaxing flow. Instead of a massage table a single bed raised several feet off the ground took up most of the tiny room. It was obviously duel purposed, a convenient height for a massage yet wide enough for two should the cash flow. Having seen the bar in daylight, Matt questioned the cleanliness of the dark room, but bedbugs were the least of his worries. Matt disrobed and climbed onto the bed. He took a deep breath, lay on his stomach, pulled the sheet up, and positioned his head comfortably on a cushioned doughnut. *God, I may need some help on this one.*

Within a minute Irina knocked on the door and walked in without waiting for a response. She closed the door and punched the button on the portable CD player. The whine of the device warming up was quickly overcome by the soft music of a Mohawk Indian playing the native flute. Matt heard the familiar sound of a zipper unzipping. He knew she hadn't opened a gym bag and suspected the quasi-medical practitioner was making herself comfortable as well. Matt decided to take the offensive. Talk is cheap, but talking adults might be too preoccupied to engage in less wholesome activities.

"My lower back is killing me. I threw it out last night. Maybe you could concentrate on that."

"You want back rub?"

"Yes."

"Just back rub?"

"Yes, just a back rub."

"I not give many just back rubs."

Matt laughed, "I suspect not."

"I know a little about how to do it, but I not really a massager." She pulled down the sheet and oiled her hands. She vigorously rubbed her hands together and placed them on Matt's back. He could feel the warmth immediately. Then she began rubbing Matt's back.

"Where are you from?"

"I am from Lviv. It is in the Ukraine."

"Are most of the girls from there?"

"Yes, all girls I know here from Ukraine. Most are from Odessa."

"How long have you been here?"

"I think several months. I not sure of time." She continued to rub Matt's back. "Does that feel better?"

"Yeah, it's helping."

"I can do more than just rub back."

"No, I'm fine with what you are doing."

"Boris would want to make sure you happy with my service."

"I'm just fine. Keep working on the back."

"You different than other men."

"How so?"

"No one want just back rub, not even Boris."

"I'm not Boris." He let her work on the lower back for a few minutes and then said, "Tell me what it's like for you here in America."

Irina continued to rub Matt's back and said nothing. She paused briefly to get more oil. As she slapped her hand on his back, Matt heard an almost indistinguishable sniffle. She continued to rub. Matt heard the noise again.

"Are you okay?" asked Matt.

Irina didn't respond but tears began to flow.

Matt turned over and sat up. Irina stood there in her underwear, her face soaked in tears. When Matt started to say something, she put her finger to his lips and shook her head. She pointed to the far corner at the ceiling. In the faint light he could make out what appeared to be a tiny microphone. Matt understood. Boris's electronic surveillance system included the rooms.

Matt nodded. "My back feels a lot better. Thanks. Maybe now if I soak it in a hot bath, it will loosen up more, and I'll be great. You're pretty talented with those hands. Maybe you should consider becoming a massage therapist full-time."

Irina smiled understanding Matt's soliloquy was for the benefit of the listening device. She leaned over and whispered in his ear, "I can meet you at eight in coffee shop of Sportsmen's Lodge. You know place?" She backed away. Matt acknowledged the invitation with a slight nod. She grabbed her dress and walked out of the room.

Matt closed his eyes and breathed a near-silent sigh. An inaudible prayer accompanied the sigh. He dressed and headed to Boris's office.

The door to the office was slightly ajar. He poked his head inside the door without knocking. Stump was sitting in front of the desk, drinking a beer. Boris was reading something and looked up when he sensed a new presence in the room.

"Hey, she is good. She loosened up my back. I think I'm going to go home and soak in a hot bath. I'll shout at you tomorrow after I talk with the attorney." Matt kept walking without waiting for a response from Boris.

When Matt was out of earshot, Boris looked at Stump. "Check him out."

"Shouldn't we have done that before you asked for his help?"

"Don't question me. It's never too late. Problems can be erased. His back loosened up a little too quickly."

"You think he's getting something on the side?"

Boris shrugged his shoulders and threw open his hands. "Something doesn't smell right. Irina gets off soon. Follow her and keep me advised."

CHAPTER FIFTY-FOUR

Matt pulled from the parking lot of the Russian Veil and headed east on Ventura Boulevard. He checked his mirrors, something that was second nature. He switched lanes twice, and he seemed clean—no tails, no cops. He then turned up a side street and drove several blocks before entering a cul-de-sac. He was clean. He grabbed his cell phone and called Dwayne.

"I think my fake backache worked. I'm meeting with one of the dancers slash hookers slash massage therapists named Irina."

"You still a virgin?"

"Yeah, I'm fine. Probably won't tell Caitlin about this latest foray, but I might have made a connection."

"Any chance it's a setup?"

"There's always that chance. Maybe she is just freelancing and didn't want Boris to know. I'll let her take the lead. She suggested the meeting and the location."

"Where are you going to be?"

"The coffee shop at Sportsmen's Lodge on Coldwater and Ventura."

"I'm familiar with the location. You think she's working out of one of the rooms?"

"I seriously doubt it. Do we have a surveillance team available?"

"Let me call SOG and find out."

"I'd love to get pictures and then follow her away."

"If SOG isn't available, maybe I can get a team together from the task force."

"Don't push it. I don't want to get burned. This could be a big step. At least get someone inside the coffee shop. I may need a witness at some point. I don't like meeting women when I'm not covered. Too many allegations can arise."

"Were you wired in the room?"

"Yeah, I had a recorder in my pants pocket. If you believe Irina, the whole thing may have been recorded by Boris. She pointed to a microphone in the corner."

"You believe her?"

"No reason not to. I know he has surveillance cameras throughout the club so I assume he has mikes in the rooms as well. I was careful in everything I said. I'm using all this as a cover to ensure my investment is safe if I'm going to be providing him backstopping for a smuggling operation."

"Just be careful with her. Who knows where her loyalties lie?"

"I understand." Matt paused in the conversation as a woman walking her dog strolled past the car. "Did you run this whole scenario by the ADIC?"

"Yeah, he was on the phone as soon as we ended the meeting."

"Make sure he understands time is of the essence."

"He knows. Let me call SOG. Stay safe."

Matt ended the call and headed back to the warehouse where he would wait until his meeting at the Sportsmen's Lodge.

CHAPTER FIFTY-FIVE

Dmitri was drawn to one of the travelers, a young Mexican girl with long black hair and dark, deep-set eyes. Her skin was smooth, not the leathery look most of the other travelers wore. She almost seemed out of place, too pretty and too young to be on such a journey. During a short break, as they sat on the open trail under the faint moon-lit sky, he introduced himself.

"I am Dmitri," he whispered.

She hesitated in her response. No one spoke during the journey. Silence was not just encouraged; it was mandated. Any noise might alert the Border Patrol.

"I am Juanita."

"Why are you making the trip?"

"Opportunity. There is little for me to do in Mexico. My aunt says there are jobs in Colorado."

"What kind of jobs?"

"It doesn't matter. I have two children. I need to care for them."

"You need to be home. Why doesn't your husband provide?"

"My husband is dead. He was in the military and killed by the drug lords."

"And now you are working for them."

"Only to get me across the border."

Oscar Cano walked over to the two. "Quieto."

MATT ENTERED THE SPORTSMEN'S Lodge parking lot from the rear entrance off Coldwater Canyon Boulevard. He drove around the back of the complex and found an empty spot east of the hotel. He parked near the coffee shop next to the bougainvillea canopy entrance. The lot was crowded, which at this hour usually meant a banquet. Two large, luxury buses were parked along the far wall. The Lodge was a frequent overnight stay for entertainers who traveled by bus from venue to venue.

Trying to be inconspicuous, Matt glanced

around the lot. He was hoping to see an SOG vehicle but saw none. He was also looking for any vehicles which frequented the Russian Veil. He didn't think Irina was setting him up, but as always he needed to be cautious. The lot was free of any familiar vehicles, friend or foe.

Matt exited his car and headed to the main entrance of the hotel. He could have entered by the side door directly leading to the coffee shop, but this gave him one more chance to subtly check the lot. Nothing noteworthy caught his eye.

As he opened the heavy, wooden, double door, he was greeted by the noise of the twenty-something generation. The lobby bar was crowded, and two near-drunks were playing pool, apparently for money or drinks because a cheer went up from those watching with each ball pocketed. The players were young, tattooed, and pierced. Their stringy, long, black hair needed washing, and Matt assumed they were no-name rockers just off one of the luxury tour busses. The women cheering had to be Valley groupies hoping to trade sex for free concert tickets.

Matt spied an older couple checking in. The middle-aged clerk behind the frosted glass at the front desk winced every time a raucous cheer was shouted. Since the couple didn't appear to be the partying type, they may have been rethinking their decision to stay.

The coffee shop was just down the hallway from the lobby. Over the course of his career, Matt met informants and even a few subjects in the coffee shop. Several years earlier he did a five-kilo coke deal with a mob associate who owned a restaurant in Burbank. Matt, pretending to be from out of town, set the deal up in a fifth-floor room of the lodge. Like clockwork the Godfather wannabe showed up with a knuckle dragger whose IQ was only a few strokes over par. They started in the coffee shop where they completed negotiations and headed to the rented room where the mob guy was to deliver the product. Once in the room Matt flashed the cash, and the errand-boy bodyguard was sent scurrying for the product. He returned in minutes with five kilos of Hollywood's drug of choice. Matt tested the white powder and gave a verbal sign to an arrest team listening to the entire transaction in the adjoining room. When they burst in unannounced, chaos exploded in the tiny motel room.

The arrest went down hard when the bodyguard tried to earn his pay after the FBI ordered him to raise his hands. Matt ended up on the receiving end of a few blows, but justice willed out in the end. Somewhere in the mix Matt managed to break a nose, only this time it was his. Caitlin didn't find raccoon eyes and bandages stretching across his face to be as sexy as Matt had hoped. But bruises heal as do broken bones, and Matt had colorful pictures to show his grandchildren someday. The mob guy received a ten-year sentence, and his genius bodyguard took a twenty-year hit for assaulting a federal officer. *Fond memories of the Sportsmen's Lodge.*

Would tonight be different?

CHAPTER FIFTY-SIX

The lodge's coffee shop was small by restaurant standards, consisting of two rooms. The smaller of the two rooms housed a counter with eight seats, two booths, and a couple tables. The larger room had about a dozen tables, some seating four, others seating two. Western artifacts and pictures of Hollywood cowboy stars covered the walls. The lunchtime crowd typically consisted of stuntmen from the golden age of television, but tonight the customers appeared to be tourists and businessmen staying at the hotel.

Three men sat at the counter, but the tables were empty. Matt walked under the archway to the larger room. Several couples were seated at tables in the middle of the dining area. He walked through the room and looked out at couples smoking on the heated patio. No Irina.

When he turned back, he saw a waif in the corner booth. She looked like a frightened runaway who might frequent Hollywood Boulevard, except her clothes were clean and her face was washed. She was almost cowering in the corner, her legs drawn up to her chest on the white leather bench seat attached to the wall. A glass of iced tea sat in front of her.

Had Matt not known she was waiting, he might not have recognized her. The heavy dose of makeup she wore at the Russian Veil was gone. Her hair was pulled back. She had an almost innocent look. She could have been the girl from the high school yearbook who didn't rate a second look.

"I afraid you not come."

Matt took a seat in the booth positioning himself to see who was entering the restaurant. He was cautious. He wasn't convinced this wasn't a setup. He wished he could rephrase his earlier comment to Boris about going home to take a hot bath. If confronted by a member of the Russian's posse, it would be hard to explain his presence in a coffee shop. It was a mistake and mistakes often have consequences. *Focus.*

"No, I came. You seemed like you wanted to talk. I thought you needed someone to listen."

"Thank you for coming. You different."

"You said that back in the room."

"You ask questions about me. Do you really want to know answers?"

"That's why I'm here."

"You not tell Boris?"

"If you don't want me to tell Boris, I won't."

"Thank you."

A waitress approached and Irina immediately quieted. A closed menu was sitting in front of the young Ukrainian.

Matt opened his menu and asked Irina, "Have you decided?"

"I not hungry."

"Sure you are. Get something. I'm buying."

Irina smiled and opened the menu.

Matt looked up at the waitress. "Give us a few more minutes." She walked away without saying a word.

After a minute of perusing, Irina closed the menu. "I have decided."

When the waitress returned, she refilled their iced teas and both ordered.

"I come first from Ukraine. I told I be secretary for movie studio. I laugh. I very good on computer but who hire me? I not speak English good."

"Who said you'd have a job in Hollywood?"

"Lady in Odessa. I answer ad in paper. My parents do not want me to leave. They say I should stay in Lviv, but I think I know better. I leave my town and I meet with her. She say first you go to Turkey. Then we get you papers for Hollywood. They say maybe I be in movies after I am secretary. I have to laugh. I say I not pretty like girls in Hollywood, but she say Hollywood need all kinds of actresses. She say I be good actress."

I hope you aren't acting now.

"How long ago was this?"

"Last year. Right after my birthday."

"How old are you?"

"I thought in this country men do not ask women their age."

Matt laughed. "Gentlemen aren't supposed to ask but men can."

Irina looked confused by the distinction, then she said, "I am eighteen."

"Tell me about the journey."

"Journey?"

"The trip. Tell me how you got from Lviv to Odessa to Turkey to Los Angeles."

Irina was quiet for several moments. At first Matt assumed she was formulating her thoughts, but then he realized she was choking back tears. Before she spoke again, the waitress appeared with their meals. She placed the plates in front of each and warned Irina her plate was hot.

"You guys got everything you need? I'll bring some more iced tea." With that she headed back to the kitchen before Matt could even respond he would like ketchup for his fries.

Matt watched her walk away and in his peripheral vision spotted Danny Garcia from the Joint Terrorism Task Force sitting in the other room drinking a cup of coffee and reading a book. Matt assumed Danny's presence meant Dwayne was unable to get SOG for the surveillance. The conversation was being recorded, but Matt welcomed another set of eyes as backup.

When Matt turned his eyes back to Irina, her head was bowed, her hands folded. She finished praying and made the sign of the cross.

"Are you Catholic?" asked Matt.

"Yes, in my country not many Catholic, but my city used to be part of Poland. Many are Catholic. When I was little girl, Pope John Paul II came to Lviv. My parents take me to see him. Many people attend Mass at great outdoor service. I always remember that day. It very special for all Catholics in my country. Are you Catholic?"

"No."

"But you are Christian. I can tell."

"Yeah, I'm a Christian."

"That is good."

She blew on the gravy of her mashed potatoes. The steam was rising from the plate. With her fork she stabbed at the broccoli and placed a piece in her mouth.

Matt got up and grabbed a bottle of ketchup from an empty table.

"So tell me more about you and how you got here."

Irina took another bite and swallowed before answering.

"I take train from Lviv to Odessa. I meet with lady who put ad in paper. She seem very nice. She tell me of all opportunities in America. I watch your movies and TV shows. I say I like them, and she say I can work with them. I say really and she say yes. She very good salesperson. So I agree."

Irina took another bite. Matt was hoping she was hungry and not stalling for time until Boris arrived. On the street you are often forced to size someone up quickly, usually erring on the side of caution. Mistakes can be deadly. Matt's general mistrust of mankind made him a frequent doubter as to anyone's good intentions. It kept him alive. He wanted to believe the tears and the prayer so he let her eat and proceed at her own pace. She swallowed, but before she took another bite, Matt said, "Then what?"

"Then I go to Turkey. She say it easier to get out of Ukraine through Turkey. Once I get there, it not like I expect. I told I must work in shop for while. Then man say he bought me. I say I not for sale. He hit me, and lady from Ukraine say I must work for him. So I go with him. He make me do things I never do. He make me be with men. I never be with man before. I cry and he hit me again and again. Some nights I am with ten men. All very bad. All smell. All have wives but want young girl. Then one night I meet man who say I can go to America. I am happy. I think I be happy here."

"And you flew to the United States?"

"Yes, I fly. I come with other girls from Ukraine. The man bring us. We stop in New York. Then we fly to Los Angeles. Once I get here, man say I sold to man in America, and now I must please men here."

Matt had heard stories of women being sold as sex slaves, but he had never encountered a female who claimed to endure such hardship. Nothing Irina said or did seemed insincere. He wanted to believe her.

"Was the man who claimed he bought you Boris?"

She nodded. "Yes, he hold all our papers."

"What papers?"

She cut the slice of chicken breast into pieces and dipped a piece into the gravy.

"They have my passport, my visa, all my identification from Ukraine. They say when I pay them back for all expenses to come here they will give back my papers."

"When will that be?"

"I do not know."

"They didn't give you a date?"

She shook her head.

"How much do they say you owe?"

"They say it cost them much money to bring me here. They say I should not agree to come i I not agree to pay back money."

"But did they ever give you a dollar amount?"

She ate several bites as Matt picked at his sandwich. She took a long drink of iced tea then nodded.

"Once they say I owe $30,000. I do not have that kind of money. I never make that much money. Now they say when I make men happy i help pay off expenses."

"Since you have been here, have any of the girls ever paid off the debt and left?"

"Boris say if we leave without paying he kill our family in Ukraine. Some girls try to leave. Others say they want their papers. They say they go to police. Now those girls are missing. They were my friends."

Tears flooded her face.

The waitress returned to the table, more inquisitive than a dutiful servant. "Is everything okay?"

"Yeah, we're fine," said Matt.

"It doesn't look fine."

"I said we're fine."

The waitress was unmoved by Matt's rudeness. "Honey, are you okay? Do you need me to call someone?"

Irina looked up. "Yes, I am fine. He is trying to help. Thank you."

With that the waitress cleared Matt's plate and walked away.

"I am sorry I cry. I do not want to work any more for Boris. I am so scared. I just want to go home. I have made many mistakes. I want parents to forgive me and let me come home. But I afraid to say anything to Boris, or maybe I be missing like other girls. Can you help me? Please, you are different. Please help me."

Matt was stunned by the request. He didn't see this coming. The tears at the club should have portended this, but he missed the signs. She was just a teenager. Of course she only wanted to go home. She wanted to undo all she encountered this past year. She wanted to start over, a clean slate. But how could Matt help without undermining the undercover operation? Even if Irina agreed to testify, the FBI wasn't ready to make arrests that evening. Was this a setup? Was Boris using her to see if Matt would admit to being an FBI agent? He was tested once by Boris with the bogus traffic stop. Maybe this was the second phase of the testing process. But the tears appeared real. She's genuine; he was sure of it, but could he take a chance and reveal his true identity?

Matt took a long sip of his drink. *God, give me some answers.*

"Will you help me, please? I want God to forgive me. I want to go home and start again."

"I believe in a God of second chances." Matt said it like he believed it.

"So you will help me?" asked a hopeful Irina.

"I'll help you, but I just don't know how yet. Are you sure Boris had something to do with the others who are missing?"

"There were three girls who work with me at club this year. Two are missing. The police find Annika shot and thrown off side of road. She, like others, want to leave and tell Boris they will go. The next day they gone, but now we afraid they go like Annika. Boris never say he kill them. I do not think Boris kill them, but I think he tell others to kill. All of us afraid."

Matt reached into his back pocket and pulled out his wallet. He took out a hundred dollar bill and five twenties. He handed the money to Irina. "Here's two hundred dollars. Rent a room for a few nights until I can straighten this out."

"Should I stay here?"

"No, this place will require identification. There's a motel a couple of miles east of here called the El Capitan." Matt took an undercover business card from his wallet and handed it to her. "They take cash and won't ask any questions. Call me tomorrow. I'll talk to Boris."

"No! You can't talk to him. If he know I leave, he may kill me."

"He won't kill you. He's a businessman and so

am I. We'll work out a business arrangement satisfactory to both of us."

"But I am afraid."

The tears that dried a few moments ago came again.

"Irina, you said I was different. I am. I'll protect you. You will have to trust me."

"Thank you, Matt." She reached across the table to touch his hand, but he pulled back. This wasn't physical, and he didn't want it to become that. There was a look of confusion or maybe even hurt on her face. Since coming to America, she only knew one way to satisfy a man. Now when she wanted to say thank you, she was rebuffed.

"You ready to go? I'll drive you down to the El Capitan."

"I walk."

"No, I'll drive you. Let's go."

Matt left money on the table to cover the bill and the tip. As they were walking out, Matt made eye contact with Danny Garcia, but there was no way for Matt to safely convey his next move.

Matt and Irina exited by the side door, avoiding the main entrance. He pushed the car remote, the lights blinked, and the doors unlocked.

As Irina entered the car, she said, "You have nice car. You must be important businessman."

"I've had some success."

Matt drove out of the lot turning left onto Coldwater Canyon. He took a left at Ventura Boulevard and drove east to the El Capitan. Had he been more alert, he would have spotted the vehicle following him.

CHAPTER FIFTY-SEVEN

The El Capitan Motel was built in the forties and at one time catered to the upper class who could afford cars and vacations. Now any out-of-town guests who showed up did so because they believed the Internet ads claiming the motel was in the heart of Studio City "where movie stars are as common as the daily sunshine." The marquee bragged of cable TV and free in-room phones; so much for luxuries. The motel room doors still had conventional locks, and the "lost keys" from decades earlier worked. On many a winter evening the homeless camped out in an empty room merely by acquiring one of the keys circulating on the street.

Matt pulled to the curb just east of the motel. "This is as far as I go. You can check in on your own. Call me in the morning and stay in the room tonight. Don't go walking the Boulevard, and don't go back to the Russian Veil."

"I going nowhere. I lock door and stay in room. Thank you Matt for helping me."

He watched her walk into the lobby and waited until she exited with a room key in her hand. As she walked toward her room, Matt pulled from the curb. He drove east on Ventura, took a left on Vineland, and headed toward the freeway and home.

STUMP AND JESSE PULLED into the darkened parking area of the horseshoe-shaped motel and stopped in front of room 15. The lot was empty. Most of the traffic was on foot, the homeless who couldn't afford cars and the prostitutes who turned tricks by the hour. It was still early in the evening, and most rooms were empty. Even those occupants in their rooms were probably drunk or high so any eyewitness testimony was suspect. Boris's two employees quickly exited the car and knocked on the door.

A quiet voice from behind the door said, "Matt, is that you?"

Stump answered in a near whisper, "Open the door."

The sound of the chain safety latch being unfastened was heard through the paper-thin doors. The men braced for their entry, predators preparing to strike.

Irina opened the door, and the two burst in with lightning speed. Irina let out a brief scream, her eyes wide with fear, but Stump quickly covered her mouth as he grabbed her and threw her to the floor. He fell with her and landed on top of the petite teenager. She hit so hard the air forced from her lungs had the power to blow Stump's hand from her mouth. Before she could catch her breath and scream, he hit her with a solid right across the face and repositioned his hand on her mouth.

Jesse stood by the door blocking the entrance and any possible egress should Irina manage to escape. But she was no match for Stump. He pulled an eight-inch homemade sap from his back pocket. The thin leather sock filled with buckshot was a dangerous weapon in the hands of a skilled technician; Stump was skilled. He beat Irina senseless, slapping her repeatedly across the face. Her head whipped back and forth with each successive powerful strike. The multiple blows fractured the young girl's skull. Within seconds her body lay motionless, the carpet stained in blood. Stump reached down searching for a carotid pulse. There was none. The Ukrainian teenager who begged for Matt's help and received his assurances was dead.

CHAPTER FIFTY-EIGHT

When Matt arrived home, Caitlin was preparing her lesson for the next day. After ten years in the classroom, she thought she had seen it all, but each day was a new adventure. This morning during recess, for no apparent reason, two boys decided to tie third-grader Isaiah Goldman to a picnic table and pelt him with rocks. Michael Hughes, who weeks earlier called Isaiah a racial slur not knowing the meaning, interceded. He grabbed the rock throwers and banged their heads together, splitting open the forehead of the larger of the two boys. Blood splattered everywhere. Children screamed and panic on the playground prevailed. The paramedics were called, and the principal was forced to notify the Board of Education who, in turn, called the attorneys. Statements were taken as were photos of all involved. Evidence tape surrounded the "crime scene." It was like an episode of *CSI:NY* as tears flowed from the victims and the perpetrators. The only one to remain stoic was Michael Hughes. "I did the right thing. They were hurting Isaiah. He needed help."

The playground monitor, a classified employee,

not a teacher, called it "vigilante justice" and wanted Michael expelled immediately. Caitlin took Michael's side. Calm eventually prevailed, but reading, writing, and arithmetic took a backseat to limiting the legal liability of the school district.

Matt kissed Caitlin and, as he headed to the kitchen, invited a long dissertation detailing her latest educational experience with what he meant to be a rhetorical question, "So how was your day?"

THE FORTY-FIVE-YEAR-OLD MARRIED MAN, father of three from Dayton, Ohio, was on a business trip. He thought he'd chance excitement in the rather mundane world of a computer software salesman. She was standing near the corner, and he succumbed to temptation. An evening of ecstasy two thousand miles from home seemed safe. Who would ever know? He had a condom in his pocket, and his wallet was locked in the glove compartment. To add to the thrill, tonight his name would be Hugh, as in Hugh Hefner. The founder of *Playboy* would be so proud.

They drove in his rental car the three blocks from the corner where she was working to the motel. He parked on the street, and the two entered the dimly lit parking lot.

The thirty-something-year-old prostitute

grabbed the key from her clutch purse as she and her trick headed to the room. As she passed room 15, she noticed the door was ajar. She kept walking until she arrived in front of 18. As she unlocked the door, she said, "Go on in, honey, and you get real comfortable. I will be there in a sec to satisfy all your desires. I just need to check on something."

Rozella walked back to the partially opened door. A quick search of the room might yield cash or something worth pawning down the street. She opened the door and screamed!

PATROL UNITS FROM LAPD arrived within minutes. The night's darkness was illuminated by the flashing red and blue lights. Paramedic units also arrived shortly after the patrol units were on the scene. The cops cleared the room and secured the site. The paramedics could do nothing but pronounce Irina dead. No amount of medical assistance was going to revive the life of the Ukrainian teenager.

The software salesman ran at the sound of the screams, but Rozella stayed until the police arrived. She worked out of the El Capitan and was on a first-name basis with most of the patrol officers on night watch. The cops let her work unless she caused problems, which was almost never. On more than one occasion she provided information to the police about the happenings on the boulevard. That was her quid pro quo for working. So even if she had run, they'd be looking for her to learn the street gossip regarding the attack. Besides, the victim's head was so beaten and bloodied, Rozella couldn't tell if the female was one of her friends who also frequented the El Capitan.

Rozella Johnson sat on the curb sobbing. She knew it was dangerous to work the streets, but never had she seen such a vicious attack.

A female detective came over and sat beside the prostitute. Before the detective could question her, Rozella said, "Who would do such a thing? Poor girl. I hope you get whoever did this. Nobody deserves to die like this. You promise me, you'll find who did this."

"We'll do our best."

"You better mean that. Just cause she may be a working girl don't mean she ain't somebody's daughter. You know what I'm saying?"

"I know."

"We ain't throwaways. Somebody cares about that girl."

"Ames," said a male detective.

The female detective rose. "I'll be right back."

The male detective handed Ames the business card found on Irina. She agreed to call the number on the card.

CHAPTER FIFTY-NINE

The undercover cell phone was lying on the night stand and began to vibrate. Matt was reading in bed with Caitlin by his side grading papers. He looked at the number and didn't recognize the 818 area code. He grabbed a recorder and turned it on.

"Yeah."

"I'm looking for Matt."

"Who's this?"

"Are you Matt?"

"It depends on who you are?" Matt could now hear a police radio in the background.

"I'm Detective Ames. I'm with the LAPD, North Hollywood Division."

"Yeah, I'm Matt. What's going on?"

"We found your business card on a deceased woman. We have no other type of identification on her. We need your help in identifying her."

"Deceased? What happened?"

"Why don't you come down, and we can talk about it?"

"Where are you?"

"I'm at the El Capitan Motel on Ventura Boulevard in Studio City."

"I think I know the place. I've driven past it a few times. I'll be right down."

• • •

MATT RACED DOWN THE 101 Freeway toward Studio City. He put the car on cruise control, set it for eighty, and called Dwayne, who answered on the second ring.

"What's up?"

"Dwayne, we've got a huge problem."

"Now what?"

"LAPD just found Irina dead in the motel where I left her."

"What?" roared Dwayne.

"I'm heading to the motel now to identify the body."

"How'd she die?"

"The detective wouldn't tell me," said Matt.

"How'd they connect you?"

"They found my business card on her. Apparently she didn't have any other ID."

"Do you think it's wise to go there?"

"I don't think I have a choice. I don't want them running a background check and finding all kinds of false flags. If they get too creative, they may blow the whole operation."

"You want me to run interference?"

"Not yet. Let's see what they have. Maybe this is a suicide or a drug overdose. I'm not going to out myself, but I think you better call Danny Garcia and give him a heads-up. The Queen Mother's going to love this latest wrinkle. This is all she needs to shut us down."

"Matt, I'll call Danny now. I think we should get him over there. He can say he got a call from an informant. At least have him on the scene when you get there."

"Yeah, that makes sense."

MATT PARKED ON THE street. The parking lot to the motel was crowded with patrol units, unmarked cars, and a coroner's vehicle. Matt spotted Danny Garcia talking with the only female not in uniform. He presumed she was Ames. Rather than look too familiar with police procedure, he approached a uniform officer near the door to room 15. He took a quick glance into the room as crime scene photos were being taken. He saw Irina's bloody and beaten body, and his stomach knotted. Rage loomed but he held his emotions in check.

"I'm looking for a Detective Ames."

The patrol officer pointed to the female with Danny. Matt headed in that direction. As soon as he got within earshot, the conversation ceased and both turned to Matt.

"Detective Ames?"

"Yeah."

"I'm Matt Wallace. You called me a half hour ago."

"Yeah." She turned to Danny and said, "I need to talk with this guy. Thanks for your help. Could you stick around a little longer?"

Danny nodded.

She then said to Matt, "Let's take a walk."

The two walked to the other end of the motel.

"We've got a dead girl in room 15. She had your business card on her. You want to explain why."

"I give out my business cards to a lot of people. I run a business. That's why they're called business cards."

Even though she was four inches shorter and about fifty pounds lighter, Ames immediately took charge. "Hey, I got a dead girl in that room. I don't need your flippant attitude."

"I didn't mean it that way. You called me but haven't given me many facts. Does she have a name? What's she look like? I thought you needed my help in identifying her. I came down as soon as you called. I'm trying to be cooperative. I need to see the girl to find out if I know her."

"We think we have a name. That detective provided some information." She nodded toward Danny Garcia. "Her name is Irina."

Matt feigned shock. "Irina. Oh no."

"So you know her?"

"Yeah, I know her." Matt ran his fingers through his hair. "Look, this is a little delicate. Please understand. I'm married. I've never cheated on my wife, but sometimes after work I stop off for a beer. Irina dances at a club I go to sometimes. I gave her my card a few days ago. She said she was looking for work. I said I could help and to give me a call. I'd put out some feelers."

"Yeah, I bet you put out some feelers."

"No, seriously, it wasn't like that. Really, I've never cheated on my wife. Irina was just a young kid. She was from one of those Russian countries. She came to the United States looking to make a better life for herself."

"In some strip joint?"

"Dancing paid the bills. You have to believe me. I never touched her."

"So how'd she get your card?"

"She came up to me when I was sitting at the bar. We started talking. It was a slow night. She asked me if I wanted a lap dance. I told her no but bought her a drink."

"You're a big spender, huh?"

"Look, I felt sorry for her. We talked that's all."

"And where did all this take place?"

"The Russian Veil."

"I know the place," said Ames scribbling the name in her notebook. "You don't look like the typical patron for a biker bar. What kind of business did you say you were in?"

"I own some real estate here in the Valley. I used to own the property next door to the bar. I'd go in there long before it was called the Russian

Veil. It's just a familiar spot. I don't go there every night, just on occasion. It was on one of those occasions I met Irina."

Matt thought he was doing a good job of selling his story and was hopeful the detective was buying it.

"Okay, that's enough for now." Ames called over a patrol officer. "Take this guy's identifying information and get an address."

"Can I see her?" asked Matt.

"No, just give the officer your information so I can get a hold of you if I need to. Then you can go."

Matt provided the address of an apartment he rented as part of his cover. Even though he spent almost every night at home with Caitlin, the address on his driver's license matched, and he occasionally frequented the apartment to give it a lived-in look.

CHAPTER SIXTY

Matt returned to his car and drove a few blocks before calling Danny Garcia, who answered on the second ring.

"Can you talk?" asked Matt.

"Yeah, give me about ten minutes and meet me in the parking lot behind the Bistro Gardens."

"Let's do this instead," Matt hesitated and said slowly, "I'll call Dwayne. All three of us meet at the warehouse in thirty."

MATT BEAT DWAYNE AND Danny to the warehouse. He kept the lights dimmed but opened the garage door so the two could pull in and not draw attention to cars parked on the street at night in a warehouse district.

Danny arrived a few minutes after Matt and parked near the far wall. As he exited his car, he said to Matt, "Dwayne just called. He's a few minutes out."

Danny walked over to Matt standing next to the garage door waiting for Dwayne to arrive. Danny noticed the dark rings under Matt's eyes. Sleep wasn't coming easily for the undercover agent.

"Are you doing okay?"

"I'm fine," said Matt with no emotion.

"Did you see the body?" asked Danny.

"Yeah."

Just then Dwayne drove in. Matt lowered the garage door after he entered. The three gathered around Dwayne's car.

Danny started, "It was bad. I worked gangs for eight years in East L.A. I saw some pretty savage beatings, but this one topped anything I've seen. Looks like someone took a ball bat to her face."

"Any doubt as to who was behind it? Is there any chance it could have been a random homicide? Maybe a john? Could she have been working and picked up the wrong guy?" asked Dwayne.

Danny said, "She had cash in her pockets. If it was a robbery, they left the money and a watch. There were no calls in or out of the motel room. It didn't look like she was working. She was fully clothed."

"It had to be Boris. I thought I was careful. I checked my mirrors. I didn't see anyone follow us from the Lodge to the motel, but I must have missed it." His voice trailed off.

"No one followed you out of the coffee shop, and I watched you pull from the lot. I didn't see any obvious tail, but they could have been waiting off Ventura or Coldwater."

Matt slammed his fist on the hood of Dwayne's car. "I told her I'd protect her." The hood gave, and when Matt removed his hand, a sizable dent was evident. Matt had seen death. He even caused it. He wasn't desensitized to violence. He lived with it every day, and it became a part of him. He killed in the line of duty, but never had he been the cause of a victim's death. His stomach twisted, and he fought to keep down his dinner. The disconnect was always tougher when working undercover.

"Where do we stand with homicide?" asked Dwayne.

"I'm not sure the detective bought Matt's act.

When did you tell Ames you gave Irina the card?"

Matt was staring beyond the conversation focused on an innocent girl lying dead on a motel room floor.

"Matt," said Dwayne gently touching the undercover agent on his shoulder.

"What?"

"When did you tell Ames you gave Irina your business card?"

"I told her I gave it to her the other night."

"Ames is pretty sharp. I wouldn't be surprised if she gets an assignment downtown with the big boys, Robbery-Homicide, when there's an opening. She said the business card wasn't wrinkled and looked fresh, as she described it. She thinks you gave it to her tonight. They're trying to put you in the room. Did anyone see you with her at the motel?"

"No, I stayed in the car when she checked in."

Dwayne interrupted, "Can we trust her?"

"Trust Ames?" asked Danny. "Yeah, I think so. She's got a solid rep at North Hollywood, and, like I said, she's on the short list for RHD downtown."

"I think maybe we should bring her onboard," said Dwayne.

Both Dwayne and Danny looked at Matt. He had his head down.

Dwayne waited a few moments expecting a

response. Matt said nothing. "Matt, what do you think? You okay with her getting cut in?"

Matt looked up. "If you and Danny think it's wise, then I'm good with it."

"Not exactly the enthusiastic response I was seeking," said Dwayne.

Matt shook his head slowly. "Dwayne, I got that girl killed. She trusted me and I got her killed."

"Matt, she's dead. But you didn't get her killed. Now we need to work even harder to put this where it belongs. Danny, when we get done here, go brief Ames. She needs to play it tight, but give her what you can. We don't need her doing a deep background on Matt and stepping in our flower bed. Matt, how do you want to handle this?"

Again Matt was slow to answer, his mind beyond the warehouse, "I'm heading over to the Veil."

"You think that's wise?" asked Dwayne.

Matt snapped, "Yeah, Dwayne, I think it's wise."

MATT CALLED CAITLIN FROM the car. "Honey, this is going to be a late one."

"You okay, Cowboy?"

"They beat her to death. I know who's behind it. Now I have to prove it."

"Just be careful."

Matt wasn't listening. "I'll see you when I get home."

"I love you," said Caitlin.

"I love you too."

CHAPTER SIXTY-ONE

Matt pulled down a side street. He had several recording devices available, which he alternated as they were downloaded by the evidence technicians. The movies had the bugs secreted in olives, but those devices were only reserved for the imagination of some Tinseltown screenwriter. When Matt first started his undercover work, the FBI was still using a Nagra for some operations. The device was the size of a thin paperback novel. The current generation of recorders was much more manageable but still not ideal. The smallest device had the least amount of recording time capability. He seldom used it because most meetings lasted beyond the time restraints. But the tiny digital recorder might prove helpful tonight. He would need to act fast once he got into the office. He turned on the device and slipped it in his shoe. He raced over to the Russian Veil.

MATT PULLED INTO THE back and made his way to Boris's office where he barged in unannounced. "Why'd you have to kill her?"

Stump jumped up from his seat as did Jesse. The security team did its job. Before Matt could react, he was braced up against the wall. "Why'd you have to kill her?" shouted Matt over Stump's shoulder.

"Strip him and check for a wire," said Boris, all the more intimidating because the delivery was so casual.

Stump started to rip at Matt's shirt. Matt was able to free his right arm and landed a solid uppercut to Stump's midsection. Stump folded, but before Matt could land a second blow, Jesse grabbed the right arm and threw Matt back up against the wall. Stump swung wildly and hit Matt in the jaw.

"Enough!" shouted Boris. "I said check him for a wire."

Jesse had Matt's arms pinned to the wall. Stump continued to rip at the shirt. Matt's bare chest lay open.

"Drop your pants," said Boris.

Jesse released his grip and Matt unbuckled his trousers. His pants fell to the floor.

"You want me to bend over so your butt boys can check for hemorrhoids," spitting blood as he spoke.

Stump threw a powerful punch to Matt's midsection. The undercover agent saw it coming and tensed enough to deflect some of the impact.

Boris shouted, "Enough! Get dressed."

Matt had trouble catching his breath. He took his time, pulled up his pants, and buttoned what few buttons remained on his denim shirt.

In a now calm voice Matt asked, "So why'd you have to kill her?"

Boris responded with a question, "Why did you meet with her at the Sportsmen's Lodge?"

He had her followed.

"She said she wanted to talk with me."

"So why did you tell me you were going home to soak your back?"

"I did go home and soak my back but not for very long. Listen, she sounded scared when she asked to meet with me. Before I got involved with importing girls into the United States, I wanted to know the full story. If she was dissatisfied with the operation, I didn't want her running to the cops or immigration. I wanted her to think I was on her side. I wanted to see what she had to say."

Boris arched an eyebrow. "And did you find out?"

"Yeah, I did, but now, thanks to you, I've got some female detective from LAPD calling me and asking questions about Irina's death. Your boys, at least I'm assuming it was your boys since you wouldn't be so stupid to dirty your hands directly, left a real mess in that motel room. At least dump the body if you're going to play assassin."

"How did the LAPD know to contact you?"

A calm settled in the office which seconds before was in controlled chaos. "Because I gave

305

her my card. Boris, she was unhappy. I wanted her to think I was on her side. I told her I was going to talk to you, and we would resolve her visa problems and immigration fees. You just can't go around eliminating every disgruntled employee with a beating. It's bad business. Sometimes a little honey makes a lot of sense."

"So why do you think I did it? The little whore was probably working the streets. You dropped her off at the motel. You think she stayed in the room. I suppose you paid for the room. How do I know you didn't go back for a little taste?"

"Boris, that's lame. I could have had all the taste I wanted in your back room and for free. Why would I rent a room and pay her for action I could have gotten here? You and I both know we're better businessmen than that. Look, you had her killed. We both know it. We both know you screwed up. I'm not interested in hooking up with a sloppy businessman who doesn't understand the basics in crisis management. Surely the KGB taught you better than that."

"I was at a bomb-making seminar when the rest of my class was taking crisis management."

Matt detected a slight smile as Boris made the comment.

"Well, if you expect me to go into business with you, I suggest you read up on problem solving. Why did you have her killed?"

The Russian slammed his fist on the desk and

raised his voice, "Enough. If you want to join me, then help me; if not, leave." His eyes bored through the undercover agent. Then in a calmer voice he said, "No hard feelings; we part as former comrades."

"Boris, I'm in. I just want to make sure you're smart."

"I am smart, my friend. Smart enough to avoid the American labor camps."

ON THE WAY HOME Matt called Dwayne. He apologized for his behavior at the warehouse before he reported the results of the meeting with Boris. Dwayne understood. No good investigator can be detached, and Dwayne knew Matt was a great investigator. Dwayne would have been disappointed had his undercover agent not taken the death of the Ukrainian immigrant girl so hard.

"Dwayne, I pushed him every way I could. He didn't deny it when I confronted him, but he never said the magic words."

"Are you still okay with continuing?"

"Yeah, I'm in and all the way. I have to stay inside his decision cycle and force him to react."

"Good. I'm glad you're in. You had me a little worried tonight."

"I don't quit, especially when an innocent girl pays with her life."

"I understand. We're not done yet."

"Not by a long shot. Where do we stand with getting on the phones and inside his office?"

"I spoke with headquarters today. They received Steve's affidavit. They say we should get it signed by late next week," said Dwayne.

"It took God six days to create the world. How come these guys who think they're God can't sign off on a piece of paper in a week?"

"Matt, you know the process."

"Yeah, I know," said Matt almost apologetic. "I would love to have heard Stump and Jesse's report to Boris after the beating."

"We'll be up on him soon. These guys are going down."

"And hard. By the way my next voucher will include the cost of a new denim shirt. Stump tried to play strip poker without the cards. I'm guessing he had playground issues at recess."

"That may have to be offset by the cost of repairing the dent in the hood of my car."

CHAPTER SIXTY-TWO

Ramon Sanchez, the principal at Caitlin's school, wanted to meet with the parents of those boys involved in the playground fighting incident. Sanchez thought a less confrontational atmosphere would be the classroom rather than his office so he set up the first appointment in Caitlin's room with Michael Hughes's parents.

The school board had a no-tolerance policy when it came to fighting. There wasn't a whole lot of wiggle room for the principal. The policy was written by lawyers and was designed more to limit the school's liability than to prevent recess violence in the elementary grades.

Ramon wanted to hear the facts before he assessed an appropriate punishment. There weren't any constitutional safeguards in this meeting, and the rules of evidence took a backseat to getting at the truth, but the principal was a fair man. Caitlin was confident he would do the right thing and minimize Michael's punishment. Had Michael somehow avoided splaying the blood of the two aggressors all over the playground, Caitlin might have been able to cover up the entire incident. Shed blood opens all sorts of doors that can be difficult to shut, especially in a public-school setting.

Michael entered with his mother and stepfather, Alicia and J. D. Pinney. As always Michael was dressed neatly. His clothes weren't expensive or even pressed, but his faded shirt was tucked in. His blue jeans were clean and, unlike even some in the second grade, were around his waist not low on his hips like an MTV rapper.

Michael's mother, Alicia, was also neat. Her

clothes may have been Salvation Army Thrift Store bargains, but she took pride in her appearance.

Both contrasted the stepfather. He was dressed like the runner-up centerfold for *Neo-Nazi Monthly*. Unshaven and unkempt, J. D. was thin, more like a meth user whose two- or three-day binges served as the ultimate diet aid. Most bikers were overweight, but J. D. was an exception. He still had a beer gut, but his arms and legs were pencil thin. He wore shorts which hung just above the calves. Both legs were tattooed in prison-blue ink of various, incomprehensible designs. His sleeves rolled up to below the elbow also revealed numerous tats while an 88 crept just above the collar.

When Ramon Sanchez introduced himself and extended his hand to Michael's stepfather, Michael stood up and also shook hands with the principal who smiled at the gesture.

Alicia shook hands but said nothing. Caitlin did notice, however, her jaw was slightly swollen and her left eye puffy. Throughout the evening Alicia kept her head lowered, less as a submissive gesture, more to conceal her apparent pain.

Sanchez tried to put the family at ease with one of those familiar "Trust me, I'm with the government. I'm here to help" speeches, but the family had little faith in anything anyone from a public agency said.

In response to the principal's inquiry, Michael explained what happened. He looked Mr. Sanchez in the eye and calmly told the story. He was straightforward and articulate, as articulate as a second grader can be when confronted by authority.

When he finished, the principal asked, "Is Isaiah Goldman your friend?"

"No, sir. We're not even in the same grade."

"But you like him, don't you?"

"No, he's a whiner. He complains all the time."

Caitlin stifled a laugh. Isaiah, the smallest student in the third grade, was a chronic complainer. If the glass was half full, that half was polluted. He was extremely bright, well beyond his grade level, but Caitlin was somewhat surprised it took the students this long to stone the perennial pessimist.

"So why did you help him?"

"It wasn't a fair fight. It was two against one. They tied him up and were throwing rocks at him."

"And you thought that gave you the right to attack those two boys?"

"It wasn't a fair fight. If it was a fair fight, I would have just watched."

"You should have contacted the yard-duty monitor."

"She was over by the swings."

Michael's stepfather stood up and began to

pace. J. D. wasn't exactly mad, maybe more adult ADD. Alicia sat quietly as the principal and Michael spoke.

J. D. said, "I'm not sure I would have come to the aid of a Jew boy, but Michael did what he was taught to do."

"I understand, but we have a no-tolerance policy for fighting. I am certain you, your wife, and Michael were made aware of that policy at the beginning of the year," said the principal somewhat nervously as J. D. toured the room.

"I can't believe you'd tolerate someone getting the crap beat out 'em," said J. D.

"That's why we have yard duties."

"Don't sound like she was doing her duty," said the biker.

J. D. was walking behind Caitlin's desk and spied pictures beneath the glass top. He stopped for a long moment and stared, then said, "Yeah, whatever, do what you have to do. I think we're done here." He pointed to his wife and with a single hand movement conveyed his intentions.

Michael and Alicia rose, and the three walked out of the classroom.

After they exited and were beyond hearing distance, the principal said, "I guess that went well."

Caitlin looked confused. "How do you figure?"

"We lived."

CHAPTER SIXTY-THREE

Oscar Cano, the veteran coyote, continued to push the weary travelers. His promise of a trip lasting a few hours was broken after the first day of travel. They were on their third day, maneuvering around mesquite and prickly pear cactus.

They traveled from the early evening until midmorning. Last night they were blocked from taking the usual route when Cano spotted headlights a few miles up the main trail. He rerouted the group, wasting time but presumably avoiding the Border Patrol or the Minutemen, a civilian border watch group. Cano wasn't sure who was behind the vehicle lights. He doubted it was vacationers, but he wanted to avoid confrontation if possible. Cano was armed but more to protect the group from predators, animal or human, than to fight government authorities. He took no chances, and the group walked an additional five miles through rugged terrain to avoid contact.

Once they found shade, they would lay up. The blistering sun made any daytime travel a fool's run. The water ran out the day before, but early that morning the coyote spotted a blue flag marking a water drum refilled semiregularly by a

Tucson-based, church-run charity. The travelers made their way toward the drum and refilled the one-gallon plastic jugs.

Snakes hid behind every rock, and only the coyote wore double-insulated work boots, offering some protection against attack.

As the party was filling the water jugs, Juanita slipped off the trail to relieve herself. She walked several hundred feet to a large clump of cactus, attempting to conceal herself from the others.

Without warning, a six-foot Western diamondback sprang from a coiled position. The hollow fangs clamped onto Juanita's right leg, penetrating the skin, releasing the poisonous venom. She screamed as an intense burning immediately surged at the site of the injury. A fang broke off in her leg as the snake released its grip and raced toward the rocks.

Most were unaware she walked off the trail and were startled by the screams. There was also a sense of anger her screams would alert authorities. The coyote and several of the men ran to the sound.

They found the beautiful traveler writhing in pain on the hot desert floor. Already weak from the journey and dehydration, she fought to avoid going into shock.

Dmitri rushed to provide aid.

"Leave her. She was stupid enough to walk among the snakes. Let her die," said Cano.

Dmitri was unfamiliar with snakebites and had no clue how to provide assistance. He pulled the broken fang from her leg. The two puncture wounds were about a half inch apart. He applied pressure but the damage was done. The venom pushed through her system attacking cells and organs. Dmitri gave her water from his jug, but Juanita quickly vomited the liquid.

"I said leave her."

Cano and the others returned to the shade of the layup.

Dmitri did what he could to minimize the panic the Mexican mother felt. He held the woman but was able to provide only minimal comfort. Since the coyote had no antivenom, it was only a matter of time. Within an hour the poison would paralyze the most important organ in her body, the diaphragm. She would be unable to breathe and death would come.

CHAPTER SIXTY-FOUR

The slender shadow moved in and out of the bushes concealing his intent. He was at the back of the school property away from any residences or businesses. He picked the darkest spot where the intermittent light poles failed to illuminate the fence. He threw a small, thick, braided rug over the three strands of barbed wire and waited a few moments to determine if his activity was detected. He then carefully climbed the chain-link fence and made his way over the razor-sharp stainless-steel security precautions. Once successfully over the top he dropped to the ground.

The school had a night watchman but no security cameras. Graffiti was the most serious problem the guard confronted. The last major break-in occurred four years earlier over the summer. The school lost a dozen computers. Since then the campus was essentially crime free.

The shadow made his way to the north side of the building. He counted down the rooms and came to Caitlin's. He checked each window, attempting to pry open one she forgot to latch. He struck out. They were all secured. He removed his sweatshirt and wrapped it around his hand and arm. Standing in front of the largest window, he swung with all his might, his arm crashing through splattering glass throughout the room. He raked his arm around the edge of the window, cleaning out the remaining chards.

The slender figure crawled through the window. He stopped at Caitlin's desk and grabbed the pictures from beneath the glass top. After thinking briefly, he lifted the glass and threw it on the floor. He rifled through the drawers looking for loose change and valuables, then emptied the contents onto the floor. He dumped over several desks and tipped a file cabinet. Papers were strewn throughout the room—perfect fuel for his next move.

He removed a can of lighter fluid from his back pocket. Popping the lid, he emptied the combustible liquid over the papers, making a trail back to the window; the pungent odor hung in the air.

Just as he climbed out the window, he spotted the night watchman, a retired schoolteacher who supplemented his pension with a part-time security job. The shadow needed another few seconds to complete his mission and make his escape. He pressed his body against the wall of the alcove waiting for the guard to pass. He could see the uniformed employee meander down the walkway humming "The Old Rugged Cross," oblivious to what awaited.

The shadow drew an automatic from underneath his shirt. The noise from the footfalls increased as the guard moved closer, but the guard was in no hurry to complete his rounds. The singing grew louder.

The shadow watched as the guard passed the alcove. The shadow began to raise the auto, preparing to fire, but in his mind he also began to sing the hymn. When the guard stepped on a piece of broken glass, he was startled and looked down. Rather than pulling the trigger, the shadow swung the weapon like a club connecting to the side of the skull.

The sixty-nine-year-old guard collapsed on the concrete walkway.

The shadow grabbed the guard's weapon, a revolver, and stuck it inside his belt alongside his automatic. The intruder then pulled a book of matches from his front pocket. He lit one match and stuck it in the book. In seconds the book exploded in flames. He tossed it into the lighter fluid trail, watched the liquid ignite and begin a race throughout the room.

As the shadow ran back to the rear fence and made his escape, the fire alarm from the classroom sounded.

MATT REACHED OVER AND turned off the lamp on the nightstand. The moon lit up the evening sky. Enough light crept through the partially opened plantation shutters for Matt to see Caitlin approach the bed wearing a white Victoria's Secret teddy. As she climbed in, he leaned over and grabbed a kiss. She returned the favor and the two embraced. The passion from their honeymoon remained, but before he could show his love again, the phone rang.

He yanked the phone from the cradle. "Dwayne, this better be important."

Matt paused for a moment, put his hand over

the receiver, and handed the phone to Caitlin. "It's Ramon."

"Why is my principal calling at 11:00 p.m.?"

"Good question. You might want to ask him."

"Ramon?" asked Caitlin. She listened for a few minutes and finally responded, "I'll be right there."

She handed the phone back to Matt. "Someone set my classroom on fire."

She and Matt got dressed and headed to the school.

POLICE VEHICLES AND FIRE engines crowded the school parking lot. A paramedic unit rushed the injured security guard to the hospital. News units were set up on the street, and reporters flooded the scene in an effort to get footage. A torched classroom was breaking news.

Matt and Caitlin edged their way through the crowd of neighbors and onlookers. Police groupies monitored law enforcement and news frequencies and flocked to any site suspected of being interesting. The crowd numbered more than fifty. Matt carefully scanned those hovering at the scene looking for a familiar face but saw none. Normally he might have badged his way to the front, but he maintained the secrecy of his FBI identity as he approached a patrol officer providing security.

"We were called by the school's principal,

Ramon Sanchez. We were told my wife's classroom was torched. Can you direct us to the detective in charge? I believe they want to talk to my wife."

The patrol officer spoke into his shoulder microphone while maintaining an eye on the crowd.

He turned to Matt. "Someone will be here shortly," said the officer.

Within a minute a detective arrived at the yellow tape and introduced himself. He lifted the evidence tape, and Matt and Caitlin walked under. Both signed the log-in sheet then followed the detective to her classroom.

Caitlin gasped when she saw the blood-stained sidewalk in front of her classroom. Matt squeezed her hand a little tighter and ushered her past the dried puddle.

Once inside her classroom she saw the devastation.

CHAPTER SIXTY-FIVE

The next afternoon J. D. Pinney walked through the back door of the Russian Veil.

The club opened at 2:00 p.m.—the same time every day. Business didn't pick up until five or six. Some of the "better" gentlemen's clubs opened at 11:00 a.m. and served a free lunch to entice businessmen and their clients. Boris catered to white trash. He saw no need to furnish free anything. The only benefit he offered was no cover charge if the voyeurs arrived before five. Once the clock struck five, a ten-dollar fee was imposed. On the weekends there was always a cover charge. Boris found a weekend cover charge didn't discourage any customer from crossing the threshold, and almost every evening the place was crowded. The economy had little impact on the clientele. Through robust times and downtimes men were willing to pay money to watch women disrobe; they would pay extra for sexual favors. Boris found the one recession-proof business in America.

J. D. knocked on the door.

"Come."

J. D. opened the door and poked his head in. "Boris, can I talk to you?"

"You are talking to me." Boris was devoted to those from Russia who followed him to the United States. He tolerated the bikers who were attracted to the club and provided a variety of criminal services. J. D. was a biker.

"I want to show you something."

"Come," said Boris motioning with his hand.

J. D. walked in and laid a picture on the desk. "Does this guy look familiar?"

Boris examined the wedding photo. It was

almost ten years old. The man's hair was short, but Boris recognized the groom. "Yeah, it's Matt. Where'd you get this?"

"This broad in the picture is Alicia's brat's teacher."

"Who is Alicia?"

"My old lady."

"Okay so Matt's wife is this kid's teacher, so what?"

"Her name is Hogan. I thought this guy's name was Wallace."

"Yes, he said his name is Matt Wallace. Thanks, I'll ask him."

"Yeah, but don't you think . . . ?"

"I said I'll ask him. Thanks. I'm busy and have important business to do." He picked up the phone and was waiting until J. D. left to punch in the number.

J. D. grabbed the picture from the desk.

"No, leave it. I'll show it to him and see what he says."

CHAPTER SIXTY-SIX

The damage to Caitlin's classroom wasn't as extensive as she first thought. When she saw the room that evening, she assumed it would be weeks before the room could be inhabitable.

Most of the mess she spied was from the firefighters who turned over furniture in an effort to extinguish all the flames and embers. The school district brought in professionals who serviced fire-damaged property, and within two days the classroom was ready for occupancy.

The investigation into the arson continued. Caitlin hadn't heard any news from Matt and was unaware of any progress the LAPD or the fire department was making. Although the teachers discussed the events in the lounge during breaks, no one could come up with a motive for the vandalism. Caitlin inventoried the equipment and everything was there; some was unserviceable, but theft didn't appear to be the reason for the illegal entry.

Caitlin's class met in the auditorium the day after the fire. She sent out notices to the parents asking for help in getting the room ready. Most of the parents worked and were unable to assist, but Alicia, Michael's mother, volunteered.

On Thursday afternoon Michael and his mom stopped by the room as Caitlin was putting new maps on the wall.

Alicia knocked on the open door as she and Michael walked in.

"Thanks so much for coming," said Caitlin standing on a chair trying to hang a map of the United States.

"We thought you could use some help," said Alicia.

Caitlin managed to level the map and stepped down from the chair. "You should have seen it the other night. I would have never thought they could get this back in order so quickly."

"What can we do?"

"Would you mind putting up the alphabet above the white board?"

For the next hour Caitlin, Alicia, and Michael worked hard preparing the room for the next day's classes. The work session was relaxed, and Alicia mentioned in passing her marriage had seen some rough times. Although she never admitted being abused, Caitlin suspected the home life wasn't ideal. J. D. Pinney was Alicia's second husband. Her first husband, Michael's father, was in the Army. Michael was in preschool when her husband's reserve unit deployed to Iraq for a second time. He died a few months after arriving in country.

Caitlin mentioned Matt's brother, a Marine, killed in Afghanistan. Caitlin knew the toll Scott's death took on the family. She could empathize with Alicia, a young mother dealing with the devastating loss of her husband.

Alicia said she moved back home to Los Angeles after Michael's father died. She married J. D. a year later.

Alicia wasn't gushing praise on her second

husband but did say he had a job and came home most nights. Caitlin never questioned Matt's love for her but in a small way could identify with Alicia's characterization of the relationship.

The conversation made the afternoon fly. Caitlin appreciated the new insights she gained into Michael's situation at home and appreciated even more the discipline he showed in the classroom.

J. D. STOPPED BY the club that evening. He stayed long enough to speak to Boris and learn Boris had not yet confronted Matt over the differences in last names. J. D. had a criminal record. He wasn't going back to prison, and he wasn't taking any chances.

CHAPTER SIXTY-SEVEN

The trail was littered with trash and human waste. Ranchers found their fences cut, animals killed, and property destroyed. One traveler was dead, and the group was still a day's journey from Three Points, Arizona, where vehicles awaited to take each to their final destinations. For some it was Iowa, others Virginia, still others Ohio. For Dmitri it was Los Angeles.

Dmitri was angry with Oscar Cano. The coyote's indifference may not have caused Juanita's death, but his attitude demonstrated each traveler was a commodity, a piece of meat merely representing profit. Cano was no humanitarian seeking to assist those subjected to poverty and oppression. It was a business, no different from the cattle drovers of the Old West. Cano's "cattle" were the people and the backpacks they carried.

Dmitri spotted the tree among the scrub brush. From a distance he could see strips of cloth blowing in the wind. As he approached, he realized panties and rags hung from the branches. His stomach tightened. The Rape Tree was real.

"Just a little longer. Around this bend and we will lay up," said Cano as the group passed the man-made warning to female travelers.

They neared the final layup. They would rest today. As the sun was about to set, they would begin the final phase, and by early tomorrow morning they would be in Three Points.

Each welcomed the rest. It had been another long night of walking. Backs ached from hunching over carrying the heavy packs. Food was now in short supply. Even those who made the journey before did not bring enough to sustain three nights in the desert. They were also out of water. No blue flags were visible; no apparent relief in sight.

The travelers dropped their backpacks with a collective sigh. Even the shade provided little comfort.

Cano walked over to one of the females. Dmitri never knew her name and never heard her talk. She kept silent the entire trip. When Cano whispered in her ear, she shook her head. Cano said something again and this time, as he completed the sentence, grabbed her by the arm and pulled her to her feet. She didn't resist or cry out. She knew the rules. Cano escorted her a few hundred feet back on the trail.

Dmitri was tired, thirsty, and hungry. He wanted to sleep, but he knew Cano's plans. Everyone did. They tried to appear as though they didn't see the coyote, but each knew Cano was escorting the woman to the Rape Tree. They remained on the ground resting for the last leg of the journey.

Dmitri kept his head down, debating his next move. He was in the middle of the desert in a foreign land he illegally entered. He was muling thirty pounds of cocaine and had no idea how to get to the immediate destination. Who would listen to him? Who would come to his aid if he acted? He couldn't count on the others. They needed the coyote in their flight for freedom. Everyone knew the rules and the costs. He put his choices on the scales of justice and watched the balance crash.

Dmitri slipped away and headed south. He saw the woman struggling with Cano. She attempted to fend off the advances, but she was exhausted from the journey. She needed her energy to survive the desert, not protect her virtue. Cano clawed at her clothing and ripped her dress. She looked down at the only piece of clothing she possessed and began a compliant cry. Dmitri had seen enough. He raced to her aid and pulled the leathery Mexican off.

"No!" shouted the woman.

Cano started to rise, flailing wildly at his attacker.

The woman again shouted, "No!"

Her screams were directed at Dmitri not the rapist.

The men wrestled each other to the ground. Cano scratched at Dmitri and tried to reach for the gun holstered on his side. Dmitri hit the coyote in the face, but without the proper leverage the blow had little impact. Cano rolled on top. As Cano spit at his attacker, Dmitri grabbed a rock and clubbed the human trafficker on the side of the head. The Mexican went limp. He would never get up again.

By now the others ran to the sound of the screams. When they arrived, they found Cano on the ground, blood flowing from the back of his head and the woman in tears, dress torn, crying into her hands.

The men were angry but not at the rapist. They

jumped Dmitri and cursed with every kick and blow they delivered. He killed their ticket to opportunity, all to protect a Mexican whore who knew the rules before the journey began. The beating was savage, and Dmitri was left to die alongside the coyote.

The travelers returned to the layup. The strongest of the group picked up the rifle Cano carried on the trip. "I've done this before. I can find Three Points. We rest later."

CHAPTER SIXTY-EIGHT

Matt arrived midmorning and pulled up to the warehouse garage door. He unlocked the back door to the warehouse and punched the alarm code into the keypad just inside the door. Pulling the heavy chain, he lifted the garage door just enough to pull in his car. Elvis was blasting through the sound system, "Suspicious Minds" . . . "We're caught in a trap."

Once he had the car in the warehouse, he turned off the ignition and as he was exiting the car, J. D. Pinney ran in.

"Hey J. D., I wasn't expecting you. You come for a car?"

The heavily tattooed biker pulled a gun from beneath his shirt.

"What's this all about?" asked Matt.

"If Boris won't ask you, then I will. How come your last name is Wallace?" yelled J. D.

"I hope the questions get tougher than this my friend. My dad's last name is Wallace," said Matt calmly and holding a steady gaze on the man with an automatic aimed in his direction.

"So how come your wife's name is Hogan?" There was anger, maybe even confusion, in the voice.

"What are you talking about?"

"Your wife is my wife's kid's teacher!"

"Say what?" said Matt trying to act confused but knowing where this was leading.

"Your wife's a teacher, right?"

"What difference does it make what my wife does?"

J. D. shook the weapon at Matt. "Answer the question, or I'm going to splatter your brains all over the warehouse."

"Hey, just calm down. I don't understand what's going on."

J. D. fired a shot over Matt's head, and it lodged in the wall on the far side of the warehouse. "Is your wife a teacher? You better answer my questions. Boris doesn't like liars or traitors. A ditch off Mulholland might be your final resting spot if you don't answer my questions."

"Okay, look, just calm down. I'll answer your questions. Yes, my wife is a teacher."

"So why is her name Hogan?"

"Who said her name was Hogan?" Matt was trying to buy time but knew a violent confrontation was inevitable.

J. D. fired a second shot, this time closer, the sound echoing throughout the building.

"Yeah, my wife's name is Hogan. That's her maiden name. She didn't want to change it when we got married. You know, she's one of those liberated broads."

"She don't look liberated to me. How come, if her name is Hogan, your name is Wallace?"

"I just answered that. Look, let me show you."

Matt started to slowly reach toward his back.

"No!"

Matt's undercover weapon, a SIG 239 was still in the car; he failed to stuff it in his waistband as he exited his vehicle.

"I'm just going for my wallet. I want to show you my driver's license and a wedding picture." Matt started to walk toward J. D. as he was reaching to his back. In a calm, almost soothing voice, he said, "I'm just going to get my wallet, J. D., that's all. I want to show you this. I think once you see my license and the wedding picture, this will all be cleared up."

Matt reached back and pulled out his wallet. J. D.'s eyes followed the leather wallet as Matt slowly moved it forward.

The two most important rules in any street

fight: always cheat and always win! A good loser is still a loser and often dead.

"You ever do something you know would trouble your mom?" said Matt.

J. D. looked at Matt, confused and unable to process the question.

In the time it took for J. D.'s eyes to roam from Matt's face to the wallet, Matt pounced. Anything can be a weapon in the right hands. He threw the wallet in J. D.'s face, distracting the biker long enough for Matt to spring forward, thrusting his left hand upward at the base of J. D.'s nose, shattering bone and cartilage. It was an odd fluidity of grace and movement. Matt grabbed for the gun, twisting it as J. D. swung wildly with his free hand. Both crashed to the ground, wrestling for control of the automatic. Matt's strength bore out. With a free elbow, Matt delivered another vicious blow to J. D.'s face then managed to twist the weapon, toward J. D.'s neck. J. D. grabbed the barrel of the weapon, and just as Matt jerked it, the gun discharged, the round powering through J. D.'s chin and out the back of his skull. A pink mist lingered in the air. This was no movie fight scene packed with dramatic tension. It was real. It was quick. It was over. Death was instantaneous; maybe he'll suffer in the next life.

Unlike J. D. Pinney's threat, it was his brains, not Matt's, now splattered throughout the warehouse.

Matt ran to the garage door and lowered it as fast as he could. How could three shots not bring a crowd? No one came running. No inquisitive tenants in the business complex. As the door closed, Matt collapsed on the floor. He was bathed in sweat, and his hands began to shake. This was not his first deadly shooting. They are never easy, but this one was personal. J. D. Pinney saw to that. This shooting involved more than just the job. This went beyond the FBI, the shooting team, paperwork, and another psychological examination by someone who never wore a badge or never pulled the trigger, at least not on the job. This involved his wife.

A million thoughts ran through his mind but foremost was Caitlin. He just shot the father of one of her students. How could he explain this to her? How could she explain it to her student, whoever that was? He blamed himself for taking a job this close to home. He should have stayed out of the San Fernando Valley. He should have stayed out of Los Angeles. Why did his adrenaline addiction have to impact the only person he truly loved? Caitlin got wrapped up in the World Angel Ministry investigation. He vowed never to involve her again and now this. The greater Los Angeles area had a population of seventeen million. Couldn't he find a couple of targets who weren't connected to his wife in some tangential way? He threw his hands to his head and looked toward heaven. How could he continue this life without losing his soul?

He had to call Dwayne, but first he had to think. He had to process all that happened. He let his shoulders drop and rolled his neck as if that might alleviate the guilt. The facts would look like an execution to the media, always happy to exploit any weakness perceived or real in the FBI.

It took several minutes before Matt pulled his cell phone from his pocket and called Dwayne. Within the hour Dwayne, ADIC Jason Barnes, and SAC Pamela Clinton arrived on the scene.

CHAPTER SIXTY-NINE

The sun baked the blood oozing from Dmitri's wounds. The cackling of chicken hawks circling overhead awoke him. Soon the animals of the desert would begin feasting on Oscar Cano's dead body. Cano wasn't the first man Dmitri killed, and if Dmitri's plan worked, he wouldn't be the last. Pain radiated through his body, and it was difficult to breathe. He assumed a rib or maybe two were broken. He crawled under the Rape Tree and attempted to get his bearings. He thought he knew where he was. He just wasn't sure how he would get where he wanted to go.

• • •

"YOU OKAY?" ASKED JASON Barnes, the ADIC.

"Yeah."

"You look like crap."

"Thanks."

"We need to shut this down immediately," said Pamela Clinton.

Both Barnes and Dwayne waited for Matt to explode, but he said nothing. There was a long pause before Barnes interjected, "Pamela, let's hear what Matt has to say before we make any decisions."

Matt proceeded to detail everything. He explained the break-in at Caitlin's school, the unnamed student, the accusations of a deceased J. D. Pinney, and his statement "a ditch off Mulholland."

All speculated he probably meant Annika, but he could have also meant Dawn Platt. She was still missing. Her body might be resting at the bottom of a mountaintop ravine.

Clinton interrupted several times, expressing her desire to terminate the undercover operation, but Barnes let Matt talk. The ADIC listened intently, understanding the ramifications of the shooting and the importance of continuing the investigation. Finally, he spoke, "Pamela, the whole purpose of this investigation is to identify the people who attacked Flip Mitchell's wife, killed the minister, and killed at least two

Ukrainian women. We have circumstantial evidence of at least one person's involvement, and I think we will soon learn of others. If there is a way to keep this operational, that is my intent. I trust my undercovers, and I particularly trust this undercover." He put his hand on Matt's shoulder. "I don't put someone in an operation like this without expecting some problems. I admit this is a problem. It's a big one, but we have overcome obstacles in the past, and we will again." The boss paused then looked at Matt, "Do you want to proceed?"

Matt's eyes were fixed on the floor, and he nodded slowly.

"I was expecting a little more enthusiasm," said Barnes.

"It's not the undercover operation. It's Caitlin. How am I going to explain this to her? I just killed the father of one of her students." Matt looked up at Jason Barnes and shook his head slowly. "She loves all of her students. I've never seen a more dedicated teacher. I just don't know how to handle this."

"Are you willing to continue the undercover operation?"

"Yeah."

"Okay, so we're agreed we continue the op," said Jason Barnes. He looked at Clinton. "Except for you. You're opposed, I know. I knew that before we came here. When Congress asks, I'll tell them you voted no." Turning to Matt and Dwayne, he said, "Now let's discuss how we handle this situation. Any suggestions?"

Clinton said, "Let's pull up this guy's rap sheet. He's served time."

Dwayne added, "Those are prison tats."

Barnes said, "Our first priority is protecting Matt. The shooting is righteous, but we can't leave the body here. That will raise too many questions with Boris."

"And his crew," said Dwayne.

"We can handle the shooting investigation in house," said Barnes. "Any ideas?"

There was an extended silence.

"Let me get a hold of Danny Garcia. He can be our LAPD liaison. He can run interference with RHD," said Dwayne.

"Why would Robbery-Homicide get involved?" asked Clinton.

"Because they investigate every officer-involved shooting in their jurisdiction regardless of the agency. They'll work with us and Danny is good."

"What do we do with the body?" asked Barnes.

"That's why we need LAPD," said Dwayne. "We cut them in now. We do the investigation here; then we move the body to some remote area and have them rule it a suicide."

"Whoa," said Clinton. "Can we do that?"

Barnes nodded. "I think we have to if we plan on

keeping Matt's credibility intact. I will take full responsibility. This can work. The wound looks self-inflicted. This guy's not going to have insurance, and if he does, we'll work with the family and the insurance company at the appropriate time. The undercover op isn't going to last forever. No insurance company I know would be cutting a check tomorrow anyway." Barnes looked at Matt. "You can chime in at anytime. Can you live with these facts if that's what we put out?"

"Sure. The way J. D. was talking he came alone, and I think he came on his own. I'm suspecting he was out to prove himself to Boris by conducting his own investigation. He was hoping to take me back to the club, forcing me to confess to my true identity."

Jason Barnes then said, "Matt, give Boris a call. Feel him out. See what he says. If you think it's safe, then we continue to march. Once we know Boris is still onboard, we put the rest of the plan into action. And Matt, regardless of what we finally decide, you and I will go meet with Caitlin and explain what happened."

Clinton added, "I'm willing to go with you. It might help having a female there."

"Thanks, Pamela," said Matt with sincerity. "I appreciate the offer, but I don't want to overwhelm my wife. Just having the ADIC in the room might put her over the top. She'll think I'm circling the drain as it is."

Everyone let out a collective laugh, more to relieve the tension than at the gallows humor.

Like every great commander, Jason Barnes assessed the situation, controlled the confusion, developed a plan, and executed it.

Matt walked back to his office and dialed Boris, who picked up on the fourth ring, "Yes."

"Hey, it's Matt."

"What is it?"

"How much longer are you going to keep the Mercedes and Honda Accord in my warehouse?"

"Why, you find a buyer?"

"No, I just get nervous one of these owners is going to report the cars stolen before you get them shipped overseas."

"If that happens, I kill the owners," said Boris with a laugh conveying more truth than humor.

"Yeah, but that doesn't keep me out of jail for possession of stolen property."

"It will not be long, maybe another day or two. By the way, is your wife a teacher?"

"Yeah."

"I did not know."

"I thought I told you that. Yeah, she's a teacher. Why? You need help with your homework?"

"No. I think I have something that belongs to you."

"What?"

"J. D. came in here the other day with your

wedding picture. He made a big deal out of the fact your wife is his stepson's teacher."

"No kidding. Small world but how'd he get the wedding picture?"

"He said he took it from her desk the other night."

"The other night or the other day?"

"The other night. What difference does it make?"

"There was a break-in at my wife's school the other night. Someone torched her room and beat up a security guard. You don't suppose that goofy piece of white trash smacked around some old man just to get my wedding picture?"

"He could have. J. D. is crazy. If he were from my country, we'd think he spent too much time sniffing the Chernobyl air after the reactor exploded."

"Well, when you see him, tell him if he wants a wedding picture of me and my wife, I keep one in my wallet. He can have it."

"Next time you come by, you can pick up the picture."

"Thanks, Boris. I'll talk at you later."

Jason Barnes, Pamela, and Dwayne came in from the monitoring room. Barnes led the discussion, "You're good to go, Matt. Let's go see Caitlin."

CHAPTER SEVENTY

The battered traveler reached Three Points, Arizona, population just under six thousand. The dry desert heat absorbed most of the sweat, but Dmitri knew his ragged clothes smelled of stale perspiration. Since he wouldn't be welcomed at many public restaurants, he looked for vending machines to meet his immediate needs. He converted his money to U.S. currency before crossing the border, but money in the desert wasn't worth much. When resources are scarce, everyone is in the same economic class. None knew he was carrying thousands of dollars on the journey.

The motel clerk accepted the cash deposit. It wasn't the Marriott but Dmitri didn't care. He needed a shower and a bed, any bed. He planned on sleeping for hours, maybe even days before he headed to Los Angeles.

BORIS BANGED ON THE door.

Matt was on the phone with Dwayne and looked out between the blinds. "Gotta go, boss, looks like I've got company. Not sure I can get the cameras activated."

Matt raced to the hallway, flipped the light

switch three times, and as the file cabinet opened, he hollered, "Just a second."

Matt turned on the machine and closed the file cabinet. He popped into the bathroom and flushed the toilet, then raced to the front door and released the double deadbolt.

"Sorry, I was making a head call when I heard you pounding. Don't get much company. What are you doing here?"

Boris looked around Matt, trying to peer in and see down the hallway. The water in the toilet bowl was still running and could be heard from the doorway. "What's a head call?"

"I was taking a dump. You're getting pretty personal."

"What kind of business doesn't keep its doors open during business hours?" said Boris, angered he had to pound several times on the door.

"The kind that doesn't like uninvited guests walking in when certain items in the warehouse are not available to the general public. What do you think I'm running here, Sam's Club? I've got great deals, but my membership is more restrictive. What do you want?"

"We need to talk."

"Show me your membership card, and I'll let you in," said Matt with a smile.

Boris raised his hand in jest as if about to give Matt a backhanded slap, pushing past Matt toward the office.

"Want something to drink?" asked Matt as he opened the refrigerator door. It was stocked with soft drinks and beer. Boris reached for a Diet Pepsi.

Boris threw the wedding picture on Matt's desk. It was wrinkled as if J. D. folded it up and stuffed it in his shirt after taking it from Caitlin's desk.

"Did you hear about J. D.?" asked Boris.

"You said he brought this to your office."

"No, some woman walking her dog found him in a vacant lot up near the 118 Freeway."

Matt couldn't tell if Boris was purposely being vague trying to catch Matt disclosing too many details of the death. *Focus.*

"What was he doing, sleeping one off?"

"No, he was dead."

"Dead? When? How?"

"Yesterday. The police are calling it a suicide," said Boris taking a sip but appearing oblivious to Matt's reaction.

"You don't believe it?"

"No, I believe it," said the Russian shrugging his shoulders and throwing open his free hand.

"How did he do it?"

"He blew his brains out."

"You said he was crazy. He must have been more screwed up than any of us thought. Did he give any clue as to why he would eat his gun?"

"No, but he's of no interest to me, and he's not the reason I'm here."

Matt was more than willing to change the subject. If Boris didn't care, Matt certainly didn't want to dwell on the death. "So what can I do for you?"

"I need access to a warehouse."

"How much room do you need?"

"I need to store a truck for a few days, and I'll need to work on it to make some modifications to it. You got room?"

"Yeah, I got room. I'm empty right now so I got room for a truck. When do you need it?" Matt leaned back in his chair and put his hands behind his head.

"I'm not sure yet. I'm just trying to get everything lined up."

"If you're talking tonight, I got room. If you're talking tomorrow, ask tomorrow. I may get containers in tonight if somebody gets lucky at a truck stop."

Boris pulled an envelope from inside his shirt. He threw it on the desk. "I am invoking what you call the six-four-three-zero-zero rule."

Matt smiled, recognizing the reference, trusting out of fear or allegiance anything anyone of Boris's size said.

"You can count it if you wish. It is five thousand dollars. I need your warehouse for a week, and I'm not interested in sharing it with anyone else. Will this cover the rent for a week?"

"You, my friend, just rented my warehouse for a week."

CHAPTER SEVENTY-ONE

Matt debated the issue with Dwayne and Steve. Both strongly suggested he not attend, but neither made it an order. Caitlin insisted she was going so Matt knew he would be there, more for protection than support. Since this undercover assignment began, his schedule was chaotic, the hours irregular, and everything seemed to be coming at once with little time to prepare or process. Most assignments lasted months, with downtime, periods of inactivity, almost boredom. To date that was not the case. Each day brought something different. Boris and his crew were worthy targets and needed to be brought down. Matt would make the time to ensure their convictions, but today was personal even though he was on the clock.

They pulled into the near-empty parking lot of the small church. At first Caitlin suggested they had the wrong day or location. Then she saw a familiar face from school, Ramon Sanchez, the principal. He came for the funeral of Michael Hughes's stepfather, J. D. Pinney.

Matt didn't say anything, but he knew they were at the right spot. He saw the surveillance van on the street covering the entrance to the

345

church. Their primary purpose was to protect Matt if the issue arose, but a secondary responsibility was to photograph those in attendance.

The tiny church sat maybe seventy-five, but there was no rush for seats. With minutes before the scheduled start, only ten people were seated. Michael and his mother were on the front pew, and the others were scattered throughout the room. Michael turned to see Caitlin and gave her a genuine smile, maybe a smile of relief. An organ played as mourners quietly sat waiting for the service to begin. A closed casket was centered in the front of the church, and the only flowers were those sent by Matt and Caitlin.

Matt worried Boris and his crew would attend, thus drawing more attention to his wife, but in a phone conversation, Boris made clear he did not celebrate the death of anyone so weak he'd take his own life. Boris must have put out the word. Apparently, no one else from the Veil chose to honor the deceased either. Had they known the real reason behind the death, the church would have been full, and those in attendance would be gunning for the undercover agent.

Matt could reflect later on the fact he killed a man and his family would suffer the indignity of a small service honoring the deceased. Each action has a consequence, and Matt's actions impacted far beyond his wingspan.

The minister walked out on schedule and began the brief ceremony designed more to comfort Alicia and her son than to praise a dead man.

Within fifteen minutes the service was over with little fanfare. Matt and Caitlin met with the family in the narthex. The twice-widowed Alicia gave Caitlin a long, heartfelt embrace yet shed no tears.

Michael was sitting on a bench by himself, and Caitlin made her way to him. She bent down and gave her pupil a hug offering condolences. They spoke for several minutes. When she rose, tears were streaming down her face.

Matt and Caitlin walked to the parking lot in silence, Caitlin trying to gain control of her emotions. Matt was bathed in guilt believing he was the cause of his wife's tears. He held the door and kissed her as she entered the car.

As he started the engine, he asked, "Are you okay?"

When the tears dried, she whispered, "Michael just told me J. D. had been beating his mother since before the marriage, but he was too afraid to tell anyone. He said he's glad his stepfather is dead."

CHAPTER SEVENTY-TWO

The next morning Matt returned from his daily race through the streets of Thousand Oaks. He finished the five-mile course in less than thirty-five minutes, his self-imposed goal for each run. As he entered the kitchen, still dripping sweat, Caitlin looked up.

"You aren't going to be happy," she said.

"Why?"

"The *Times* has an article on the al-Dirani sentencing and the case."

Matt gave a quick read of the article and was livid. "What an idiot!"

"Who?" Knowing the answer.

"The Queen Mother." He let out an expletive and headed to the bedroom, ripping off his running clothes as he walked down the hallway.

Matt showered quickly. As he was toweling off, Caitlin walked into the bedroom.

"You okay?"

"Yeah, I'm fine. She has no concept of what it's like to work the streets. That crap she told the *Times* was for one reason only, to further her career. It served no other purpose."

"Maybe she thought it would put the FBI in a better light. You guys need all the positive publicity you can get. After all, you did stop a terrorist attack. The *Times* is quick to jump on the mistakes. She just took the opportunity to sing the Bureau's praises for a change."

"You mean sing her praises, don't you?"

"Are you jealous she didn't mention your name?" Then a smiling Caitlin said playfully, "Mommy, look at me. I got my name in the paper."

Matt offered a weak smile as he threw on a pair of jeans and a faded Polo shirt.

"But how will my mom ever be able to brag to her friends at church how her little boy kept the world safe for democracy if no one knows it was me?"

"I'll tell Mommy you really are a hero."

"Thanks, but you know why I'm mad."

"Yes, I do and I'm sorry. She is an idiot."

Matt kissed Caitlin and started to leave. She grabbed him and pulled him toward her. The two embraced for an extended moment and kissed passionately.

Caitlin said, "Hurry home tonight."

"Can we consummate the marriage?"

She winked. "If you get home before I fall asleep."

"Just wear something sexy to bed. I'll handle the rest. Besides, you can sleep through it if you want."

She feigned disgust, "It's all about you, huh, Cowboy."

"You got it babe."

• • •

MATT ARRIVED AT JERRY'S Famous Deli on Ventura Boulevard in Woodland Hills. Dwayne was waiting on the patio, coffee in hand.

Before either could exchange anything close to a greeting, Matt was waving the folded *Los Angeles Times* and said, "She's an idiot. At least in her case we know the lobotomy worked, but why put her in a position of responsibility? Can she not keep her mouth shut when the press starts sniffing around? Why not just release our ops orders? Save the reporters from doing all that digging."

Dwayne shook his head. There really wasn't too much to say. Matt was saying it all.

Ibrahim Saleh Mohammad al-Dirani, AKA Dr. Ibrahim or Ismad, a Muslim extremist from Egypt, was snagged in an FBI undercover operation last year. A medical doctor, al-Dirani infiltrated World Angel Ministry, a Christian charity treating children injured in war-torn countries. Matt spent months undercover at the charity. Al-Dirani and his American-born, home-grown terrorist girlfriend were the statistical successes of that operation. Al-Dirani's original target was the Israeli consulate when the vice president was scheduled to visit. A series of mistakes resulted in the terrorist changing his plans at the last minute. Matt prevented the detonation of a dirty bomb at the Century City

Renaissance Hotel on the evening of the planned attack. A lot of lives were saved and a terrorist act prevented. The U.S. Attorney for the Central District of California never sought the approval of the Attorney General to file the matter as a capital case. The powers in Washington refused to give the Egyptian doctor and his supporters the satisfaction of martyrdom status. Yesterday al-Dirani was sentenced to life without the possibility of parole. He will spend the rest of his life at the United States Penitentiary, Administrative Maximum in Florence, Colorado. Known as Supermax, al-Dirani joins Zacarias Moussaoui, dubbed the twentieth hijacker, and Richard Reid, the shoe bomber, in the nation's most secure federal prison. The U.S. Attorney's Office, the FBI, and every agency represented on the Joint Terrorism Task Force were present for a press conference following the sentencing, all praising the other for a job well done. All taking the glory for what could have been another devastating attack on U.S. soil.

The *Times* article covered the sentencing and press conference, but then it went further. Pamela Clinton gave an exclusive interview to the *Times* reporter. She detailed the undercover operation conducted by the JTTF, discussing Matt's assignment. She reported for the first time the potency of caesium-137, the ingredient making the explosive device Matt disabled, a dirty bomb. In fact, the solution was extremely weak. Although strong enough to cause panic, it would not have been fatal had the bomb been detonated. The dirty bomb just wasn't all that dirty. But even more troubling than releasing that information, she said, "The FBI, the lead agency at the Joint Terrorism Task Force, avails itself of all investigative techniques, including under-cover operations, which are ongoing as we speak in an effort to protect the citizens of Los Angeles." She then confirmed the Bureau uses wiretaps, phone traps, national security letters, as well as undercover agents to stop terrorist attacks before they happen. "The agent who thwarted this attack is busy currently assisting our Joint Terrorism Task Force in another undercover investigation. We are fortunate to have such dedicated employees willing to risk their lives for our nation."

In other words, she told the world the FBI had an ongoing undercover operation with the same operative.

"At least she didn't release your name as the UC in the current operation," said Dwayne.

"Oh, that's a big relief. I can just see this reporter doing all he can to identify me and, when he does, expecting to be imbedded otherwise, he splashes my name, picture, and operation across the front page of tomorrow's paper."

"Matt, she was wrong."

"Of course she was wrong. I hope Barnes hangs her butt out to dry. She deserves to be fired. Can't we do something?"

"I'll talk to the ADIC. Do you want to pull out?"

"Get real. I'm not quitting. I might frag the Queen Mother the next time we cross paths, but I'm not quitting."

CHAPTER SEVENTY-THREE

The back door to the Russian Veil was open, but the bar was closed. Boris was airing out the stale smell of alcohol. He and an electrician were rewiring the sound system to the stage where his Eastern European beauties nightly satisfied the basest cravings of American men. Boris heard a car pull into the parking lot. He wasn't expecting anyone so he stopped and walked toward the door, waiting for his uninvited visitor to enter. He heard a car door slam and quick-paced footsteps pounding the blacktop.

Dr. Ubadiah Adel al-Banna, a jihadist doctor practicing in the United States, walked in with a folded paper in his hand. "Did you see this article in the *Times*?"

"Not here. We go into my office to discuss business."

They walked to Boris's office, the doctor still waving the paper. Boris closed the door and Dr. U shouted, "Did you see this?"

"Not even a good morning from my terrorist friend," said Boris, unwilling to take the doctor or his cause seriously.

"Knock off your idea of communist humor. Did you see the article?"

"Yes, I saw it."

"So what is your answer?"

"My answer is, yes, I saw it."

"No, this article says the caesium-137 was so diluted it would have never killed anyone even if the bomb was detonated. I want some answers. We paid you good money, and you obviously took advantage of us."

"Dr. U, please come here," said Boris in a smooth, calming tone.

The Syrian-born physician walked toward Boris waving the newspaper, his eyes piercing and his hands shaking in anger. When Dr. U got within arm's length of the Russian, Boris grabbed him by the arm and spun him around and threw him into the wall. Dr. U hollered a series of Arabic obscenities, but the screaming did little to deter the Russian. Boris braced the doctor with one arm and with the other began groping at his clothes, frisking him for a wire. Boris reached into the doctor's pockets, emptying them of keys and coins. He threw the wallet on the floor and removed an iPhone from its holster. Boris carefully examined the device until he was satisfied it was as advertised. He then slammed it to the floor where it burst open.

"What are you doing?" screamed the doctor, this time in English.

Boris continued the search until he was satisfied. He then grabbed the doctor by the shoulders, lifted him off the ground, and spun him around. The 5'8" doctor was dwarfed by Boris's 6'4" frame.

"You don't come into my home and accuse me of doing anything illegal. Do you understand me?"

"Do you think I am wearing a wire? Do you think I would work for the infidels? Surely you know me better than that!"

"Like, I'm going to trust you? Listen, I read the article. I had no idea how potent the solution was." Boris was a professional liar, a skill he perfected working as an intelligence officer for Mother Russia, as he called his homeland. With all the seriousness the moment required, he said, "I bought the product from my people. They assured me it would do the job. How can you trust the American press? Maybe they wrote the story to prevent a panic. Maybe the FBI or the CIA lied to the reporters. Do you expect this administration to tell the American public how they almost allowed a city to be destroyed by a weapon of mass destruction? I stand by my people, and if you want to continue to do business with me, you will stand by me."

Boris was a salesman. With complete spontaneity he sold the Arab on his sincerity. Integrity never entered the calculus.

"Maybe you are right."

"Maybe?"

"No, you make sense, my friend. I should have believed you before I believed the Crusaders and their stooges, the Zionist American press."

Dr. U offered his hand in a conciliatory gesture. Boris grabbed it and pulled the doctor toward him, giving him a Soviet bear hug.

"Are we still on for Friday?" asked Boris.

"When I read the paper this morning, I wasn't certain. But you have reassured me. Thank you for your explanation. We are still on for Friday."

"Good, I have already made many arrangements. I will be ready."

"Excellent, so will we," said Dr. U.

CHAPTER SEVENTY-FOUR

Boris stood at the open door and directed the driver as he backed the truck into the undercover warehouse.

Matt was surprised. He wasn't sure what type of truck he was expecting to store, but this was a

Marine MTVR, a medium tactical vehicle replacement. The all-terrain truck with six-drive wheels had a seven-ton off-road capacity, thus its common name in the Marine Corps, a seven-ton.

"Where'd you get that?" asked Matt.

"I have my connections," said Boris.

"It's a Marine Corps seven-ton."

"How would you know?"

"I watch the History Channel, and I can read the small print on the side of the truck. Just because I got a D in high school chemistry doesn't make me stupid."

"I bought it at the auction up in Barstow."

"Boris, I'm serious. This better not be stolen. I'm not interested in bringing the Feds in on my operation."

"I have a bill of sale."

"Anyone can phony up a bill of sale."

"I'm telling you my people bought it at the auction. I have no interest in alerting the Feds either, and by the way I got an A in chemistry."

Matt pointed to the two stainless steel SIXCONs, military storage tanks, in the bed of the truck. He knew what they were from his time in the Marine Corps but didn't want to appear too knowledgeable. "What are these?"

"That, my friend, holds my new liquid diet aid."

Matt laughed, "I'm sure this is some nontaxed fuel, smuggled in from Russia without additives, sold at bargain-basement prices to that independent guy down the street."

"You understand my marketing and sales plan."

"So how long does it stay here?"

"Not long. I have to make some modifications, and then it will be ready. The sale will be completed on Friday night. The truck will be gone Friday afternoon."

CHAPTER SEVENTY-FIVE

Had a committee been formed to select the least desirable spot for the Los Angeles Greyhound Bus Depot, it could not have done better than the East Seventh Street location. Walking just a few yards in any direction from the terminal put you in the middle of an urban combat zone.

The Greyhound bus, an aging MC-12 Americruiser, pulled into the lane marked J. The bus was on time which, considering L.A. traffic, was a minor miracle. For many the journey would be described as long and uncomfortable; for Dmitri it beat the hike from Sasabe to Three Points. The seats were padded, and the toilet in the restroom at the rear of the bus flushed. Compared to his trip across the desert, toilet paper beat the alternative so he had no complaints. Besides, traveling by bus suited his needs. Security was minimal, not like an airport or some train stations. Even with a boarding in Tucson and a transfer in Phoenix, no one checked his identification. He was illegally in the United States, and the authorities didn't seem to care. If he was successful, he was certain his presence would be of interest to officials at some level of the government, but there would be no record of his entry or exit.

Dmitri left Tucson around 9:30 p.m., and the thirteen-hour trip included seven or eight stops. Dmitri lost count and slept most of the way as did many of the passengers. With his arrival in L.A., another leg of the mission was complete. Now he needed to get to West Hollywood where a friend of a friend, whom he'd never met, lived.

He exited the bus and was immediately greeted by the smells of rotting fruits and vegetables courtesy of a produce company across the pavement. He made his way to the entrance of the one-story building made of split-face concrete blocks. Painted a two-tone red and white, the sign above the entrance to the passenger terminal read, "Welcome to . . . Bienvenidas a . . . Los Angeles, CA." Everything at the depot was written in English and Spanish. Had the sign not told him, he might think he was still in Mexico. He entered through the double doors and made a quick stop at the restroom on the right. More unwelcome smells greeted him. One of the urinals was running continuously, and another had an out-of-order sign draped across it in English and Spanish. He sloshed through the puddle forming on the floor to the third urinal where he hoped to avoid any splashback. The towel dispenser was empty so he used the only working electric blower. *This is Los Angeles? I was expecting more.*

Before Dmitri approached the large, matronly woman standing behind the information counter, he stopped at a vending machine, dropped in seven quarters, and purchased a Coke. He took a strong pull on the plastic bottle before asking his question.

"How do I get to West Hollywood?"

The gray-haired lady wearing glasses and not appearing too interested in Dmitri's question continued straightening some travel folders and bus schedules on the counter. Dmitri feared his accent might cause him communication problems in the United States, but after only a brief time in the bus depot, he realized his English was better than most.

He repeated the question. "How do I get to West Hollywood?"

She looked up almost annoyed at being disturbed. "I don't know."

"But you are information."

"I know what I am. I don't know how to get to West Hollywood."

"Is there anyone who can help me?"

She shrugged her shoulders and pointed to the exit door. "Try the cabbies. They can get you anywhere."

He shook his head as he walked to the exit, past the bank of pay phones, each occupied. He was used to service like this in his country, but from all he read, he assumed America was different.

Once outside he saw the taxi stand on the street to his right. He walked only a few feet before a brown-skinned, battered man approached with his hand out asking in broken English for spare change. Dmitri ignored him, and the man continued walking, asking the next person out the door.

Three taxis sat ready, the drivers under a tarp to ward off the late-morning California sun.

"How much will it cost me to get to West Hollywood?"

Two of the drivers were talking to each other in Arabic, but the third looked at him and responded, "Do you have an address?"

"Yes," said Dmitri, pulling out a piece of paper from his pocket. "Near the corner of Fairfax and Santa Monica Boulevard."

The driver didn't even hesitate with a quote, "Around thirty-five dollars."

"Oh."

"Get in. I will take you. We can leave now."

"No, that is too much. It did not cost me much more than that to get here from Tucson."

"But you are not where you want to be. You want to be in West Hollywood. I can get you there."

"Not for thirty-five dollars."

As Dmitri spoke, he spotted a city bus heading west on Seventh Street stopping a block from the bus depot. He didn't know how long or how much, but he knew the bus would be cheaper than the cab. Dmitri walked to the street, crossing over. A small market was open and he walked in, purchasing beef jerky, several candy bars, and another Coke. After paying for the items, he stuffed them in his pocket and headed up the street to the bus stop. He only waited a few minutes. The next leg of his journey consisted of a long circuitous bus ride including several transfers. Within a few hours he would be in West Hollywood.

CHAPTER SEVENTY-SIX

The military truck was nestled into the warehouse, safe for a time.

Boris would be over later to install the detonation device. He still didn't know the target but assumed it wasn't in the middle of nowhere.

Dr. U wanted the truck to explode when detonated not upon impact. Whatever the target, a suicide driver made more sense thought Boris. Find some Palestinian willing to self-detonate, seeking seventy-some virgins, teach him to drive, and let him plow into the building. The al-Qaeda Wahhabis learned how to fly. Surely the terrorists could place some willing soul into a local truck-driving school. But Boris loved tinkering. He loved the idea of designing a device which would trigger the fuel-laden truck to explode.

The Russian gangster racked his brain to decide how best to invest his money to gain from the next domestic terrorist attack. Boris assumed the economy would be impacted adversely. If the terrorist attack were big enough, stock markets would crash. Should he sell or short? But short which stocks? Which industry would be impacted? Without knowing the target, it was difficult to predict. With the right move his portfolio could explode with wealth just as jihadist millionaires profited from the last attack on U.S. soil. America would be on its knees again. He would get paid for devising the explosive device, and he would profit from betting the right way on the market. It doesn't get much better than that for the Soviet sociopath.

MATT ARRIVED AT THE warehouse at 9:30 a.m. He set up the recording equipment and awaited his guest. Just as he sat down to read the morning paper, his cell phone rang, and he looked at the caller ID.

"Hey, what's up, boss?"

"I thought you were going to call me," said Dwayne.

"I was, but I figured I'd wait until he left. I don't have anything to report now."

"Did the truck get there?"

"Yeah, it got here yesterday afternoon around four."

"Any idea what's going on?" asked Dwayne.

"Not really. It's a military seven-ton with two SIXCONs in the bed. He told me it was full of fuel and tried to laugh it off when I told him my insurance didn't cover gasoline explosions."

"What did he say to that?"

"Nothing. He just said it was safe."

"What do you think?"

"I'm guessing it's a tax scam. I figure it's unregulated gasoline they smuggled into the country and are going to sell it to these independent stations around town," said Matt leaning back in his chair.

"There's a pretty big profit in that if you can maintain the volume, but how many gallons of fuel are we talking?"

"A SIXCON holds about nine hundred gallons of fuel."

"So we're holding eighteen hundred gallons at the

warehouse. Hardly seems worth all the mystery."

"Dwayne, Boris won't waste his time on anything not generating a profit. He's a gangster entrepreneur. This isn't a not-for-profit crime syndicate. He's making a bundle in some way."

"When does he arrive?"

Matt looked at the recently installed Mickey Mouse clock hanging on the far wall. Mickey's tail doubled as a pendulum and swung back and forth. The clock was more of a subtle commentary on Matt's opinion of FBI management than a humorous conversation piece, even though he assumed it would draw a comment or two from even the most hardened criminals. "He should be here in about ten minutes."

"Call me when he leaves. I'm trying to see if we need to expand the scope of the undercover operation order again."

"You got it."

CHAPTER SEVENTY-SEVEN

Boris arrived at ten sharp, just as he promised. Matt watched him through the tinted office windows. The Russian removed a large satchel from the rear hatch of the Escalade and awkwardly carried it to the front door. The first knock was civilized; the second louder. Matt decided to let him pound on the door a couple more times before answering. Since the undercover car was parked in the warehouse, Boris couldn't be certain Matt was in the office. *Turn up the stress.*

After several solid slams on the door, Matt hollered, "I'll be right there. I'm on the phone." He waited a few more seconds, then walked to the door. As he opened it for Boris, he said, "I'm sorry, I was on the phone and had trouble getting the guy to shut up. Come on in."

Boris grumbled something, maybe in Russian, maybe in English. Matt couldn't understand it, and it probably wasn't worth repeating.

"You want some coffee? I just put on a fresh pot."

"No," said Boris as he headed down the hallway into the warehouse lugging the satchel.

Matt followed. "You need some help carrying that? You seem to be having problems, big guy."

Boris's answer was in English and understood.

Matt laughed. "My mother would wash your mouth out for using potty talk."

Boris repeated his response while stopping in front of the restroom. The Russian put the satchel down, walked in, and closed the door.

Matt took a quick peek inside the oversized bag but saw only tools on top. Before he could root through the bag, the toilet flushed. Matt backed away quickly and stood by the door to the warehouse.

Boris closed the door as he walked out of the restroom and grabbed the bag.

"You wash your hands?" asked Matt.

Boris repeated his "potty talk" response as Matt held open the door to the warehouse. "Listen, I've got some calls to make. Do what you gotta do, and if you need me, just holler."

The Russian walked in, and the spring-loaded interior door slammed shut as Matt returned to his office. Unsure what Boris was up to, Matt knew every move Boris made in the warehouse would be video recorded. Thanks to the Constitution and without wiretap authority, an audio recording would be illegal unless Matt was present. For now Boris could feel secure in a nonthreatening environment doing whatever he needed to do. Questions about the Russian's actions and intentions could come later.

MATT SAT AT HIS desk and continued reading the *Los Angeles Times*. After finishing the sports section, he opened his laptop and accessed the current news. Another typical news day, nothing worth noting. Civilization was on its last leg according to every pundit on either side of the aisle. He was anxious to get out to the warehouse to see what Boris was doing but didn't want to appear too eager. Matt's eyes were reading the computer screen, but his mind comprehended little. Finally he shut the laptop and headed down the hall.

Boris's cell phone was ringing in the warehouse. Matt stopped and placed his ear to the door. He couldn't make out much of the conversation, but Boris seemed agitated. Matt could make out "Do it now and don't argue with me."

Fearing Boris might be talking about eliminating another dancer, Matt debated his next move but only for a second. It was chancy and illegal, but he flipped the light switch three times and entered the tech room. Then closing the battered file cabinet, which acted as a door to conceal the monitoring room, Matt grabbed the headphones and could now clearly hear Boris's side of the conversation.

"You are not listening. I said sell everything."

There was a pause.

"What part of my instructions do you not understand? When I say everything, I mean everything. I am getting out of the market."

There was another pause. Matt listened intently for any footfalls, worried Boris might come back into the office and catch him monitoring the conversation, a violation of the Queen Mother's mandate and Boris's constitutional rights.

Boris continued the conversation more agitated after listening to the caller, "I may buy back in a week or two; it depends. I may invest my money elsewhere. But if you don't follow my instructions, I will have to wait to jump back into the market until after attending your memorial service. I hope I am making myself clear. Sell everything now! Think of it as my financial Armageddon. By this time tomorrow you will have liquidated my entire portfolio. Is that understood?"

With that Matt heard the spring door slam. Boris was in the hallway!

Matt threw down the headset and thought for an extended second.

"Matt," came a call from the hallway.

The undercover agent spied the pipe running across the open ceiling. He jumped up and chinning himself, climbed onto a support beam running the length of the warehouse. He inched his way over to the restroom and dropped. He caught his breath, flushed the toilet, brushed off the cobwebs, and walked out into the hallway.

"I need a broom and something cold to drink," demanded the Russian returning to the warehouse.

"Sure."

Matt walked back to his office, relieved he dodged another bullet, grabbed two Diet Pepsis from the refrigerator, a broom from the metal cabinet, and headed into the warehouse.

The Russian said nothing as Matt handed him

the soda can. Boris popped the top and took a long gulp.

Matt looked at the truck. Nothing stood out as different from its appearance before the Russian's arrival. "Everything okay?" asked Matt.

"Everything is fine."

"What have you been doing? The truck looks the same. I was expecting to find a souped-up monster truck ready for the Speed Channel's next event."

"I merely had to tinker with the odometer so when I sell it on eBay I can advertise it as low mileage."

Matt gave the Bear a confused look, and Boris let out one of his patented laughs. The Bear swept around the truck gathering trace pieces of evidence: wire clippings, metal shavings, crumbs of a white, claylike substance. He put the accumulations in a clear plastic bag and tossed it in the satchel. When he finished sweeping and he finished his drink, he prepared to leave.

"I will return Friday afternoon at 3:00 p.m. Be here and don't be late."

"Have you ever known me to be late? I'll be here tomorrow afternoon and Friday afternoon. You can count on it," said Matt.

"Do not touch anything and allow no one in the warehouse. I paid for an exclusive rental of your property."

"That's my understanding as well. The five thousand bought you a week."

Boris nodded. "Thank you for allowing me to store the truck here."

"You want to go grab some lunch?" said Matt.

"No, I have to get back to the club. Maybe some other day."

As Boris hustled out of the warehouse, Matt noted the satchel was a little easier for the big Russian to manipulate.

As soon as the Escalade left the parking lot, Matt slammed the double dead bolts on the front door into place and raced back to the warehouse.

He did a once-around the truck trying to observe any modification. He saw nothing. He climbed on the step to the front door and looked inside; his eye caught a minor object which seemed out of place but hardly alarming. Stepping from the cab, he bent over to view the belly of the seven-ton. When he pretzeled his body beneath the vehicle to size up the undercarriage, he froze, then backed out slowly. He grabbed a chair, pulled it alongside the truck, looked inside the bed, and then ran to his office.

CHAPTER SEVENTY-EIGHT

"**C**an you get over here now?" The urgency in Matt's voice was evident.

"What's going on?" said Dwayne.

"I have no idea. I hate to even say this, but you better clue in the ADIC. This is way beyond our pay grades."

"I'll have to tell the Queen Mother."

"Do what you have to do."

"Do you want us to come there? Isn't that a little dangerous?"

"No, you need to come here. I'm not sure you will believe this. You need to see the truck. Call me when you're a minute out, and I'll open up the back. And Dwayne . . ."

"Yeah."

"I'm not sure how much time we have."

DR. U WAS WAITING in the parking lot behind the Russian Veil when Boris pulled up. The doctor jumped out of his Range Rover. "Are you ready?"

"Not here," said Boris exiting the Escalade. "Wait until we get inside."

Once they entered Boris's office, the Russian grabbed a beer from the refrigerator and offered one to Dr. U who shook his head. "You guys amaze me. You don't drink, but you'll blow up innocent women and children."

"No unbeliever is innocent. Is the truck ready?"

"It is ready. Are you?"

"Our man will be here soon."

"So now do you want to tell me the target?"

Dr. U offered an evil smile.

"I don't believe you plan on blowing up a truck in the middle of a K-Mart parking lot. What's the mission? We have no secrets."

Dr. U. continued his smile. "The Zionists are having a fundraiser. We plan on raising our own fun." The Syrian doctor laughed at what he believed to be a play on words.

"I thought the Germans told bad jokes. I'm not exactly sure you Islamic radicals have a future as stand-up comedians."

Dr. U frowned.

"Oh yeah, I forgot. You aren't a religious fanatic."

"Even American political correctness no longer insults our beliefs. Why must you persist?"

"I like to watch you pout. So what's the target?"

"Have you heard of the Maccabi Electra Tel Aviv?"

"No."

"They are from Israel."

"I'm not stupid. I didn't think they were from Sweden. The Tel Aviv kind of gave it away."

"It is a basketball team. They are coming Friday night to play a charity basketball game against the Los Angeles Lakers. All of the money will go to support the Migdal Ohr."

"And that is what?"

"The world's largest orphanage."

"Where?"

"In Israel."

"No, where are they playing?"

"The Staples Center. The arena seats twenty thousand. The event is almost sold out, and the sponsors are donating a thousand seats to the American military. Every Zionist supporter in Southern California will be there. Americans will long for the days of 9/11 when only three thousand infidels died. Fort Hood will merely be a hiccup. We will bring even greater devastation to the Big and Little Satan all in one massive explosion. We shall rain fire and death on the infidels."

"I bet right!" said a laughing Boris with a perverted joy in his voice. "How will you get the truck close enough to detonate?"

"We have carefully studied the building. We know where we must go. There is an underground entrance off Georgia Street. It will provide access to the belly of the structure. Inside, our people will secure the exits blocking anyone from escaping. We will succeed."

"Perfect. The C-4 will work better in an

enclosed environment. The flames from the exploding fuel will melt the steel underbelly of the arena. Wow! Unbelievable, if you can pull it off."

"If Allah wills, we will succeed."

Boris smiled. "If Allah wills, I'll succeed."

CHAPTER SEVENTY-NINE

Matt tugged on the chains of the overhead garage door as it opened. He was getting pretty good at rapidly pulling the steel links and opening the door in seconds. Dwayne pulled in, and the Queen Mother followed with the ADIC in her passenger seat. Matt just as quickly lowered the door, allowing it to slam to the ground.

They sprang from their cars and hustled over to the military vehicle where Matt was now standing.

"What is this?" said Pamela Clinton.

"A truck," said Matt with a condescending tone evident to all but the Queen.

"So Matt, what's going on?" asked Jason Barnes.

"I'm not sure. That's why I wanted you and Dwayne to see this. According to Boris this thing is loaded with fuel. At first I assumed he was selling untaxed gasoline or smuggling in fuel without the state required additives."

"If that's true, I think it goes beyond the scope of the undercover operation. We need to get that corrected immediately," said Clinton, interrupting and continuing to look at the vehicle as if she were a patron at the children's museum.

Matt ignored her. "I overheard him mention on his cell phone a financial Armageddon, and he was getting out of the stock market at least for the short term."

"Sounds like he's expecting a major impact on the economy," said Barnes.

"We need to modify the scope of the operation," said Clinton ignoring the real issue.

Barnes looked at her and in almost a whisper said, "Give it a rest."

Pamela Clinton was stunned. Her face said it all. She was the special sgent in charge of the terrorism section of the Los Angeles Field Office of the FBI not merely some street agent. No one dare tell her to "give it a rest." Matt thought he saw her upper lip quivering and a tear forming. *Oh for crying out loud, man up!*

Jason Barnes made no effort to assuage the wounded pride of his SAC. More important matters demanded his immediate attention.

Matt said, "The truck is involved." He then bent over and signaled for the three to do the same. "Take a look at this." Matt pointed to what appeared to be a green rope running from beneath the truck bed to the cab. The rope was pulled taut and attached to the belly of the truck by several eye hooks. "That's det cord."

Matt straightened up and led Dwayne and Jason Barnes around the back of the seven-ton. The Queen Mother was still squatting, trying to look under the truck without getting on her knees. From her position she couldn't see what the others observed. "I'm still not seeing it."

All three ignored her.

The men stepped up on some improvised scaffolding Matt made on the side of the truck. He pointed to the base of both SIXCONs. Attached to each was a plastic box about the size of a Tom Clancy hardback novel. The boxes were somewhat concealed from overhead but visible if you craned your neck. The det cord observed from the belly of the truck fed into the plastic boxes. The men looked at one another without saying a word, gripped by the knowledge they were staring into the face of potential mass destruction.

Matt directed the two to the cab and pointed to the twelve-volt power receptacle on the dashboard. "A military seven-ton isn't going to have a cigarette lighter."

The Queen Mother finally caught up, still not finding the det cord or seeing the plastic boxes attached to the SIXCONs. "Why wouldn't a military truck have a cigarette lighter? Soldiers smoke."

All three ignored her.

"Do we need to get someone over here to dismantle this?" asked Dwayne.

"What?" said Pamela Clinton now circling the truck.

"I could get Warren and Holdanak over here," offered Dwayne.

"Are they back?" asked Jason Barnes.

Special Agent Tim Warren graduated from the Naval Academy, spent eight years as a Navy SEAL, specializing in explosives, and was a top expert on anything that went boom. He and his FBI partner Bill Holdanak, a former Marine Corps combat engineer, returned from a four-month deployment to Afghanistan where they helped train the Afghan National Army to disarm improvised explosive devices, commonly known as IEDs. The once crudely made bombs now gave way to highly sophisticated devices manufactured in Iran and Syria. Their expertise was welcomed by the American and Afghan military but needed once again by their employer, the FBI.

"They got home this past weekend," said Dwayne.

"Then get them over here. I suspect this is equipped to detonate upon command not impact," said Barnes. "It wouldn't take much to throw the economy into chaos even if this exploded in the middle of the Disneyland parking lot, but is anyone aware of some type of event scheduled this weekend?"

Dwayne shook his head as Clinton was still trying to come to grips with the issue at hand; the confusion on her face was hard to mask.

Matt thought for a moment without responding, then said, "The Staples Center."

"What about it?" asked Jason Barnes.

"An Israeli All-Star team is playing the Lakers in a preseason fund-raiser Friday night. I read this morning in the *Times* the game is sold out with a thousand tickets going to the military. What better way to strike a blow to the Crusaders and Zionists!"

"That makes a lot of sense, but how or why would Boris be tied to terrorists?" asked Barnes.

"Boris is a gangster capitalist," said Matt. "He'd whack his grandmother if the price was right. He's a fan of no one but himself."

"Get Tim and Bill over here, and let's get whatever this is identified," said Barnes.

Dwayne walked toward the hallway to place the call, fearful a cell phone might somehow detonate the device.

As Dwayne was walking, Matt hollered to him, "Remind them not to drive that four-door cop mobile over here."

Dwayne nodded.

When he returned, he said, "They'll bring the Expedition and be here in thirty."

Matt continued to eye the truck. "We can sit in my office until they come. There's not much we can do here."

"Have you run a 10-28 and 29?" asked Barnes, referring to motor vehicle records for registration and warrants.

"I haven't called it in yet. I don't have access to a computer out here. He claims he bought it at auction," said Matt.

"He may have, but you know the Marine Corps. They don't survey anything unless it's on its last leg. I seriously doubt you can drive a seven-ton off the auction lot. You buy two or three and hope between the multiple vehicles you've got enough working parts to make one serviceable truck for the annual July 4 parade. Dwayne, get the 28 and 29 run. Let's try to figure out who this rig belongs to and if it's stolen. It might give us a lead or two," said Barnes.

"We really should get working on the paperwork to expand the scope of the operation," said Pamela.

"Good idea," said Matt almost imperceptibly shaking his head. "Let me put you up in the other office, and you can start the process." Pamela was shocked Matt agreed with her assessment of the problem and was willing to assist her. He ushered the SAC to the other side of the warehouse where a cramped room housed a small desk and telephone. Dwayne and the ADIC looked at each other and could barely conceal grins. The Queen Mother had no clue she was being shuffled off to Buffalo, a place many in L.A. wished she would land.

Matt unlocked the door and allowed the SAC entrance. Maybe a month of dust and cobwebs covered the desk and telephone. Matt grabbed a towel and began wiping, stirring up more mess than existed before his efforts. "Sorry about the mess. We never use this room, but it will be quiet so you can call D.C. and get the process started."

"Thanks, Matt. You've really been helpful."

Matt closed the door on his way out and returned to Dwayne and the ADIC.

The three retreated to Matt's office and reviewed the surveillance tapes detailing Boris's activities as he modified the seven-ton.

CHAPTER EIGHTY

Tim Warren and Bill Holdanak arrived before the top of the hour and pulled the Expedition into the warehouse. A chill wind blew through the open door portending the danger before them. Everyone exchanged pleasantries, but this wasn't the time for grips and grins. Matt filled the two in on Boris's latest actions and the review of the surveillance tapes.

"Where'd this guy get a seven-ton?" asked Tim.

"It was stolen from the Marine Corps Reserve Center in Encino yesterday," said Dwayne, who learned of the theft from the computer records check.

Tim walked around the vehicle, examining the exterior and crawling underneath. He touched nothing as he made his assessment.

"That's det cord running the belly of the truck and leading into the attached boxes. I don't see any obvious traps. Based on everything you've said, I think it's safe to take a closer look. If you guys want to go for coffee, we'll understand, but I'm not too worried about this thing going boom."

"But you never know," added Bill with a coy grin.

Pamela Clinton emerged from the dusty closet where Matt secreted her. He wasn't the only one who forgot she was still at the warehouse. A huge smile covered her face. "We got the expansions on the undercover project. We can continue."

All but the ADIC ignored her. He said, "Thanks, Pamela, it's great to know we're on the right track administratively."

Matt faked sincerity. "Pamela, Tim was just saying he thinks the truck is safe, but there is always a chance for an explosion. We decided to stick around. We'll leave it up to you if you want to head back to the office."

He could see her swallow hard trying to come up with a way to extricate herself from a potential career-ending firebomb. She was at a loss for words, a situation which seldom arose. Several seconds of an uncomfortable silence filled the warehouse as she slowly pushed a stray lock of hair behind her ear.

"Let me get back to Westwood. I'll get all the approvals and modifications in place. We don't want to give OPR any chance to second-guess us."

"I think that's a great idea," said Matt, rushing to open the warehouse door.

"I'll make sure the ADIC gets back to the office," said Dwayne.

The Queen Mother was out of there in a New York minute as the real work of the Bureau continued.

"At this point I'm more concerned with determining what we have than preserving a potential crime scene. Are we agreed?" asked Tim.

Everyone nodded as Bill stepped on the oversized rear tire and climbed into the bed of the truck. Tim followed. They both carefully examined the handle on the twelve-inch-cap on top of the SIXCON. There were no wires or attachments. Bill popped the handle and lifted the lid. The distinct smell of jet fuel permeated the warehouse. He dipped a foot-long wooden blade inside and pulled it out. The liquid had the oily consistency of kerosene-based jet fuel.

"This is JP8. The military uses it in the diesel engines of most tactical ground vehicles."

Bill then examined the contents of the second SIXCON. It was also JP8. The two containers held eighteen hundred gallons of a fuel which burns hotter than gasoline.

Tim squatted between the two containers and carefully snapped the top to the plastic box attached to the forward portion of each SIXCON—the contents, an off-white pliable substance resembling modeling clay.

"With both boxes I'm guessing we have at least a pound and a half of C-4. This will cause quite a bonfire for the homecoming rally," said Tim as he jumped down from the truck. "Any idea of the target?" asked Tim now crawling under the vehicle.

Matt said, "We think the Staples Center, Friday night."

With his right hand Bill rubbed his eyes and pinched the bridge of his nose before speaking. "I'm not sure how they plan on getting it to center court, but C-4 works better than TNT in an enclosed area. Your guy knows what he's doing. When Ramzi Yousef put together the first World Trade Center bombing in '93 he used a Ford Econoline packed with ammonium nitrate soaked in fuel oil. In the Oklahoma City bombing McVeigh used over a hundred bags of ammonium nitrate fertilizer, fifty pounds each. This is much more efficient assuming you can get close to the structure."

Tim emerged from beneath the truck. "It looks as though the det cord is linked to the power receptacle on the dash." He then opened the driver's side door and entered the cab. Peering underneath the dashboard, he assessed the situation, emerged, and carefully removed the cigarette lighter. Holding it up, he said, "This is the detonator. It's been modified for the twelve-volt auxiliary power plug. Push it in, and when it heats up and pops, the det cord is primed. Within seconds all this goes boom."

The five returned to Matt's office to discuss a strategy. Matt pulled a six-pack of Pepsi from the refrigerator and each took one.

"He's picking it up on Friday afternoon. We can assume they plan to detonate it Friday night, which makes the Staples Center a logical target. It doesn't make much sense to leave it parked in front of his house all weekend for an early Monday morning explosion. He's going to leave it here as long as he can until he needs it. I figure we have two days, but we need a plan, and we need to implement it soon," said Matt.

"This isn't the same as Dawn Platt's Nissan. We can't very well substitute another seven-ton," said Dwayne.

"I don't think we have to," said the ADIC.

"First we need to install a tracker and a kill switch just to be safe. First thing Friday morning we have SOG sitting on this, and when the driver picks it up, we take it away."

"But you still have a moving bomb bouncing on the freeways," said Dwayne.

"Not if we substitute the explosives," said the ADIC. He looked at Tim. "Can you do that?"

"Sure, I can switch Play-Doh for the C-4. I use it all the time at the bomb tech seminars, and I've got training det cord in the Expedition."

"We can disable the detonator," said Bill.

"That still leaves eighteen hundred gallons of jet fuel in the SIXCONs," said Matt.

"We could switch them out and replace them with water," suggested Dwayne.

"That might take some slick maneuvering," said the ADIC. "I can call over to the reserve unit and see if they can accommodate us."

Matt balked at that idea. "We have to minimize the activity here. Boris may be back and forth protecting his bankroll. And I'm concerned how he got a seven-ton and two SIXCONs in the first place. I'm not sure you just drive off the lot at a Reserve Center. He might be in bed with the Marine equivalent of Fort Hood's Major Hasan; somebody over there may be playing both sides of the ball."

"Trust but verify," said Jason Barnes.

"It worked for Reagan," said Matt.

"Good point," said Barnes. "Tim and Bill, do what you can as fast as you can, and let's see where we stand by close of business today."

MATT MADE IT HOME by eight, somewhat miraculous considering the events at the warehouse. Caitlin begged his presence so he made the effort. The sun had long set, but he welcomed the serenity of the condo regardless the hour. When he walked in the door, he was greeted by the sights, smells, and sounds of dinner, candlelight, and soft music.

Caitlin walked out of the kitchen and looked radiant. Without saying a word, she threw her arms around him, and they kissed forever.

When he finally stepped back and looked at her, he said, "Do you have an announcement?"

A tear rolled down her cheek. "You're going to be a daddy."

He grabbed her again, and the embrace lasted a lifetime.

CHAPTER EIGHTY-ONE

Driving a borrowed Honda, Dmitri moved slowly along a crowded Ventura Boulevard. The curb was thick with parked cars, and he was seeking an opening. From a block away he spied a man exiting the club, crossing the street, and entering a pickup. Dmitri arrived at the spot just as the pickup pulled out and maneuvered the Honda to the curb.

Dmitri exited the car and waited for traffic to clear before running across the street. Jesse was working the door on another beautiful L.A. afternoon. Dmitri hesitated at the entrance long enough for Jesse to spot the newbie.

"You interested? We've got some beautiful women inside," said Jesse.

Dmitri looked at him without saying a word.

"Better step in now, pal. At five we start a ten-dollar cover charge. Right now it's free. But in an hour you'll wish you would have saved that ten spot to put toward a lap dance."

Dmitri walked in and was immediately drawn to a girl dancing on stage. She was beautiful and athletic. His eyes fixed as she maneuvered around the pole in a suggestive, rhythmic dance, but there was a vacant look in her bleak, dark eyes. The kind he saw in men who spent too much time on the front lines of war. The woman was going through the motions in a detached, orderly way. Six men sat along the edge of the stage, beers in hand, lusting at a woman just an arm's length and a few dollars away.

Dmitri took a few steps toward the bar, still concentrating on the dancer. He bumped into a waitress carrying drinks for several patrons.

"Hey!" she said trying to prevent the drinks from spilling, spills that would come out of her paycheck not Boris's profits.

"I am sorry," said Dmitri in strongly accented English.

The waitress provided a weak smile and replied in Russian, "It is okay."

Dmitri walked over to the bar. "What do you have?"

The bartender picked up on the accent as well and answered in Russian, "Probably anything you want. You are new here, no?"

Dmitri nodded and ordered a Zhigulevskoye. The bartender extended his hand across the bar and introduced himself. "My name is Peter."

"I am Dmitri."

"You must be true Russian to order Zhiguli. How about Baltika?"

"Yes, Baltika is fine. Do you have Krepkoe?"

"No, just Klassichesko."

"Then the classic will do."

"What brings you to Los Angeles?"

"I have important business."

"Everyone has important business," said Peter as he wiped down the bar. "While you are in here, you should meet many beautiful women who work in bar. They are all from Ukraine and Russia. They very good. Boris let me try out many. It is included in my salary, what Americans call part of compensation package." He winked.

"So where is Boris?"

"He around. He often stay in back room. Sometimes he come out. You know him?"

"I hear of him. Some friends say to look him up when I get to America. They say he big man in U.S."

Peter laughed, "Boris is big man wherever he is. He weighs maybe 150 kilograms."

"I was told he built like bear."

"In fight I think he beat the bear," said the smiling bartender.

"They say he drive big important car."

"He drive a black Escalade Cadillac, a big car for a big man. Is your business with Boris?"

"I would like to meet him."

"Let me call back in office. Maybe he come out. It still early. Maybe he not busy."

Peter picked up the phone behind the bar next to the register. Dmitri couldn't hear what Peter was saying. The loud music blaring from the speakers made eavesdropping difficult. When Peter hung up the phone, he turned to Dmitri. "He said he has someone in office, but he would come out soon."

Dmitri nodded, picked up his beer, and moved to the stage. He sat at the only open seat which gave him a clear view of the door to Boris's office. The seat next to Dmitri was occupied by a man who spent more on alcohol than personal hygiene. Even his desert travelers smelled better, but Dmitri needed the vantage point and took the seat next to the Unwashed.

The dancer spotted Dmitri, a new patron at the stage. She made her way to him, undulating to the music as she moved closer and closer. Dmitri's neighbor began hooting as she moved ever so slowly. In between shouts his breathing increased, huffing like an asthmatic sprinting toward the finish line. Before the dancer could get close, the Unwashed lurched forward, grabbed the young dancer, and pulled her toward him.

A near panic ensued as the other dancers screamed. Two bouncers sprang from the shadows. They grabbed the Unwashed and began to rip at his extremities. His cries meant nothing to the security team. The beating was quick, savage, and public. Its purpose was to not only convince the attacker he was never welcome again but to serve as a lesson to any observer: you must pay before you play.

Dmitri was content to watch the savagery, his focus on the patron getting a lesson in strip-bar etiquette. When Dmitri looked up, he realized the yelping of the Unwashed caught the attention of management. The door to Boris's office was open. Dmitri quickly scanned the room and saw the behemoth giving orders, a man from the Middle East by his side.

Enough. Dmitri left fearing the police would be called. His immigration status didn't allow for interaction with the authorities. He would wait to meet the Bear.

CHAPTER EIGHTY-TWO

Matt arrived at the undercover off-site around four-thirty preparing the final steps for tomorrow's betrayal. He spent most of the day at the JTTF catching up on the mounds of FBI paperwork accompanying every investigation. He also got what he believed to be a well-deserved workout at Gallo's Gym. Fernando Perez was working out at the same time. Matt wanted to thank him for the third round knockout at Caesars which brought a great deal of credibility to the undercover op but decided to let the future champ learn of his contribution when Matt published his memoirs in about fifteen years.

Matt was in the warehouse examining the seven-ton. Tim and Bill replaced the C-4 with Play-Doh and rewired the det cord using the training substitute. The lighter was disabled. It looked perfect. The SIXCONs were still filled with fuel, but without some type of detonating device, the truck was relatively impotent. The tech agents concealed a tracking device and kill switch, Caitlin was pregnant, and all was right with the world.

Matt decided not to liquidate his retirement

account but assumed Boris had, hoping the Russian had created his own financial quicksand with enough of a paper trail to connect him to the conspiracy.

SOG would be set up first thing in the morning, and the plan was for the surveillance team to follow the driver until the target was identified. Everyone still agreed the Staples Center made the most sense, but nothing being reported by the CIA or NSA identified an event or a venue.

Matt was admiring the work of Tim, Bill, and the tech agents. He double- and triple-checked to ensure no one left any telltale signs demonstrating the plot had been uncovered. He spied nothing out of the ordinary. The phone in his office rang, and Matt ran from the warehouse to pick it up, assuming it might be Boris. It was Dwayne.

"Steve just heard from Houston. They located Dawn Platt."

"She's alive?" asked Matt.

"Yeah, she said Jesse was ordered to kill her, but Andy, the guy you call Stump, grabbed Jesse's gun and said he would do it. He drove her around back of an abandoned building. He fired a round into the car, cut his arm, and smeared his blood on the seat. Then he kissed her and said he'd have to keep the car. He told her he would tell Jesse and Boris he disposed of the body in an elevator shaft in the building. He gave her some money for the car and for a plane ticket back to Houston. He said if she kept her mouth shut she'd live. He also told her he was going to move to Houston in a few months to be close to her."

"Amazing, ain't love grand."

"Not quite. She's willing to testify against Jesse and Stump. Detective Ames over at North Hollywood said the slug they found in Dawn's car matched the ones that killed Annika and Benjamin Hobbs. Ames is putting together the paper to pick up Jesse and Stump later this evening. Danny Garcia will be a part of that. You don't by any chance have an idea where our boys will be?"

"My only guess would be the Veil," said Matt, then with sarcasm dripping from every word, "Are they picking up anything on the wiretap yet?"

"Don't be a smart aleck."

"Did you ever get any word from headquarters on getting up on the phones or Boris's office?"

"They said maybe by tomorrow we'll have the approvals."

"Will that be before or after the Staples Center blows up?"

"I hear you."

"If I hear from Boris, I'll see if I can pick up anything on the whereabouts of Stump and Jesse. What about Boris and the murders? Does Ames have enough to connect him?"

"It's still weak. Maybe if either flips, we can tie him up. It sounds like Stump has an incentive to cooperate. We may be able to link it all up into a RICO indictment, but we'll let LAPD have the first shot. Ames has been very cooperative. I want to make sure she gets all the credit she deserves. We can always use another friend at RHD."

"Did she get selected for Robbery Homicide?"

"No, but Danny says this puts her over the top."

"Good, that takes me off the hook. I was the only common denominator for a couple of 187s."

"Yeah, 'homicide suspect' doesn't look good on your resume."

CHAPTER EIGHTY-THREE

The Thursday afternoon sun was preparing to set, and there was a touch of cool wind blowing through the open driver-side window. Dmitri lowered himself in the seat and was barely visible from a distance beyond the width of the street. His mission was singular in nature. He needed to speak with Boris without the henchmen who often accompanied the Russian. Dmitri was patient. He traveled half a world. He would wait however long it took for the one-on-one meeting.

He watched the men as they walked up to the door. Jesse stood out front, sometimes acting as the roper, always as the gatekeeper. Men reached into their pockets pulling out tens, paying the fee for an evening of gawking. His country was no better. Many were exploited in his country, but why would men living in the freest nation on earth sanction the virtual imprisonment of teenagers? Where was the populace rage?

Dmitri spotted the black Escalade as it pulled from the back lot, down the side driveway, and prepared to turn onto Ventura Boulevard. Boris was behind the wheel, his Middle Eastern friend in the passenger seat. At least he wasn't in the company of his regular entourage. Dmitri started the engine and prepared to follow the Russian to his ultimate destination.

He watched the Cadillac lurch forward as Boris gunned the engine, pulling out into traffic. A horn blared, the driver unhappy with Boris's attempt to enter the crowded commuter traffic pattern. As soon as the Russian pulled into the lane, he slammed on his brakes to avoid hitting the car in front. Now it was Boris's turn to sound the horn, as if car horns ever did anything to improve rush-hour traffic in Los Angeles. Boris and his passenger began a journey inching their way down Ventura Boulevard. Dmitri pulled into traffic and followed from a safe distance.

At one point Dmitri fell too many cars behind

and was stopped at a red light as Boris continued through the intersection. Dmitri kept a close eye on his target. Thick traffic prevented Boris from escaping. Thanks to the stop-and-go traffic, by the time Dmitri's light changed, Boris was stuck at the next light.

It made little difference whether you traveled by side streets or freeways; the traffic moved at a snail's pace. Rush hour in L.A. started decades earlier and would end when the car joined the likes of the dinosaur. Dmitri feared being lost at another light so he crept ever closer to the Cadillac.

After Boris drove several miles, he signaled and turned. The traffic moved faster as the two cars headed north. Boris would often race from one green light to a red one at the next intersection. Regardless of how fast he drove, he never outdistanced Dmitri's Honda.

They made their way through the San Fernando Valley. Dmitri had no idea where he was and paid little attention to the street signs. He just knew Boris remained a few cars ahead. After several miles the Escalade signaled again and turned left onto a dead-end street leading to an industrial complex.

MAINTAINING AN UNDERCOVER MIND-SET for months at a time was exhausting. Fighting bad guys and bureaucrats took its toll. Matt was drained and not excited about battling bumper-to-bumper traffic in the evening commute. Before heading home, he decided to pull out the Bible from the locked bottom drawer. He was working his way through the Old Testament, the Minor Prophets, and the verse from Amos practically jumped off the page, "But let justice flow like water, and righteousness, like an unfailing stream."

The phone rang before he could fully digest the words. He assumed it was Dwayne calling back and started to answer with a smart remark when he spotted the caller ID.

"Hey, Boris."

"I am glad you are still there. I'm bringing a potential buyer to view the truck."

"I was just getting ready to leave. Can this wait until tomorrow?"

"No, leave the back door unlocked. We will come through the alley. It won't take long. We are just down the street," said Boris abruptly as he hung up the phone without waiting for a response.

Matt raced out to the warehouse and unlocked the back door. He stopped briefly to scan the truck one more time to ensure no evidence of the FBI's tampering was visible. When he returned to his office, he punched in Dwayne's number. "Boris just called. He's on his way and bringing someone with him. I couldn't put him off, and before I could ask about Stump and Jesse, he hung up."

"With this traffic I'm not sure I can get anyone over there to cover the meet. SOG is set up for tomorrow. All their teams are at LAX this afternoon helping to cover the Israeli basketball team."

"I'll be okay. I'll call you after they leave."

"I'll still try to get a team over there. This obviously has something to do with tomorrow."

CHAPTER EIGHTY-FOUR

Within a minute of ending his call with Matt, Boris entered through the alley door of the warehouse and raised the garage door. He pulled the Escalade in and both men exited. They began to circle what once was merely a military truck but now a mobile weapon of mass destruction. Boris pointed out the plastic boxes attached to the base of both SIXCONs and the det cord running along the belly of the vehicle.

"Once he activates the cigarette lighter, he has only minutes to clear the building. If he runs, he will live to fight for your cause another day. If he walks, he martyrs himself. Personally, I would work on my sprinting between now and tomorrow."

"We will have our shahid on the inside locking

the exits blocking the escape of the infidels," said Dr. U.

"I guess they will be the martyrs if they don't escape."

"You understand our beliefs."

"So when are you joining them and taking the bridge over Jahannam to Paradise?"

"When I am called."

Boris smiled. "I like your deep pockets so I hope you aren't called anytime soon. The primer cords are timed to ignite simultaneously. The entire truck will explode in an instant. The explosion alone should bring down the building, but the fuel will splatter throughout the lower level. Fire will spread with the fuel."

A dark smile overtook Dr. U's face. "Many will die from the explosion, many from the fumes, and many from the flames. It is the perfect device to bring maximum devastation to a weak nation. With twenty thousand dead, the World Trade Center will be a mere footnote in their history books."

"I can't guarantee the number but many will die. A message will be sent."

"And received," said Dr. U almost giddy with anticipation.

"And received," Boris repeated the words slowly. "Who is your driver?"

"We have a man who is experienced. He needs the money but also supports the cause."

"A win-win. If he lives, he gets to spend the money with his family. If he dies, he gets seventy-some virgins."

"Yes," said Dr. U, not sure he appreciated the Russian making fun of his religious beliefs.

"Aren't you guys running out of virgins? It seems like you've been sending a lot of martyrs to their deaths."

"Do not make light of Allah and our beliefs. You will need him someday."

"You mean when the Mahdi returns? Assuming any of you religious zealots are correct, I'll enjoy my time on earth and take my chances in hell."

Matt entered the warehouse and crossed the room. "Sorry, been on the phone."

He looked at Boris and spied his visitor. Matt continued walking but his stomach twisted. He was face-to-face with Dr. U.

Matt knew the eyes could betray everything. Could he see recognition in the doctor's eyes? But Matt had to guard his own eyes as well. A year earlier he met the doctor at World Angel Ministry. The FBI never identified the Syrian-born doctor as part of the terrorist cell which infiltrated the Christian ministry, but to Matt's knowledge the doctor was never cleared. You can't prove a negative. You can prove someone is a terrorist. You can't prove he is not. Tonight Matt had circumstantial proof Dr. U was a terrorist or at least a keeper of very bad company.

Regardless, if Dr. U remembered Matt as a volunteer at the clinic and read the *Times* article, it might be best to act rather than react. Matt's weapon was hidden beneath his shirt. He brushed his back to feel the reassurance of the 9 mm in his waistband. He was poised, ready to explode should the situation warrant. *Never ignore what you see, waiting for your brain to engage. Watch the eyes.*

"Matt, this is Dr. U. He's a friend of mine who is investing in my fuel project."

Matt extended his hand.

"Have we met?" asked the doctor.

"Maybe so. I hang out at the Veil. You might have been waiting in line behind me for a lap dance." Matt's smile continued.

Boris laughed. "Dr. U refers to my girls as temptresses and whores. His religion does not allow him to partake of such debauchery."

"Neither does my wife," said Matt.

Matt could tell the doctor wasn't satisfied with the response and was sizing up the undercover agent. Life was in the balance.

"Boris, let me close the garage door. I've got nosey neighbors," said Matt heading to the door. It suddenly hit him. He forgot to activate the video recording devices. *Idiot, exhaustion is no excuse. Focus!* He needed to work his way back to the hallway. He risked getting caught trying to activate the machine, but he needed Dr. U on tape. It's the best evidence, maybe the only evidence, linking him to the conspiracy. Before Matt took another step, he glimpsed a man out of the corner of his eye.

A screaming Dmitri rushed into the warehouse brandishing a CZ 75, the Czech Republic's most popular combat handgun.

"What the . . . ?"

"Everybody stop, don't move," said Dmitri waving the automatic at the three. Then he said, "All of you over there." Dmitri signaled with the weapon he wanted the three men to move closer together next to the tanker. The intruder was nervous; his hands shaking, his voice quivering.

"So what is it? Do you want us to stop or to move? Don't give conflicting messages when you're waving a cannon around," said Matt in a calm but confident voice trying to defuse the situation.

"Move. Now!"

The three moved closer together.

Boris said something in Russian and Dmitri responded.

"Let's keep it in English, fellows," said Matt. "I want to make sure everyone is on the same page and there are no more surprises, so English only."

"Shut up. You talk too much," said Dmitri.

"Only when some nut comes running into my

warehouse waving a gun around. What is it you want?" said Matt slowly.

"I want him." Dmitri pointed at Boris.

Boris said something in Russian.

"English. Say it in English," insisted Matt in a louder than normal voice.

"He kill my daughter!" shouted Dmitri.

"Your daughter?" asked Boris.

"Yes, my Annika. You bring her here from Ukraine."

"I never brought your daughter here," said Boris lying to a member of his extended family of enemies.

"Your people convince her you make her big Hollywood star. You trick her to travel to Istanbul, then bring her to United States on work visa. She think she become actress. She tell us how excited she is to come here. Then when she arrive, you take her passport and visa. You say she must work for you before she can work for movies. You say she must take off clothes and sleep with men to pay back all you pay to bring her here."

Matt heard the story before. Irina painted a similar picture of horror and deceit. Matt saw the focused rage in the eyes of a father seeking not revenge but justice. *But let justice flow . . .*

"You are wrong," said Boris, his voice betraying fear.

"You are liar. My daughter is good girl before

404

she meet you. She call us crying, asking for help, asking for money to buy her back from you. I sell everything I own for my child, but before I get her money, I get call. My daughter dead. They find her shot at bottom of hill thrown from side of road. I promise my wife I come to America to find man who killed our Annika."

"I had nothing to do with her death," protested Boris weakly.

The Russian bear's courage was waning, a slight quiver in his voice. Sweat sprouted from his forehead and soaked his collar. The man who surrounded himself with supplicants and yes-men was now on his own, his posse nowhere to be found. His only chance was a Syrian doctor who did not appear eager to martyr himself.

"Shut up! Do you know what it is like to lose your only child? My wife cries every night. We sacrifice our daughter so men can lust at our most precious gift. We have lost everything because of your lies!"

"You better listen to him, Boris. I don't understand fuel tanks, but I'm guessing a bullet into that SIXCON, and we are all destined for closed caskets. Crispy critters don't make for good viewings at memorial services."

"Shut up, all of you!"

"Now I know," said Dr. U looking at Matt. "You worked at World Angel Ministry. Boris, this guy's an FBI agent. It was in that article in the paper. He's the one who disarmed the bomb at the hotel."

"FBI?" said Boris looking at Matt with confusion, then contempt.

Even though Dmitri was from the Ukraine, he understood; the FBI was a federal law enforcement agency. He would take no chances. With the precision of the military training he received years earlier, he fired three shots in rapid succession.

CHAPTER EIGHTY-FIVE

Boris collapsed to the warehouse floor, his body gasping for life, but even the cool concrete provided no comfort. All three shots were fatal.

Dmitri stood there, his mission complete, his target down, but his world now imploding.

Dr. U ran as soon as the shots were fired, and Matt gave chase without concern for Boris or the Ukrainian father. The industrial complex was open, and there were few places the doctor could hide. He ran east toward the street but then headed north into a neighboring complex. Dr. U had no idea where he was running, just away from the man he now knew to be an FBI agent. The Syrian was no match for the experienced runner. Matt closed quickly. Dr. U rounded the corner of a building and disappeared briefly from Matt's view.

Matt had been in enough foot pursuits to know better than to run without purpose around any corner. Matt stopped short of the building. Although his ears were ringing from the shots in the warehouse, he listened for footfalls or breathing or any signpost his quarry was near. He heard nothing.

Breathe, slow and deep; relax even in the midst of chaos. Matt did a sneak and peek around the edge of the concrete edifice. Dumpsters in front of each unit lined the alley separating two buildings. Since the pavement was clear, Matt assumed the doctor was hiding behind one of the green metal trash containers on either side of the alley; the rusty oil barrels were too small to conceal the Middle Eastern jihadist.

"Give it up, doctor."

There was no response.

"Give it up. I'm not even sure why you ran. I guess you could always argue you feared for your life. A jury might buy that argument. It's not an indicia of guilt."

Nothing. Matt was coaxing any response to locate the enemy. Locate, close with, and destroy. The mission of the Marines was now his mission in the industrial park alley.

"Come on, doctor. This isn't some Third-World

battlefield. We can't just shoot you. Ibrahim could have had a trial had he wanted one. Why don't you come out, and we can discuss this?"

"Maybe I don't want to discuss it."

Keep him talking.

Flattened with his back against the wall, Matt welcomed the coolness of the concrete through his shirt. "In that case we have a standoff. I can't walk away."

"Why not?"

The sounds were echoing off the buildings, and Matt still wasn't clear which container hid the terrorist.

Matt had been here, in his mind and on the street; not this alley, not this target, but he had been here. He knew the difference between the serenity of the classroom and the explosive setting of an urban battlefield. Violence wasn't just a controlled abstract for the range or the ring; it was a reality. For those who experienced combat, life has meaning the weak will never understand. Matt understood and would once again do battle!

"Doctor, we both know you are part of a conspiracy to destroy America."

"America will destroy itself. It is a civilization in twilight unless it submits to the laws of the prophet."

Matt identified the container.

"Then come on out. I can guarantee you a pretty big platform. You won't get some military tribunal. You'll get a federal district court, press conferences, truTV, CNN. The *Los Angeles Times* would love an exclusive. Think of the exposure."

Matt slowly edged his way down the side of the building outside the view of the doctor hidden behind the dumpster. Matt was seeking cover behind the container on the opposite side of the alley.

"The word says, 'Prophet, make war on the unbelievers and the hypocrites and deal rigorously with them. Hell shall be their home; an evil fate."

Matt was behind the container across from the terrorist physician. He remained quiet as Dr. U continued his diatribe. "Only the sword can save us."

The doctor was ranting the same propaganda screaming from the jihadist Web sites supporting Takfir, a sacred license to kill.

"Slay the idolaters wherever you find them. Lie in ambush everywhere for them. Accept the word or die."

As soon as Dr. U said die, Matt moved to a firing position across from the terrorist.

Matt could see the doctor leaning up against the container, a mini-Glock gripped with both hands, his arms extended. Matt didn't have a clear shot, only of the extended arms. Dr. U shouted out more verses from the Koran. "And if you are slain, or die in the way of Allah, forgiveness and mercy from Allah are far better than all they could amass."

Dr. U took a quick peek around the container. He spotted Matt across the alley and fired wildly, the sounds echoing in explosive dissonance.

Before Dr. U could get off a second volley of shots, Matt ran forward, sighting his target, aiming lower than normal, knowing he tended to shoot high in low light. Matt fired twice: once to the chest, once to the head, blood pouring from both wounds.

The life drained from the doctor's eyes as his body slumped down the side of the trash container, a fitting place for his death. No longer would the Syrian doctor terrorize America. But the plot to destroy the Staples Center died as well, a plot known only to the doctor, Boris, and a few anonymous Shahid who will live to fight another day.

Matt rushed forward, kicked the doctor's weapon beyond reach, and placed two fingers on the carotid artery. There was no pulse. In a near whisper and with contempt, Matt uttered, "*Allahu Akhbar.*"

CHAPTER EIGHTY-SIX

Grabbing the mini-Glock, Matt raced back to the undercover warehouse.

When he arrived at the open garage door, he took a quick peek around the wall seeking to find Dmitri, knowing the Ukrainian was armed and dangerous. Matt was stunned by what he saw.

Annika's father was seated on the floor watching Boris lying in a pool of blood, Dmitri's weapon resting on the floor a few feet away.

"Get your hands up," hollered Matt.

Dmitri complied immediately, his body in complete surrender.

Matt carefully approached in a combat-ready firing position, keeping an eye on Dmitri's hands and the weapon. When close enough, Matt kicked the weapon away, and the Czech-made automatic skidded across the floor.

Matt was confused by the submissive murderer staring at his victim. "Why are you still here?"

"I wait for you," said Dmitri softly.

"You waited for me? Why?"

"The man say you FBI."

"Right, I'm an FBI agent."

"Then I wait for you. I come to this country only to kill man who kill our child. I not come to

411

make FBI mad. I do not want to force you to look for me. If you not here in warehouse, I would have run after stopping this man's evil, but now you know me. It would not be right to make you chase me back to Ukraine."

"You have a strange sense of justice."

"The only justice I seek is man who kill my daughter."

"And you found justice?" said Matt as he slowly lowered his weapon.

"Yes, I find justice," said the now meek Ukrainian.

Matt saw pain and resignation in a loving father's face.

Sirens wailed in the background as the FBI agent contemplated his next move. Knowing he never activated the recording machines in the warehouse, Matt slid his undercover weapon in his waistband and said, "Then I think you better go."

"What do you mean?"

"You better leave before more FBI agents arrive. You've suffered enough. Go back to your wife and try to find peace."

Dmitri didn't move.

The sirens were getting closer.

"You don't have much time. You've got a thin minute before the people who don't allow choices arrive."

The Ukrainian stood up and extended his open

hand. The two shook hands, then Dmitri pulled Matt toward him, gave him a heartfelt hug, and fled the warehouse.

After watching the father race into the alley, Matt sat down against the wall and blew a slow breath. When Dwayne arrived, Matt would tell a diluted truth: Dmitri killed Boris; Matt chased down Dr. U and shot him in the alley after taking fire; when Matt returned to the warehouse, Dmitri was gone.

Matt looked toward heaven as if seeking approval. None came.

He grabbed his cell phone and punched in Dwayne's number. "The warehouse is secure. Targets down."

Caitlin said God was a God of second chances who could "erase our failures and betrayals. It's a matter of what you are willing to live with." Matt made his choice. Now could he live with it?

The words of the prophet Micah echoed in his head. "He showed you o man what is good and what does the Lord require of you but to do justice, love kindness, and walk humbly with your God."

Matt struggled with humility. He didn't always love kindness. But at least for today he did justice.

He hoped God agreed.

ACKNOWLEDGMENTS

Thanks to Selma Wilson, president and publisher of B&H Publishing Group, Oliver North, my "Commanding Editor," and Gary Terashita, my executive editor, for your friendship, support, and confidence in this former undercover agent. Thanks to John Thompson, Julie Gwinn, Kim Stanford, Jean Eckenrode, Jeff Godby, and all the great people at B&H. I'm proud to be part of the team.

To Bucky Rosenbaum, my agent and friend.

To Daniel Combs, Chele Stanton, Chris Burgard, Becky Towle, Ryan Wilson, and Monika Baker for your input, feedback, encouragement, and support.

But most of all, thanks to a gracious God, who blessed me with parents who served as role models and a wife who stood by me through a lifetime of undercover stories. Thanks, God, for the two greatest children a dad could ever want, who married wisely and provided grandchildren who melt my heart and bring a smile to my face.

Center Point Publishing
600 Brooks Road ● PO Box 1
Thorndike ME 04986-0001 USA

(207) 568-3717

US & Canada:
1 800 929-9108
www.centerpointlargeprint.com